Praise for Donna Grant's Sons of Texas novels

"This first-class thrill ride will leave readers eager for more."
—*Publishers Weekly* (starred review) on *The Hero*

"Dangerous, steamy, and full of intrigue."
—*Booklist* on *The Hero*

"Grant's dizzying mix of danger and romance dazzles . . . off-the-charts chemistry and a breath-stealing plot."
—*Publishers Weekly* (starred review) on *The Protector*

The Dark Kings series

"Grant's ability to quickly convey complicated backstory makes this jam-packed love story accessible even to new or periodic readers." —*Publishers Weekly* on *Fever*

"A sweet and steamy romance." —*Fresh Fiction* on *Fever*

The Dark Warrior series

"The world of the Immortal Warriors is a thoroughly engaging one, blending powerful ancient gods, fiery desire, and touchingly human love, which readers will surely want to revisit."
—*RT Book Reviews*

"Sizzling love scenes and engaging characters."
—*Publishers Weekly*

The Dark Sword series

"Grant creates a vivid picture of Britain centuries after the Celts and Druids tried to expel the Romans, deftly merging magic and history. The result is a wonderfully dark, delightfully well-written [series]. Readers will eagerly await the next Dark Sword book."
—*RT Book Reviews*

"Another fantastic series that melds the paranormal with the historical life of the Scottish Highlander in this arousing and exciting adventure."
—*Bitten by Books*

"Will keep readers spellbound."
—*Romance Reviews Today*

ALSO BY DONNA GRANT

HEART OF TEXAS SERIES
THE CHRISTMAS COWBOY HERO
COWBOY, CROSS MY HEART
MY FAVORITE COWBOY
A COWBOY LIKE YOU
LOOKING FOR A COWBOY
A COWBOY KIND OF LOVE

THE DARK KINGS SERIES
DARK HEAT
DARKEST FLAME
FIRE RISING
BURNING DESIRE
HOT BLOODED
NIGHT'S BLAZE
SOUL SCORCHED
PASSION IGNITES
SMOLDERING HUNGER
SMOKE AND FIRE
FIRESTORM
BLAZE
HEAT
TORCHED
DRAGONFIRE
IGNITE
FEVER
INFERNO

THE SONS OF TEXAS SERIES
THE HERO
THE PROTECTOR
THE LEGEND

THE DARK WARRIOR SERIES
MIDNIGHT'S MASTER
MIDNIGHT'S LOVER
MIDNIGHT'S SEDUCTION
MIDNIGHT'S WARRIOR
MIDNIGHT'S KISS
MIDNIGHT'S CAPTIVE
MIDNIGHT'S TEMPTATION
MIDNIGHT'S PROMISE
MIDNIGHT'S SURRENDER

THE DARK SWORD SERIES
DANGEROUS HIGHLANDER
FORBIDDEN HIGHLANDER
WICKED HIGHLANDER
UNTAMED HIGHLANDER
SHADOW HIGHLANDER
DARKEST HIGHLANDER

THE REAPERS E-NOVELLA SERIES
DARK ALPHA'S CLAIM
DARK ALPHA'S EMBRACE
DARK ALPHA'S DEMAND
DARK ALPHA'S LOVER
DARK ALPHA'S NIGHT
DARK ALPHA'S HUNGER
DARK ALPHA'S AWAKENING
DARK ALPHA'S REDEMPTION
DARK ALPHA'S TEMPTATION

HOME FOR A **COWBOY** CHRISTMAS

DONNA GRANT

St. Martin's Paperbacks

First published in the United States by St. Martin's Paperbacks, an imprint of St. Martin's Publishing Group

HOME FOR A COWBOY CHRISTMAS

For information, address St. Martin's Publishing Group, 120 Broadway, New York, NY 10271.

www.stmartins.com

ISBN: 978-1-250-82026-6

Our books may be purchased in bulk for promotional, educational, or business use. Please contact your local bookseller or the Macmillan Corporate and Premium Sales Department at 1-800-221-7945, ext. 5442, or by email at MacmillanSpecialMarkets@macmillan.com.

Printed in the United States of America

St. Martin's Paperbacks edition / November 2021

10 9 8 7 6 5 4 3 2 1

Chapter 1

Light flashed behind Emmy's eyelids, the rocking of the SUV lulling her. It was too bad she couldn't sleep. She was bone-weary. The kind of exhaustion that sapped every bit of good out of life.

"We're almost there."

She opened her eyes at the sound of Deputy US Marshal Dalton Silva's voice. Emmy straightened in her seat and glanced his way. Dalton wore a white Stetson that covered his short black hair. His deep brown eyes were solemn, intense as they met hers.

They had been on the road for over fourteen hours straight, backtracking and taking several different roads to throw off anyone who might try to track them. And someone would definitely come after them.

Emmy was sick of being in the vehicle, but it was the only thing between a future and certain death. So, who was she to complain?

"You should've let me drive more," she told Dalton. "You're worn-out."

"It's my job."

She drew in a deep breath and slowly released it as she looked out the passenger window to the scenic view. The sun shone in the clear blue sky, giving her a stunning view of the white-topped mountain range. A light dusting of snow had fallen overnight, but it was already melting under the bright rays of the sun.

If she had to hide, this was as good a place as any. She hadn't been too keen on Dalton's idea, but when backed against a wall, a person did everything they could to stay alive.

"It's just until after the first of the year," Dalton said as if reading her thoughts.

"They found me in three days this last time."

Dalton shifted in his seat and leaned his right elbow on the center console. "No one but me knows where you'll be."

No one should have known the times before, but they had. A chill raced down Emmy's spine when she thought of the gun barrel that had been pointed at her head. The feel of the cool metal against her skin, her would-be murderer's uneven breathing. Had Dalton not unexpectedly checked on her that night, she'd be dead.

"I'm going to find the leak," Dalton vowed in a voice rife with anger and unease. "I'm going to find them and put an end to things."

She swiveled her head to look at the marshal. "That may cost you your life."

"We're the good guys, Emmy. Or at least we're supposed to be. Whoever is leaking your information needs to be reminded of that. I'm no fool, though. I'll be careful."

She quirked a brow. "How do you plan to do any of that if you aren't returning to the office?"

It was one of the reasons she had agreed to this trip. After Dalton shot and killed the assassin sent after her, he had pulled her after him out of the hotel to his company vehicle and sped away. To her shock, Dalton had pulled into a parking garage and parked the car. They had jumped out and rushed away from the SUV. He then led her through the streets of Denver, telling her when to keep her head down and when to put her back to a camera so they couldn't be picked up. That took them to an old, beat-up truck with tinted windows.

He reached into the back of the cab and pulled out a black duffle bag, tossing it onto her lap and ordering her to look through it. There were hats and wigs of all styles inside. Emmy made her choice. Surprisingly, it made her feel somewhat shielded.

Dalton swapped his Stetson for a ball cap, pulling it low. Then they drove away, Denver in the rearview mirror. On the road, he laid out a reckless, wild plan to take her to Montana. First, they would travel east, then south, then west, and finally north to big sky country.

Emmy had no idea if the plan was good or not. All she wanted was to stay alive. Dalton had saved her life. Maybe she was naïve to believe that she could trust him, but she knew she wouldn't get very far on her own. So, she did everything he told her.

Every few hundred miles, they stopped at places he had other vehicles waiting. Inside each were three burner phones still in their packages. Dalton would open one, dial a number and simply push a button. Emmy later learned that those calls were to individuals who would make sure their previous vehicle disappeared. She didn't ask how. She didn't care if it meant that she lived to see another day.

She raised her brows, waiting for him to answer her question. Emmy knew if he returned to the marshals' office in Denver, it would only be a matter of time until someone figured out what he had done with her.

"Don't worry about me. I'm not stupid." He snorted and

shook his head. "I know it doesn't appear that way. I suppose I put too much trust in my fellow marshals, but now I'll be looking into everyone with a fine-tooth comb."

"Just don't get yourself killed. You're the only one I trust."

He shot her a crooked grin, his eyes filled with resolve. "I won't fail you. You have my word."

She forced a smile and looked straight ahead. She was apprehensive about her next stop, but she wouldn't be unarmed again. Dalton had given her a knife that she kept on her person. Would it be enough? Only time would tell.

The look of glee on the man's face when he came to kill her had chilled her blood. She had been sport to him, and people like that would never stop hunting her. And her enemies had plenty of time to track her down again.

Which meant a living Hell for Emmy. Time spent scared out of her mind and wondering when they would come for her.

"Dwight's place is the safest location for you. He's ex-FBI and Homeland Security. He'll know exactly how to keep you safe while I plug the leak."

Emmy hoped so. But if he didn't, then she had a plan of her own that included the weapons and one of the burner phones Dalton had given her so they could contact each other in case of emergency. She wouldn't be at anyone's mercy ever again. If she had to run and hide, then she would do it. Not only because she wanted to testify against her old client but also because she didn't ever want to feel as helpless and frightened as she had when death had come calling.

The SUV slowed, pulling Emmy from her thoughts. Dalton turned off the paved road. A fence ran for miles on either side of the drive, extending in all directions. The pastures were empty as the land undulated gently, adding to the already striking scenery.

"Riverlands is an eleven-thousand-acre ranch," Dalton

explained. "Dwight has cattle, horses, and even alpacas. Portions of the land are farmed for hay."

She licked her lips. "Sounds nice."

"It's been in his family for four generations."

Emmy grunted, no longer able to find words. She was so tired. Now she wished she had slept during the drive, but she'd wanted to be alert to aid Dalton during their escape.

When the two-story log cabin came into view, Emmy's heart started beating wildly. The closer they got to the house, the more she began to doubt Dalton's plan. The ranch was remote, but that wouldn't stop those coming for her. It would only put everyone at the ranch in harm's way.

Before she knew it, Dalton had put the SUV into park, but he didn't shut off the engine. He looked at her and covered her hands in her lap with one of his. "Do you trust me?"

She nodded.

"I trust Dwight."

God, how she hated this. Emmy swallowed, though it was difficult. She was about to reply when movement out of the corner of her eye caught her attention. She slid her gaze slightly to find a tall man walking out onto the porch to lean against one of the log columns. He wore a thick jacket and a black Stetson and held a steaming mug in his hand.

Dalton followed her gaze and nodded. "That's Dwight."

She couldn't see Dwight's face clearly, but she saw the clean-shaven lower half of it. If things were different, she would've been keenly interested to see the rest of him. Dwight lifted the mug to his lips and drank as if he had all the time in the world.

"I'll give you a few moments while I go speak with him," Dalton told her.

She quickly grabbed Dalton's arm before he could leave. "I do trust you. You saved my life, but . . ."

"I know," he said softly, understanding in his brown eyes.

"I've handled a lot of people in the witness protection program, but this is the first time anything like this has happened. My job is to ensure that you stay alive to testify, and I plan on being right beside you when we walk into that courtroom."

Emmy released him and sank back against the seat. "I'll be out in a moment."

Dalton exited the vehicle. A gust of cool air hit her as he closed the door behind him. She turned to look out her window and spotted a barn and a nearby pasture where a mare and her foal grazed. Emmy took in the valley and the mountains in the distance. She could just make out a waterfall. The tranquil beauty of it all brought a smile to her face.

Sooner or later, she would have to meet Dwight. This was where she would be for the foreseeable future. There was nowhere else. Dalton had asked for her trust, and she would give it to him.

Finally, after a deep breath, she opened the door and stepped onto gravel. She could sense the gazes of both men as they grew quiet. Her knees knocked a bit, but the feel of the knife and cell phone gave her courage. She lifted her chin and walked around the front of the vehicle to the porch steps.

Before she could greet her new host, a dog trotted toward her. She eagerly paused and bent over on the steps to pet the Australian Cattle Dog, noticing that his collar said: *Sam*. The instant her fingers slid into his mottled fur, a mixture of blue, black, and tan, she felt some of her stress dissipate. She liked his big, pointed ears and the solid black patch over his right eye, giving him a roguish look. The dog gazed at her with the most soulful dark eyes she had ever seen.

Until she looked up and found herself drowning in blue eyes that belonged to none other than Dwight Reynolds.

She forgot to breathe as she stared at him, taken aback by not only the color of his eyes but also the intensity in them.

Handsome didn't come close to describing the man before her. He had a rugged appeal, the kind that made people fall for cowboys, time and again. He was tall, and while his jacket hid his body, it couldn't hide his broad shoulders. She spotted dark brown hair between his hat and the collar of his jacket. She ran her gaze over his strong jawline and chin, his razor-sharp cheekbones, and a firm mouth that curved slightly at the corners.

"Ma'am," he said and tipped his hat to her.

This man wasn't playing cowboy. He was authentic, down to his drawl. Something about him made her want to hand him her troubles. Was it his deep voice? The drawl? It could be his gorgeous face or those penetrating eyes. Or maybe it was the ranch. She couldn't explain why—or when—her apprehension about Dalton's plan began to dissipate, but it did.

She forgot about the dog as she straightened and glanced at Dwight. "Hi."

"Emmy, this is Dwight Reynolds. Dwight, Emmy Garrett," Dalton introduced them. Then, to Dwight, he said, "I owe you for this."

"You don't owe me anything. I'm the one who owed you," Dwight corrected.

Emmy shivered and fought to keep her eyes open. If she let herself, she could've gone to sleep right then and there. It must have been noticeable because Dwight turned his blue eyes to her.

"Consider my home yours. Take your pick of rooms upstairs. Let me know if there's anything you need," he said.

"Thank you."

"You're safe here," he added, his look sincere, his manner honest.

Emmy nodded, drowning in his eyes. She believed him. She didn't know why, especially after everything she had been through. But she did.

Suddenly, she wanted nothing more than to be alone. She had kept everything inside while on the road with Dalton, but it was all about to boil over, and she didn't want an audience. She turned to the marshal. He opened his arms, and she went to him.

He briefly hugged her, whispering, "Keep the weapon and phone on you at all times."

She leaned back and looked into his dark eyes. "I will. Thank you."

"Everything is going to be all right."

She smiled, knowing the promise was an empty one. He had no idea what he was up against or how deeply the betrayal went in the marshals. "Be safe."

Dalton flashed her a smile. "Always."

Emmy licked her lips as she looked at Dwight. She wasn't sure why she kept looking at him. Maybe because there was a thin thread of hope that she might actually come out of this alive. He gave her a nod and another soft grin. She hadn't wanted to smile in days, but she found her lips softening in response.

Her body felt weighed down as exhaustion pulled at her, despite how good it felt to be in Dwight's presence. She forced her attention away from her good-looking host as she walked to the door. Once in the house, she was surprised to find the dog trotting beside her. She was mildly astonished that the home wasn't decked out with stuffed animal heads everywhere. In fact, it was tastefully decorated with paintings of running horses, other western themes, and historical black-and-white pictures from the Old West.

A quick glance showed a thick fur rug before the massive fireplace. The floor was wood, the sofas brown leather, but he had flashes of color in the red and cream rugs and pictures. The house had to be about four thousand square feet, but it felt homey.

A nudge against her leg reminded Emmy of the dog. She absently petted his head and thought about getting a look at the rest of the house, but her fatigue took precedence. When she saw the stairs, she walked to them with heavy feet. They seemed to go on forever as she climbed, showing four doors once she reached the top.

Emmy ended up taking the first on the right simply because of proximity. She barely made it into the room as it was. She glanced out the window that faced the mountain and saw the waterfall. The soothing blues of the room made her relax even more.

Emmy leaned against the wall and removed her boots, her eyes drifting closed. She cracked them open to set the footwear near the door, hoping she hadn't tracked any dirt into the house. The dog sat just outside the room, watching her. She gave him another rub behind his ears, then closed the door, locking it before shuffling to the bed. She sat down and let her shoulders droop.

Then the tears came.

She buried her face in her hands as she let the past fourteen hours wash over her.

Chapter 2

The last thing Dwight expected when he got up that morning was to have a voicemail from an old friend. He couldn't remember the last time he had heard from Dalton Silva. Dwight had listened to the succinct message several times, noting his friend's tense tone.

Dwight stayed close to the house since he wasn't sure when Dalton would arrive. He had been pouring coffee when Sam's head popped up from where he lay near the door. That alerted Dwight that someone was pulling up the drive. Less than two minutes later, the small tan SUV rolled to a stop.

With his coffee in hand, Dwight looked out the window and spotted his friend's profile. Dwight walked onto the porch. His interest piqued when he saw a woman in the vehicle with the marshal. After a few moments, Dalton exited the SUV.

His old friend hadn't changed much in the five years since they had last seen each other. Dalton's hair was shorter, and his face had a few more lines. Otherwise, he was the same. There was a genuine smile on his lips when he faced Dwight.

"It's good to see you," Dwight said as his friend walked

onto the porch. They shook hands, and there was no denying the relief in Dalton's eyes.

"You're a sight for sore eyes," Dalton said.

Dwight glanced inside the SUV to see the woman who had remained behind. Her blond hair was cut blunt to her shoulders. "You look like you've been on the road for some time."

"A little over fourteen hours." Dalton released a long, tired breath and glanced at the vehicle. "I'm in a world of shit. I hate to put you in this position, but I need help. *She* needs help."

"I've always told you, I'm here for whatever you need. What can I do?"

Dalton ran a hand down his face, his weariness coming through. "There's a leak in my department. The woman with me is set to testify against one of the biggest mob bosses in Denver. It was only by chance that I stopped by her hotel last night to check on her. I found a man with a gun against her head. The marshals who were supposed to be guarding her were nowhere to be seen."

"Damn. She's lucky."

"And scared shitless. This will be her fourth place. The department chose the three others. If there's even a chance she survives until the trial, I had to bring her somewhere no one would think to look."

Dwight took a drink of his coffee as he turned over everything he'd just learned. "You chose right. Were you followed?"

"I changed vehicles every few hours. I also went different directions to ensure no one could follow us."

Dwight quirked a brow. "But?" Dalton was too good at his job for there not to be a *but*.

"I'm going to keep driving. I'm headed to a safe house until the trial. If anything should happen, or if you can't keep her that long—"

"She can stay as long as needed."

Dalton parted his lips to say something just as the passenger door opened, and the woman stepped out. Dwight's gaze locked on her tall form. She wore a dark green sweater, light jeans that encased her long legs, and boots. With her short hair, it allowed him to see her long, graceful neck. Then she turned her head to face them.

Dwight was taken aback by her startling beauty. Large eyes the color of autumn leaves swept the area. Her lips were wide with just the right amount of plumpness. When that mouth of hers turned up in a smile as Sam went to her, it was like a punch in Dwight's gut. Then, she looked straight at him.

For a heartbeat, he forgot his name. And in that instant, he noticed two things—her vulnerability and her strength. Finally, he found his voice.

Her softly spoken, "Hi," was lilting. That's when he noticed the dark circles under her eyes. The protector in him immediately wanted to swoop in, but the wariness around her told him that now wasn't a good time.

Dalton introduced them. Dwight could've stared at her all day, but her shiver reminded him that she was without a coat. He motioned to the house, and she said a farewell to Dalton. All the while, Dwight stared at her, taking in every beautiful detail of his guest.

Then she looked at Dwight once more. He didn't know what prompted him to promise that she would be safe, but the minute the words were out of his mouth, she gave him a soft smile. It was so unexpected, so raw, that he could only stare like a tongue-tied teenager as she went inside the house with Sam at her side.

Dwight pulled in a shaky breath, trying to understand the emotions running rampant inside him. He swallowed and looked at his friend. Dalton continued staring at the door long after Emmy had gone inside. "She'll be fine here. I'll make sure of it."

"I know." Dalton ran a hand down his face in exhaustion.

"Why don't you stay for a bit? Eat and rest before you head out."

Before he'd even finished, Dalton was already shaking his head. "I'd love to, but I need to get back on the road."

"How about some coffee for the trip?"

"Now that, I'll take you up on."

To Dwight's surprise, Dalton didn't come inside. Dwight filled a thermos full of coffee and brought it to his friend.

"She hasn't slept in days," Dalton told him.

"Understandable."

Dalton moved the thermos from one hand to the other. "She's a kind soul, and she's stronger than she looks."

"We'll be fine. I'll take care of her. I promise. Right now, I'm a tad more worried about you."

"It makes me sick to my stomach to think someone would betray those in the marshal service."

Dwight nodded. "It might be more than one person. And it might go higher up in the chain than you want to consider."

"I've already thought of that. I can barely think of anything else between the leak and getting Emmy here."

"You've completed one job. Rest easy on that. That gives you time to focus on the other."

Dalton removed his hat and scratched his head before replacing the Stetson. "Getting her back will be another matter."

"We'll cross that bridge when we get to it."

"Right. Right." Dalton's dark eyes met his. "Thank you."

Dwight shook his head. "Like I said, I owe you."

"Then we're even."

They weren't even close as far as Dwight was concerned, but he'd save that argument for another time. "Is there anything else I can get you?"

Dalton shook his head. "I won't call unless there's an emergency."

"We'll do the same."

They shook hands again before Dalton got in the SUV and drove off. Dwight took a deep breath and entered the house. It was quiet. He went to the foot of the stairs and looked up, listening for sounds that Emmy was moving, but there was only silence. Hopefully, she was resting. He spotted Sam gazing down at him from the landing. Dwight chuckled at his dog, but he didn't blame him. If he were able, he'd be up there lying next to Sam, waiting to see if Emmy needed anything.

"I can't do that, though," he mumbled to himself.

Dwight retraced his steps and went to the kitchen, where he heated leftovers from the night before for lunch. He sat at the table and ate while looking out the window. When the meal was done, and his plate had been rinsed and put in the dishwasher, he made his way to the barn. He worked nonstop until evening.

When he returned to the house, Sam was still at the top of the stairs. The minute the dog saw him, he rushed down and out the doggie door. It wasn't long before Sam was back inside and up the stairs again, resuming his position.

"Looks like someone has a crush," Dwight said with a chuckle.

He took off his jacket and hat by the back door, hanging them on hooks. Then he went to the kitchen and washed his hands before taking out some steaks to cook. He wasn't sure if Emmy would be down, and since he knew she was tired, he wasn't going to knock on her door and disturb her if she was sleeping.

After dinner, he sat before the fire in the living room with a book in hand. No matter how hard he tried, he couldn't concentrate on the story. His mind kept going over everything

Dalton had told him. Whoever Emmy was testifying against was clearly ready to do whatever was necessary to remove her as a witness.

Dwight set aside his book and rose, heading to his office. He opened the laptop and checked the motion sensor cameras he had situated around the ranch. He'd put them up a few years earlier when he had some trouble with his alpacas going missing. He not only caught the culprits, but he also found that a mountain lion had set up a den not far from one of his barns.

He lived close to wildlife that, in his opinion, had just as much right to the area as he did. Unlike some ranchers, he didn't go out and kill the animals, but he did take steps to ensure that his livestock wasn't harmed. Sometimes, he was successful. Other times, he wasn't. But living where he did meant a delicate balance.

He had another five cameras in his office that he could put up, and now that Emmy was there, it was time he did just that. In fact, he wished he had better equipment. He couldn't go into town and get upgrades without causing a stir. Field Point had a population of only six thousand, and everyone knew everyone else's business.

The less attention he brought to himself—and therefore his ranch—was what he needed to keep in mind. A river separated his land from his neighbor's on the right. A gorge formed the border to his neighbor on the left. The mountains made up the rear of the property. But if someone wanted onto the ranch, they'd find a way.

Dwight raised his gaze to the ceiling. He hadn't heard any movement from above. If it weren't for Sam, he'd be worried that she had snuck out as he worked. Dwight pulled out the other five cameras and set them on his desk to deal with in the morning.

Since he couldn't focus on reading, he decided to take care

of some administrative work for the ranch. When he looked up again, it was almost ten. He pushed back from his desk and walked from the room. He locked the doors and turned off all the lights before heading to the master bedroom on the main floor. Sam's collar had a chip in it that allowed only him to go in and out of the doggie door, and Sam had access to that anytime he needed it.

Dwight left his door open a crack. Sam had slept with him since he was a puppy, but this might be the first night that didn't happen. Dwight wasn't angry, though. He found it endearing that his dog recognized that Emmy needed safeguarding.

After a hot shower to wash away the day's grime, Dwight slipped between the covers and lay down. His eyes wouldn't stay closed, however. He looked at the ceiling, all kinds of questions about Emmy and the people she was testifying against running through his head. He hadn't thought to ask Dalton about that—not that it mattered. Whoever these people were, they were criminals. The fact that the US Marshals Service had been brought in as protection for Emmy said how important her testimony was to the prosecution.

His thoughts turned from the criminals to Emmy and her brush with death. He had spent four years in the military before joining the FBI, then moving to Homeland Security. He had been trained for battle in various formats, but even though he hadn't had a gun stuck to his head, it had been traumatic. He could well imagine how it affected Emmy.

The way Dalton had spoken of the event, he had arrived mere seconds before the assassin pulled the trigger. No wonder Emmy was suspicious of everyone. Dwight was surprised she trusted Dalton. But Emmy had to rely on someone in a situation like this. It was good that she'd put her faith in Dalton.

Dwight knew what a good man he was. The lengths Dalton

had gone to in order to see Emmy safe proved that his friend's core morals hadn't changed over the years—though the leak within the department might color his vision a bit.

Dwight cleared his mind, intent on sleep. When minutes passed, and he found it difficult to shut down his thoughts, he threw an arm over his eyes. Not even that helped. He tossed and turned for hours. Finally, around two, he got up and walked the house. It had been years since he'd had such a sleepless night.

Sam came down the stairs and sat with him in the living room. Dwight got his book and read until he couldn't keep his eyes open anymore. As he made it back to his bed, he grinned when he heard Sam follow him in and then turn and head back upstairs.

The last thought Dwight had before falling asleep was that Emmy would be at the ranch for Christmas.

Chapter 3

The sound of birds chirping woke Emmy. She rolled over and saw that the sun was just breaking the horizon. Or was it lowering? She honestly didn't care. She lay on her back and stared at the ceiling as she slowly came awake.

It no longer felt as if her body were weighed down. She stretched and sat up. Spotting her jeans in a wadded pile on the floor, she vaguely remembered trying to take them off when she had gotten up to go to the bathroom connected to her room. She'd gotten tangled in the legs and had nearly fallen. Not far from her pants lay her sweater, socks, and the wig.

She pushed her fingers through her hair and yawned as the smell of bacon wafted through the air. Her stomach growled in response. Emmy tossed aside the covers and jumped out of bed. She hurried to dress before stopping in the bathroom to make sure her hair wasn't sticking out everywhere. She smoothed the wavy, tangled, frizzy locks as best she could, then went downstairs.

Except Dwight wasn't there. A plate of bacon and warm biscuits sat on the stove. Emmy grabbed a piece of bacon and wolfed it down, along with a biscuit. After three more strips of bacon, she poured herself some coffee and leaned against the counter, delighting in the food and caffeine.

She quite liked the kitchen. It meshed well with the openness of the house. The dark gray cabinets, white quartz countertops, and stainless-steel appliances were nice, but she was in love with the rectangular kitchen table that seated six. It looked like reclaimed wood, but she suspected it wasn't store-bought. It might, in fact, be heirloom.

Dalton had told her that the ranch had been in Dwight's family for generations, but someone had obviously taken it upon themselves to keep the inside of the house updated. She hadn't paid too much attention to her en suite bathroom since she had been half-asleep. She certainly would look more closely the next time she went upstairs.

She sniffed, wrinkling her nose. She needed a shower—just as soon as she finished stuffing her face with the delicious meal. As she munched on another perfectly cooked slice of bacon, she turned to look out the kitchen window toward one of the barns. Her gaze locked on Dwight as he opened the gate to the pasture with a bucket in one hand and a rope in the other.

The sorrel mare lifted her head when she heard the gate. When the horse saw Dwight, she started toward him, the sorrel foal with its white forehead star following quickly. Emmy was transfixed as she watched Dwight set down the bucket so the mare could eat. He spent time petting the horse while the colt remained close to its mother before venturing nearer to Dwight. He never put the lead on the foal, simply let it get used to him and the rope.

Emmy finished her coffee and rinsed the cup before putting it into the dishwasher. Then she searched the cabinets for some containers for the leftover food. Once it was in the fridge, she took one last look at Dwight and the horses before going upstairs.

That's when she saw the pile of clothes near her door. They had been on the opposite side so she hadn't spotted them when she went downstairs. There hadn't been time to pack anything when Dalton had spirited her from the hotel. Nor had they dared to stop for anything more than gas and food on their trip. But Dalton must have told Dwight that she didn't have anything—not even a jacket.

Emmy bent and lifted the clothes before taking them into her room. She used her foot to shut the door behind her. After setting the pile on the overstuffed chair, she made the bed so she could spread out the clothes.

There were two pairs of jeans in different sizes, three long-sleeved shirts, two plaid flannel button-downs, and a sweater. There were also socks and a thick coat. Emmy held the jeans up to her. They were on the short side, but they would do. In the meantime, she would wash her clothes, including her underwear.

She went to the bathroom and stripped. In the sink, she washed her bra and panties and left them to dry. Then she pushed back the shower curtain and turned on the water for a shower. Just like in the kitchen, Dwight had modernized the bathroom. It was nice without being overdone. The cabinets were navy, bringing in the blue from the bedroom. The granite counter was beige with flecks of brown, copper, and various blues. The floor was the same wood as throughout the house. Two of the walls were wood, but the other two were decorative stone.

Emmy sank her bare toes into the thick navy rug before the tub. She found towels rolled up in a basket. Another look around uncovered small bottles of shampoo, conditioner, and soap—just like in a hotel.

When the water was the right temperature, she got in and sighed as she stepped beneath the spray. She stretched her neck, rotating her shoulders to work out some of the knots that had formed. The heat from the water worked wonders.

She couldn't let her guard down completely. She might be in the middle of nowhere, but that didn't mean she couldn't be found. Still, she would enjoy this moment while she had it. Emmy poured the shampoo into her palm and then worked it through her strands, lathering. She washed her hair twice before letting the conditioner sit as she scrubbed her body four different times.

No matter how much she cleaned herself, she couldn't wash away the fear of her near-death experience or her escape from Denver. Emmy sighed and rinsed her body and hair. When she turned off the water and pulled back the curtain, steam filled the room. But she felt much better after the shower.

Drying off, she wrapped the towel around herself and then twisted her lips at her underwear. She didn't want to put them on wet, but the thought of going without wasn't an option. That's when she looked beneath the sink and found a blow-dryer. A smile graced her face as she plugged it in and alternated between drying her panties and bra and her hair.

Her underwear dried quickly. She opted to layer the long-sleeved shirt and the sweater. It helped to hide the fact that she wasn't wearing a bra. The socks warmed her icy feet. She then tried on the longer of the two pairs of jeans. They were a little tight around the waist and stopped well above her ankles, but they would do. She shook her head as she looked down. She'd always had trouble finding jeans for her long legs.

She put on her boots that were fine for walking on city streets but wouldn't do much good out on a ranch. But, they were shoes. Next, she gathered the dirty clothes and went to the laundry room that she'd seen downstairs. Once the clothes were in the washer, she dusted off her hands and looked around.

"Now what?" she asked herself.

She walked to the kitchen window, hoping Dwight was still with the mare, but he was gone. She moved from window to window, scanning the area for some sign of him. Emmy debated whether to go outside and look for him. She felt safe within the house, and that wasn't something she'd expected. Because of that, she wasn't too keen on leaving it just yet.

"All right," she said with a sigh as she turned to the house. "If I'm going to stay here, then I'll pull my weight however I can."

The problem was, the house was already tidy. And she wouldn't know where to put anything anyway. She found a duster after a brief search and brandished it in triumph. She didn't particularly enjoy cleaning, but she hated being idle more.

"Housework it is," she declared.

Emmy started in the living room, where she wiped down every picture, every piece of art, and every table. Then she stood before the two large bookcases filled with books of all genres and subjects. She had to use a chair to reach the top. She carefully removed each book and wiped it down before replacing it.

As she got to her feet after finishing the first bookshelf, her head turned at the sound of a flap closing. The dog rushed her, tail wagging and tongue lolling. She squatted down to pet him. That's when the door opened, and Dwight filled the entrance.

Their gazes locked for a brief moment before his eyes went to her hair. Emmy touched it, wondering what was wrong, then she recalled the wig.

"This is me," she said about her dark waves.

"I like it better than the blond."

He closed the door and removed his hat and coat to hang on the hooks near the entrance. Only then did he turn back to her. This was the first time she had seen him without his hat, and it left her breathless.

It wasn't just his blue eyes that seemed to pull her in. Her gaze followed his hand as it raked through the long strands of his dark brown hair then shoved it out of his face. The sun had bronzed his skin, and small lines graced his lips and eyes. His mouth was wide, a bit too full, but damn if she didn't like it. His nose had a bump on the bridge, letting her know that it had been broken at least once.

She had thought her sleep-deprived mind might have made him more handsome than he really was, but it was clear that Dwight Reynolds was, in fact, gorgeous.

"I was beginning to wonder if you would ever wake."

Emmy swallowed, jarred out of her thoughts by his deep voice. "How long did I sleep?"

"Two full days."

She raised her brows in surprise. "I had no idea."

"I see you found breakfast."

"The smell woke me," she said as she straightened and wrinkled her nose. "Apparently, I was starving."

He nodded, his gaze lowering to the dog. "Sam's quite taken with you. He stayed outside your door most of the time."

Her heart melted as she smiled down at the dog and gave him another rub on his head. "I have to admit, I'm quite taken with him, as well."

"I said it before, but it bears repeating. You're safe here. I have cameras around the ranch to help me keep track of wildlife and would-be thieves. I put up another five the morning after you arrived. I'll show you how to view them from the laptop in my office. You need to feel safe, and being able to see everything will help with that."

She had seen his office but hadn't dared to venture inside. "I appreciate it."

"I'll show you after dinner, if that's all right."

"That's fine," she said with a nod. He was going out of his way to make her feel comfortable. She hadn't expected that, but she was grateful.

Dwight walked to the kitchen sink and washed his hands. As he dried them, he turned to her. "You don't have to clean."

"I don't feel right doing nothing."

"You can do whatever you want. I don't want you to think you have to do anything. When you're ready, I'll show you around the property. I have a handful of people working for me, but I'm keeping them away from the house for now. If they come near, I'll let you know so you can stay inside. But, Emmy, you aren't a prisoner."

She shifted her feet, uncomfortable with the turn of the conversation. How could she explain to him that those after her had put her in exactly that position? She decided to just let it be for now. "I know."

"I don't think you do, but I hope you come to see me as a friend. I'm sure Dalton told you about my job history. I'm capable of protecting you and keeping you out of harm's way."

"It's not that I don't think you're capable. These people will stop at nothing to ensure I don't testify. They've proven that."

Dwight twisted his lips as he tossed the towel onto the counter. "Dalton went to great lengths to make sure that no one could track either of you. He didn't tell me where he was going, and I didn't want to know. The property is pretty isolated. There are ranches on either side of ours, and a mountain between us and the town. Also, getting there takes thirty minutes to an hour, depending on the inclement weather that pops up. With the snow already here, not too many people will be driving over the mountain who don't have homes here. It's a dangerous road unless you know it."

Emmy looked out the window at the clouds dotting the sky. The snow had already melted from when she arrived, but it was November. And there were acres of land and miles of highway between her and Denver. Did she dare to think that she might be safe? That she might make it to the first of the year? Returning to Denver would be another matter entirely, but she hadn't thought she would live to see that, so she hadn't thought too much about it at all.

Until now.

"Hungry?"

Her head swung back to Dwight. She couldn't seem to look away from his blue eyes. They were magnetic, hypnotic. Mesmerizing. They made her unsteady, as if he could see straight into her soul. Emmy blinked and yanked her gaze away, shaken by her thoughts.

His stare caused her to realize that she hadn't answered his question. She thought back and remembered his query. "Yes. I could eat."

"Sandwich okay?"

She started toward the kitchen. "It is. Can I help?"

He shook his head without looking at her and went about making the sandwiches. Emmy looked around nervously, fidgeting with the duster. She hated awkward situations. What could she say? What should she do?

She hastily returned the duster to where she had found it and reentered the kitchen to wash her hands. With nothing else to do, she pulled out a chair at the table and sat. Try as she might, she couldn't make herself look anywhere but at Dwight Reynolds. The man was . . . mouthwateringly gorgeous.

"Cheese?" Dwight asked.

It was one of her favorite things to eat. "Yes, please. Whatever you have. I like it all."

"Mayo? Mustard?"

"I'm good with whatever."

He looked at her over his shoulder and grinned. "Both, huh?"

She returned his smile. "My father loved mayonnaise. My mother loved mustard. They switched off who made my lunches in the morning, so I got used to both."

"Interesting," he mumbled and went back to preparing the sandwiches.

In no time, he set a plate in front of her. He opened the pantry doors and retrieved a bag of barbecue chips and Cheetos and raised a brow, silently asking which she preferred. Emmy pointed to the Cheetos. He grinned and handed her the bag before sitting down.

They ate in silence for a time. It was something Emmy was used to. When she had been put into WITSEC, there was always at least one marshal near her. She ate some meals by herself, others with the marshals.

"Thank you for the clothes," she said, just remembering.

He swallowed as he nodded. "It isn't much, sorry. Dalton told me you didn't have a bag. I can get you anything else you need. Those are my sister's. She comes by a couple of times a year. It won't seem odd at all for me to be buying things for a woman since I do it for her."

Emmy broke a cheese snack in half. "Actually, there are a couple of things I need."

"Make a list. I can go into town for them."

"Thank you. I'll pay you back as soon as I have access to my funds again."

He waved away her words. "Don't worry about any of that."

She was tired of talking about herself. "What's your sister's name?"

"Victoria."

"What does she do?"

Dwight smiled. "She's the vice president of a bank in Billings."

"You're proud of her."

"I am," he admitted with a grin. "We've had our issues, as all siblings do, but we're really close. It's too bad she can't come in while you're here. I think the two of you would get along great."

Emmy glanced at her plate as she laughed. "Please tell her I appreciate the loan of her clothes."

"If Vic were here, she'd buy you an entire wardrobe. She's a giver. If she hears someone needs something, she'll give them that and more." He jerked his chin to the kitchen. "She's the one who helped me with the remodel. It was taking me longer than I wanted, trying to handle it all myself. One day, I came in from the barn, and she was here with all kinds of samples so I could figure out what I wanted. Then she ordered it and set up installation."

"She sounds amazing."

"She is, but don't ever tell her I told you that," he said with a grin.

Chapter 4

He had to get ahold of himself. Dwight had seen Emmy's beauty when he first met her, but now, after she had rested and sat smiling at him, he was utterly enamored. Her shoulder-length caramel waves framed her face with the right amount of seduction and allure. The dark circles under her eyes were gone, and her smile made his heart skip a beat.

It had been a while since he'd had a woman, but his attraction took him aback. It was visceral, primal.

Unrelenting.

Dwight inwardly shook himself. He had to get control. And quick.

"I, uh, I do want to help out while I'm here. I'd offer to cook, but, trust me, you'd regret it. I freely admit that I know nothing about cooking. I was never interested in it, no matter how much my mother tried to teach me. The few times I tried were disastrous."

He fought not to smile at her heartfelt words. "Thanks for the warning. I have no problem cooking."

"I'll do everything else, though," she added. "Clean. Wash. Whatever."

"That's kind of you, but you don't need to."

A pained expression came over her delicate features. "But I do. If I'm not busy, then I think about what happened in Denver. I think about them coming for me. I *need* to stay busy."

He nodded, seeing the truth in her pale brown depths. "All right. There's a hamper in the master if you wish to do some laundry. I live here alone, so I don't make much of a mess."

"Thank you," she said with a grateful smile.

They went back to eating, silence once again reigning. When he finished, Dwight rose and brought his plate to the sink. He started to rinse it when Emmy cleared her throat behind him. He set the plate in the sink and turned to her with a smile.

"If you'll get me that list, I'll head into town. There's a big storm coming in tomorrow evening. I'd rather not chance being on the road if it hits early."

"Of course." Emmy rose.

Dwight took the magnetic pad of paper stuck to the fridge along with a pen and handed it to her. As she wrote down what she needed, Dwight noted that Sam watched her intently.

"Here," she said, not meeting his gaze as she handed the paper to him.

He read it over, noting that she had put brand names beside the things she needed. It wasn't until he came to the last two items that he found himself looking at her.

She wrinkled her nose. "Maybe it would be better to buy those online?"

"It'll be easier to get them in town."

"You sure?"

He smiled. "Do you have any particular colors or anything?"

"It doesn't matter. Whatever you find."

Dwight folded the paper and put it into his wallet. He wrote his cell phone number on the pad and put it back on the fridge before walking to the hooks to put on his coat and hat and then reaching for his keys hanging nearby. "My number is there if you need to call. Lock the door behind me. Sam will stay with you. I shouldn't be longer than two hours. If I'm held up, I'll call the house and leave a message."

"Thank you."

It had been a really long time since he had felt the need to protect the way he did with Emmy. He gave her a nod and walked from the house to his truck in the garage. Once he'd backed out and was on the road, he called his sister.

"Hey," Vic answered cheerfully. "You don't usually call until evening. What's going on?"

"Nothing is going on."

"Right. Spit it out," she stated.

He hesitated for a moment. "I need a favor."

"Of course. What do you need?"

"I . . . well, I need to buy women's panties."

There was a beat of silence before Victoria burst out laughing.

Dwight rolled his eyes as he made his way up the mountain. "Let me know when you're finished."

At his comment, she laughed even harder.

It took another full minute before she calmed herself. "Sorry," she said, but he could hear the smile in her voice. "I was unprepared for that statement. Took me completely off guard."

"Mm-hmm," he murmured.

"Want to fill me in on why you need to buy such things?"

He wrinkled his nose because he'd known she would ask that. "I can't get into details. I'm doing a favor for someone in a bind."

"Does this someone in a bind have a name?"

"Emmy."

"Oh," Vic said, drawing out the word. "What a pretty name. Is she pretty, as well?"

Dwight clenched the steering wheel. "She's fucking gorgeous."

"Ah. She must be for you to admit it in such a way."

"Don't even think about matchmaking, Vic. This isn't the time."

She snorted loudly. "There is always time for that."

"Not when her life is on the line."

"Damn. So, I take it this favor is from your old days."

"Yeah," Dwight answered.

Victoria sighed, all the teasing gone from her voice as she said, "Tell me what details you can."

"She came with nothing but the clothes on her back. I let her borrow some of yours, but the pants are a bit short."

"She needs a little of everything, then."

"That she does."

Victoria was silent for a heartbeat. "Okay. How about this? Get a few of the basics that she's asked for, but also send me the list. I'll buy some things here and then drive down in a couple of days. It's a good time for me to visit."

"That's a lie. You've got that big client coming in that you need to prepare for over Christmas."

"True, but I'm ahead on things. And it's nothing for me to take a long weekend. Besides, it might do Emmy good to have another female around."

"Maybe you can get her to leave the house."

"It's that bad, is it?" Victoria asked.

Dwight reached the top of the mountain and rounded the curve to begin the descent. "It is. I can't share anything over the phone. You need to make sure you don't repeat any of this."

"I can't believe you just said that," she snapped. "Of course, I won't. Now, tell me. How do my tops fit her?"

"Okay, I guess. Maybe a little small. It's the jeans I noticed."

"Was it only the length in the pants?"

Dwight tried to think back. "I believe so."

"I'll get a few different things. It's not a big deal to return anything. How far are you from town?"

"About another twenty minutes."

"I've got to head into a meeting in a sec. I gather she's going to need some panties for the next few days. Don't get her granny panties."

He was appalled at the words. "Is there such a thing?"

"God, yes," she said. "Get her a three-pack of cotton bikinis. Did she ask for bras?"

Dwight tried not to think of her breasts. "Yes."

"Do I need to go over that?"

"I'm not an idiot. I have dated, you know. I can figure it out."

Victoria laughed. "Let's hope so. I'll start shopping tonight and be there in a couple of days.

"You're the best, sis."

"And don't you forget it," she said with a smile. "Love you, big brother."

"Love you," he replied before disconnecting.

By the time Dwight reached town, he felt better about the entire situation. He pulled into the lot and parked. Inside, he grabbed a buggy and went straight for the women's section. He pulled out the list, snapped a picture of it, and sent it to Victoria. Then he got the package of panties his sister had told him to. The bras were another matter entirely.

He'd had no idea there were so many styles and colors. It wasn't as if he paid much attention when he walked past them. He went up and down the aisles, trying to imagine which ones Emmy would want.

His phone dinged, alerting him to a text. As if his sister could read his mind from miles away, she wrote: BEIGE AND BLACK BRAS ARE BASIC.

He sent a quick thanks and began looking for Emmy's size in those two colors. There were still different styles to choose from, but the narrowing down of colors helped tremendously. Once he'd chosen those items, he hurried to pick up the other things he knew Emmy would need immediately.

Thirty minutes later, he was back in his truck and on his way home. He paused, realizing that it had been years since he had been in such a hurry to get back.

Chapter 5

Emmy stood in the doorway of the master bedroom and looked inside with Sam beside her. The same rock that accented her bathroom walls had been used to create the fireplace. Massive, exposed beams ran along the ceiling, creating depth and giving the room dimension. A cream rug with vibrant colors through its design covered the wood floor. The king-sized bed sat against one wall with its tall headboard and simple, off-white comforter.

But it was the wall of windows showing off the picturesque mountains that caught her attention. She moved slowly into the bedroom to the two chairs and small table set before the windows. The leather chairs looked comfortable, but she didn't want to sit and put her back to such grandeur.

Having lived in Denver her entire life, she was used to mountains—or so she thought. This view was breathtaking.

She forced herself to turn away from the windows and looked for the door to the bathroom. Her mouth dropped open when she saw it. The floor had been covered in various-sized travertine tiles. One wall was wood with two darker wood vanities. The counters were a deep gray and black quartz with white rectangular sinks.

The shower was an open-concept design with rocks of various dark colors. There was even a rock seat in the stall, along with a rain showerhead above and two other showerheads on either side. She turned and spotted the freestanding soaking tub on the opposite wall with a leather chair next to it. And next to it was the hamper. Emmy glanced into the tub, thinking how great it would feel to relax in there with a glass of wine. Then her gaze moved to the shower as she wondered which showerhead Dwight preferred.

The minute that thought went through her mind, she grabbed the wicker hamper and carried it to the laundry room as Sam trotted beside her. But if she thought that would get her mind off Dwight, she was wrong. Lifting out each piece of clothing only made her think of him more.

Somehow, she got through it and tossed her load into the dryer as she put his in the washer. She turned it on, then quickly went back to dusting the other bookshelf. Sam lay down before the fireplace and rested his head on his paws as he watched her.

When she finished, she put away the duster and went to the sofa, sinking into it, surprised that it was so comfortable. Sam walked to her and stared until she patted the couch for him to jump up.

"I hope you're allowed up here," she told him. "If you aren't, I'm blaming you."

In response, the dog plopped down beside her and rested his head in her lap. Emmy ran her fingers through his soft fur. She loved dogs. She had always wanted one, but her schedule had never allowed it. She didn't think it fair to leave a dog inside an apartment all day. Now, however, she was getting her fill of having a dog—and she feared she would never be without one again.

Her lids grew heavy. Emmy didn't fight to keep her eyes open. She leaned her head back while continuing to pet Sam. She found herself comforted. As she lay there contemplating the peace she felt, she realized that it wasn't just one thing. It wasn't just the ranch. It wasn't just Sam. It wasn't just Dwight. It was a combination of all three, and it had somehow eased the huge stress ball she'd been carrying around.

Of course, catching up on sleep had helped. Yet, that was only a portion of it. Her mental state hadn't been good since she had gone to the district attorney with what she knew. She could've stayed quiet. Could've kept what she knew to herself and allowed a murderer to go free. But she never would've been able to live with herself.

So, she had made the decision to go to the DA. They had immediately put her into witness protection. No one should've known about her, but given the laws that said the state prosecutors had to turn over all evidence to the defense, she was hunted almost immediately.

Sam's head suddenly jerked up. Emmy opened her eyes and looked at the dog. His head was turned toward the door, his ears perked. After a moment, he leapt from the sofa and hurried through the doggie door. Emmy rose and followed him to peer out the window. She saw Sam on the edge of the porch, his tail wagging as Dwight's truck pulled into view.

She watched Dwight as he parked the truck in the garage, then climbed out with some bags in hand. As he drew closer to the porch, she unlocked the door and opened it for him. He wore a smile in greeting.

"Good thing I went when I did. The storm is moving in quicker than expected," he told her.

Emmy shivered at the cool air that followed him inside. She quickly closed the door behind him and trailed him into the kitchen, where he set the bags on the table. "Thank you for this."

"It was no trouble at all."

She wasn't so sure about that, but she wouldn't argue. She was just grateful to have more underwear. After she dug through each bag, she took out the pack of panties and opened them. Five wasn't a lot, but they would do.

"I'm going to go put these in to wash. I think your load of clothes is finished anyway."

He nodded as he shrugged out of his coat.

Emmy got her clothes out of the dryer and folded them. Then she switched Dwight's from the washer to the dryer and started it. Her panties were the next to load. Once they were in to wash, she returned to the kitchen to find that Dwight had taken everything from the bags, including the two bras he'd bought.

"I hope those are okay," he said, glancing at the garments. "If not, I can return them."

"They'll do perfectly," she replied with a smile.

Emmy had never been embarrassed about underwear, but something about having a man buy her bras unsettled her. It almost seemed . . . erotic. Or maybe she was so crazed from nearly dying that she had, in fact, lost her mind. Why else would thinking about bras be stimulating?

"Are you all right?" Dwight asked with a frown.

Emmy swallowed, the sound loud to her ears. "Yes. I'm fine."

"You're flushed."

"Just my thoughts getting away from me."

His frown deepened as he studied her. Finally, he relented. "How were things while I was away?"

"Quiet," she answered. "Sam stayed with me. I have to say, your master bedroom and bath are stunning."

That made his lips soften into a grin. "Vic kept telling me

that the bedroom needed to be an oasis, of sorts, and that I should go all out."

"Did you?"

He chuckled and shook his head. "No. I did take some of her suggestions, though."

They stared at each other, the awkwardness making Emmy nervous. She gathered her items. "I think I'll take these upstairs."

"I'm going to get back to work then."

He grabbed his coat and went outside. Sam looked between her and Dwight before bolting out the doggie door to follow his master. Emmy smiled after the duo before continuing up the stairs. She set her things in the bathroom on the counter then went back downstairs and got a couple of the plastic bags. She didn't have any luggage. Her next best thing would be bags to haul everything in when she left.

She had to chuckle to herself. Not too long ago, she hadn't believed that she would live even this long. Now, she was actually thinking about making it to the beginning of the year. She still had a long way to go, but maybe Dalton's words had sunk into her hard head. Maybe she had a real chance of staying hidden on the ranch.

The image of the gun barrel two inches from her face flashed in her mind. In an instant, the calming thoughts were gone, and terror filled her once more, her anxiety shooting through the roof. She backed herself into a corner and wrapped her arms around herself before slowly sliding to the floor.

"I'm safe," she whispered. "I'm safe, and the gunman is dead."

Dalton had made her say those words over and over as they sped out of Denver. They hadn't worked then, and they weren't working now. She buried her face in her hands and tried not to cry, but it was useless. The tears came in a flood.

She sobbed, her shoulders shaking. She didn't understand how she could have been fine and then knocked on her ass with fear again.

She had no idea how long she sat crying before the tears finally dried. But the panic didn't subside. She took several deep, calming breaths that helped, but the thought of leaving the bathroom was too much for her to even consider.

Emmy remained in the corner with her legs drawn up to her chest and her mind sorting through all kinds of thoughts—few of them good. She was back to the panic that had clamped its cold, bony hands around her when the man had busted into her hotel room and pulled the gun. She closed her eyes and recalled how he'd forced her to her knees.

How he'd smiled in triumph as he said, "You forgot where your loyalties lie."

Her heart had jumped into her throat. Time had slowed, her life flashing before her eyes as she realized that she hadn't done any of the things she had wanted to do. There had always been one reason or another to put them off. It became crystal-clear how much of her life she had allowed to pass her by. And it was all going to end.

All she could think about was whether she would feel the bullet enter her brain before she died.

She heard sniffing and a soft whine that pulled her out of her musings. Then she heard the soft thud of footfalls as Dwight walked up the stairs. Sam's nails clattered on the hardwood as he moved out of the way onto the rug that ran the length of the hall.

Dwight knocked softly. "Emmy? Dinner's ready."

Dinner? How long had she been up here, lost in the fear?

Sam pawed at the door, whining again. She wanted to get up and open it because she knew if she put her arms around the dog, she'd feel much better. But she couldn't move.

"Emmy?" Dwight called again, a thread of worry in his

voice. "Can you let me know if you're okay? Sam wants in bad. He's acting like he needs to get to you. Do you mind if I let him in?"

"Please," she forced the word as fresh tears came.

She watched the knob turn and the door open just enough for Sam to squeeze in. He rushed to her. He didn't lick her face, didn't try to climb on her. He simply stood beside her and let her wrap her arms around him as she pressed her cheek against his fur and cried. Sam inched closer, and she held him tighter.

The tears quickly passed this time, and just as she had known, her breathing calmed. No longer did she feel as if she were back in the hotel room, about to die. Sam had helped to steady her. He had reminded her that she was somewhere else.

"Thank you," she whispered to the dog.

She sniffed and lifted her face. He turned his head to her and started panting. The parting of his lips made it look as if he were grinning at her. Emmy couldn't help but smile back.

"You're an amazing dog, Sam. Thank you."

He nudged his cold, wet nose against her cheek and lay down before her. She climbed to her feet and washed her face. When she looked at herself in the mirror, she was able to stare back at her reflection without flinching.

She turned to Sam. "Ready? I think Dwight is going to want some answers."

Sam jumped up and trotted to the door before looking back at her, waiting patiently. Emmy walked to the door and opened it. The dog bolted downstairs, but she took a moment for another deep breath before following him.

Chapter 6

Dwight kept looking up the stairs, waiting and wondering. He knew what had happened to Emmy, but he wasn't sure she did. At least, she had allowed Sam to enter. He'd dealt with his own post-traumatic stress, and Sam had been a part of his healing. The dog had an uncanny sense of when someone suffered from the disorder.

He kept the food warm, hoping Emmy would be up for a meal. Dwight finished checking the Brussel sprouts he had in the oven, and when he looked down, Sam was there, his tongue lolling and his tail wagging. When Dwight didn't immediately give him any food, Sam looked toward the stove, then back at Dwight.

"You're too damn smart for your own good," he told the dog and cut him a small slice of chicken.

Sam wolfed it down, then turned his head toward the stairs. Dwight followed his gaze to find Emmy.

He smiled, noting the strain around her eyes. "Hungry?"

"I am, yes. Sorry to keep you waiting."

"Don't worry about that. Grab a plate and come help yourself. There's lemon-rosemary chicken, garlic-roasted Brussel sprouts, and a salad. I tried to cook healthy. Wasn't sure what kind of food you like."

She grinned at him as she approached with a plate. "The bad kind. Cheeseburgers, hot wings, potato wedges, and the like."

"Wish I would've asked sooner," he said.

"This smells delicious. I'm not against healthy food, but it's easier to get the other kind."

He watched her put the food on her plate. "Maybe in the city. Not so much out here. If I want pizza, I have to drive into town."

"You should get your own pizza oven. I hear that's a thing now."

He rolled his eyes. "Please don't ever mention that to my sister. She's been threatening to buy me one for a year now."

"Why are you against it?"

"Because all I'd eat is pizza."

Emmy laughed. The sound was light. Breezy. And completely caught him off guard. Dwight found himself staring at her, unable to look away. He had to physically force himself to turn around. Even then, he was aware of her, of her every movement. He fixed his plate, barely paying attention to what he was doing.

He sat across from her at the table. Her light brown eyes regarded him silently. The color resembled that of a fawn's coat. Her thick, caramel-colored waves tumbled around her shoulders. He wondered if she knew how incredibly sexy her hair was. Did she spend hours getting it to look like that? Somehow, Emmy didn't strike him as that kind of woman. Which meant that her hair was in its natural state.

Suddenly, he wanted to touch it, to run his fingers through it.

"Thank you," she said.

He blinked, jerking back to the present. "For what?"

"For not asking me what happened upstairs."

Dwight grabbed his fork and put a sprout into his mouth as he shrugged. He swallowed before saying, "That's partly because I don't need to ask. Though you probably aren't aware of it since the incident just happened, you're suffering from PTSD. And it's perfectly normal after someone tries to kill you."

She looked down at her plate, moving the Brussel sprouts around. "The . . . whatever that was upstairs . . . came out of nowhere."

"And they will. Sam helped me with mine."

Her eyes snapped to his. "Yours?"

"Few in the military don't have PTSD. Compound that with my time in the FBI as well as Homeland Security, and you can well imagine how bad it can get. People don't have to be in the military or do the jobs I've done to have PTSD. It occurs for any number of reasons. As you've discovered. Sam was always aware when I had an attack. He helped me through it. The way he was acting to get to you told me you needed him."

Emmy licked her lips. "I did. I wanted to get up and open the door, but I couldn't."

"If you'll allow him, Sam will do wonders to help."

"I felt it today with him. I was in a good place. I even felt safe. Then . . ."

She trailed off and looked away. But she didn't need to finish. Dwight knew what she was thinking about. He said no more as he went back to eating. After a few seconds, she did as well. The silence wasn't hard to bear, but Dwight wished he had something to fill it if for no other reason than to help put Emmy at ease. But he needn't bother since Sam stood beside her, his head resting on her lap as he looked adoringly up at her.

"He's an unforgiveable beggar. It's my fault," Dwight admitted. "I can't say no to those eyes of his. And he knows it."

"I can't say no to him, either," she said with a smile as she gazed at the dog.

With the meal done, Dwight rose and began clearing the dishes. Emmy was suddenly beside him, gently taking them from his hands.

"I'll do them," she said.

He relented and backed up a few steps to give her better access to the sink. While she took care of the dishes, he put the leftovers into containers to be eaten later. Then Dwight stood at the back door and held out a jacket for her.

She eyed him. "Are we going somewhere?"

"The porch. It's a little chilly, but it's still nice. I won't be able to say that in the morning."

Emmy slipped on the coat while Dwight zipped up his jacket. He opened the door and waited for her to go ahead of him. Once outside, he moved around her and motioned for her to follow him to the side of the house that had the best views of the mountains. It also happened to be the side the master was on. An L-shaped outside couch with tall heaters on either side awaited them.

"Oh, wow," she murmured when she saw the seating area.

He turned on the heaters then rubbed his hands together. "If these aren't enough, there are blankets."

She sat and stared out at the mountains. The sun was gone, but a little light remained. Soon, the moon would rise and bathe the mountains in its bluish light. Dwight observed her expression of surprise, appreciation, and admiration of the beauty that was Montana.

"This is incredible. If I were you, I'd be out here every night," she said, never taking her gaze from the view.

Dwight smiled as he sat down. "I'm out here more often than not. Especially in the mornings with the sunrise."

"Even in winter?" she asked, finally looking his way.

"All seasons. I don't claim to stay out long when the temperatures dip too low, but there is something about looking at that view that reminds me why I live here."

She nodded slowly. "I can understand that. I'm used to mountains having grown up in Denver, but this place far exceeds it."

"You're comparing a city to the country. Two different beings."

"You say that as if they're alive."

He shrugged, twisting his lips. "In a way, they are."

"And you prefer the country."

Dwight looked out over his land. "Growing up, I couldn't wait to get out and see the world. I've been all over. Seen the largest cities, visited the tiniest towns. Then I came home. What I realized was that I'm not trying to catch up with everyone else here. On this land, tending the ranch, I'm in step with the universe. Everything makes sense." He swung his gaze to her. "Now, I'm not saying there aren't hardships because there are. A lot of them. More than I like to admit. Cities have conveniences, but what I have here far outweighs any of that."

"When I had my attack tonight, do you know what I remembered?"

He was shocked that she'd brought it up. "What?"

"When the man forced me to my knees, and I realized he was going to kill me, it hit me that I hadn't done any of the things on my list."

"List?" Dwight asked with a frown.

She shrugged and snuggled deeper into her coat. "I have a list of places I want to visit, things I want to do, food I want to try. Call it a bucket list, if you like."

"I see," he replied with a nod.

"I'd been making that list since before college. During

that moment before death, I realized that I hadn't marked one thing off that list. That's not how I wanted to live my life."

"You have a second chance now."

She smiled softly before looking back at the mountain. "Once the trial is over."

"There's no need to wait that long."

Emmy shot him a dubious look. "And what's that supposed to mean?"

"We've got weeks before Dalton comes to take you to the trial. I'm sure you recall some of what's on that list. Tell me. Let's see if we can do a few things."

"Really?"

"Really."

Her gaze softened. "I've never met a man like you, Dwight Reynolds."

"You just needed to get out of the city."

She laughed again. Dwight loved the sound. All he wanted to do was keep making her laugh.

Chapter 7

Snow fell in thick sheets when Emmy looked out her bedroom window the next morning. She showered and dressed in a new pair of panties and bra. She chose her jeans, another long-sleeved shirt, and a plaid flannel. Once her socks and boots were on, she went downstairs. This time, she woke early enough that Dwight was still in the kitchen.

"Morning," he said with a bright smile and surprise in his blue eyes.

She grinned. "Morning. That's a lot of snow."

"Yes, it is. I'll spend most of the day in my office, catching up on paperwork."

"Anything I can do? And before you answer, remember how I said I like to stay busy."

He chuckled before drinking his coffee. "There is some filing that needs to be done."

"I'm sure there is a lot more, but we'll start with filing."

"There are blueberry muffins," he said with a nod to the plate next to the stove.

Emmy's eyes widened. "You bake, too?"

"I can, but I prefer not to. I bought those yesterday when I went into town."

She laughed and made her way to the muffins. "I was about to say that you must not be real if you baked those."

"Is it so odd for men to bake?"

"Not at all. But you're different."

His dark brows drew together. "Why is that?"

"You're a rancher, a warrior, a cook, and a bodyguard for me. That's a lot more than most people have in their entire lives. It seemed too unfair to add baker to that list, as well."

Emmy was rather surprised at how chatty she was that morning. Whatever the reason, she enjoyed it. She grabbed a still-warm muffin and took it, along with a mug of coffee, to the table to eat. The instant she sat, Sam was there, begging for any scraps that might find their way to him.

"Do you have family back in Denver?" Dwight asked.

Emmy shook her head. "I was an only child. My father passed of a heart attack when I was sixteen. I lost my mom a few years ago when a drunk driver crashed into her car."

"I'm so sorry. No extended family? Aunts? Uncles?"

"Two aunts on my father's side, but they never really wanted to have anything to do with us. My mom was also an only child. The good thing about not having any family is that I don't have to worry about the people going after them, as well."

Dwight nodded as he leaned back against the counter. "True."

"What about your family?"

"My parents retired and handed me this place," he said with a wry smile. "They had plans to tour the world. On their second week of this extravagant vacation, the tour bus they were on went off the side of a mountain in Peru. There were no survivors."

Emmy set down the uneaten portion of her muffin. "That's horrible. I'm sorry for both you and your sister."

"We had to travel to Peru to claim their bodies and bring them home. It was an ordeal in itself. Our government had to get involved. It was long and messy. But we brought them home where they wanted to be."

"You have Victoria."

He wrinkled his nose and jokingly said, "Don't remind me."

"I always wanted a sibling."

"I've heard that from everyone who is an only child. And I'm sure you've heard those with siblings say they would've rather not had any."

Emmy nodded. "Exactly. We always want what we don't have, I suppose."

"That's how it goes."

"This ranch has been in your family for generations. Are you going to keep that going?"

"You mean, am I going to marry and have kids?" he asked with a smile.

Emmy shrugged half-heartedly. "Yes."

"I'm not against it."

"Is my being here going to cause problems for you? I mean, that is, if you're seeing someone," she hastened to add.

He turned and rinsed the empty mug before placing it in the dishwasher. "My last serious relationship ended about four years ago. She liked me, but she didn't like the ranch."

"Didn't she realize that you and the ranch are a package?"

"She did in the end," he said with a sigh.

Emmy regretted asking since it seemed to have drudged up some bad memories. "I'm sorry."

"Don't be. She wasn't the woman for me. The brunt of

producing an heir isn't just on me, though. There's Vic. She's been dating Ted for six years now. I thought they might get married, but she told me she's against it. Said there's no reason for all the formality of it."

"What do you think?"

Dwight eyed her for a moment. "I think it depends on what the couple wants. I see why some choose to get married. I also see why others decide against it. There are still legal forms that can be filed to get the same results as marriage. There are pros and cons to both, and it depends on who you ask."

"Well, if that wasn't a roundabout answer, I don't know what is," Emmy said with a laugh.

He shrugged. "It's how I feel. I want my sister to be happy, and if what she has makes her happy, then who am I to tell her it's wrong?"

"The more I learn about you, the more I'm beginning to think you're a unicorn."

His brows shot up in his forehead. "A unicorn?"

"You know. The mythical beast."

"I know what a unicorn is. How does that pertain to me?"

Emmy finished her last bite of muffin before saying, "It means that you have qualities most women swoon over. You're the type of man women everywhere search for and can't find."

"Is that right?" he asked in a soft voice, his blue eyes boring into her.

"It is. With the right marketing, I could have women lined up for miles just to meet you. You'd have your pick of a wife."

Dwight lifted his hands in surrender. "I'd rather do it the old-fashioned way."

"Yep. Definitely a unicorn," she murmured as she followed him to his office.

When he took the chair behind the desk, he became ultra-focused on the tasks at hand. He handed her a stack of papers and pointed to the filing cabinet. Emmy went through the stack quickly. That's when she discovered there was another stack, and another, and another. By the time she finished, the pile on the credenza behind him had been cleared.

While he answered emails, she opened and sorted the mail he'd handed her. There were bills to be paid, but there was also money coming into the ranch from those who had bought cattle, etcetera. A check from someone who had leased one of Dwight's pastures for their herd. Another from a farm who had purchased some hay.

Emmy put the mail into two stacks and handed it to him when he was ready. He took the bills due and asked her to match up the payments coming in to the invoices he had. It was menial work, but she loved it. It took her mind off other things and kept her busy. And she was learning things about a working ranch that she hadn't known.

Since she had known nothing, she learned quite a bit.

More than anything, she truly enjoyed herself. Dwight shared stories about the ranch and kept the conversation going all morning until lunch. She was, in fact, disappointed when they paused to eat.

"Don't worry," he told her. "There's a lot more to do."

"I like the sound of that."

He shook his head as he laughed. "I've never known anyone who actually wanted to do this kind of work."

"I'm not like most people."

"There isn't anything wrong with that."

She looked up at him to find Dwight's blue eyes locked on her. His gaze reflected the sincerity of his words. "Thank you."

He gave her a nod and rose to leave. Emmy glanced

around, happy that she had been allowed to spend the time helping. It had taken her mind off other things, which was exactly what she needed.

They had a quick lunch, but just as they were returning to the office, Dwight's cell phone rang. Emmy heard a man's voice but couldn't make out the words. Dwight's brow furrowed as the conversation continued.

"I'll be right there," Dwight said and hung up the phone. Then he looked at her. "One of the calves is stuck. I've got to help my men."

"Of course. Go. I'll be fine."

Dwight put on his coat and hat, then paused at the door to look back at her. "I don't know how long I'll be. The storm could make things worse."

"I understand."

Sam sat between them, looking from one to the other as if he couldn't decide what to do.

Emmy liked having the dog with her, but she suspected that Sam was also a working dog. "Take Sam."

"He should stay with you," Dwight said.

"You need him."

After a moment, Dwight nodded and called Sam's name. Then they were out the door. Emmy locked it behind them, then turned and let out a sigh. She went back to the office and finished what she had been doing. Unfortunately, that only ate up about thirty minutes. She needed some music to help fill the silence, something other than the whining wind as it blew around the house.

She looked for a radio of some kind but came up empty. That's when she saw the black smart speaker. It was angled on the table in the living room behind some ivy. She had nearly missed it. Emmy asked it to play some feel-good music. A smile pulled at her lips when the first beats of

Stevie Wonder's "Superstition" filled the air. She bobbed her head as she made her way to the laundry room and found the duster once more.

The next hour crawled by as she wiped down each spindle of the staircase and dusted the four rooms upstairs. Hoping to eat up more time, she cleaned each of the bathrooms, even though they were already spotless. She tidied her room, then went back downstairs.

Her gaze immediately moved to the door. With the music playing, she wouldn't have known if anyone walked in. Emmy told the speaker to lower the volume as she checked the back door locks. Everything was as she had left it.

She tested the front door, as well as the side entrance. Those were locked, as well. But that wasn't enough. She went to the windows, examining each to see if someone had tried to open them, while also looking at the snow outside to see if there were any footprints. Her growing fears eased some when she found nothing. But they didn't subside entirely.

Emmy wrung her hands as she turned in a slow circle. Anxiety bubbled within her. Another attack was coming. She dragged in mouthfuls of air, trying to get oxygen to her lungs. Sam wasn't around for her to cling to, and she couldn't always count on the animal. She had to focus her mind on something else. Anything else.

Her gaze landed on the cabinets. With shaking hands and legs so weak she wasn't sure they would hold her, she made her way over by supporting herself with anything she could lean on. When she reached the cupboard, she opened the first door and began slowly and meticulously removing each item, placing it on the kitchen table.

When the cabinet was empty, she wiped down the inside and then put everything back exactly as it had been. Each time the memories of her near-death rose, she acknowledged them and then let them and the emotions pass. It was something she remembered from a meditation she had once done.

It took considerable effort, but it seemed to be working—this time, at least. But Emmy couldn't relax yet. With the first cabinet done, she reached for the second.

Chapter 8

Denver, Colorado

"What do you mean, you can't find her?" Joe Roma demanded from behind his desk. He couldn't remember the last time he had been this furious. Or the last time his men had failed him.

"We've looked everywhere, boss," Orso answered.

Joe looked the hitman over. He stood tall, his black hair liberally laced with gray. His dark eyes were hooded. He had laugh lines around his mouth, but Joe had never seen him crack a smile. Orso had worked for the Roma family for two decades now. Orso's work was art. He went in quietly and left before anyone even knew he was there. Joe should've sent him to begin with. But he had wanted to give his cousin a chance to redeem himself in the family's eyes.

"Emmy didn't shoot Paulie," Orso stated. "There was someone else there."

Joe leaned forward and placed his elbows on the desk. Orso had spent years as a Denver police detective, and he had friends who were still cops. "You examined the scene?"

Orso shrugged, his lips twisting. "After every abbreviation in the book had their look at it. But it was clear by the way Paulie fell that the shooter stood at the entry. Paulie wouldn't have allowed the woman to get near the door once he was in the hotel room."

"Did one of the cops suddenly develop a conscience and return to stop him?"

Orso shook his head. "You paid them handsomely to leave their posts. They won't be saying anything."

Joe flattened his hands on the desk and pushed to his feet. "I've got to tell Paulie's wife that he's dead. Worse, Emmy is out there, and if she isn't found, she's going to testify against me. Then, everyone will know that the Roma family is back in business. We've kept things quiet since Arturo died in '06. We'll have everyone breathing down our necks again."

"And you'll be in jail," Orso stated matter-of-factly.

Joe held the hitman's gaze. "That's right. Everything I built after my uncle died will have been for nothing."

"Then I need to get out there and find Emmy before she ruins us all."

"You have no idea where she is."

Orso's lips twisted again. "We couldn't get to her handler. Dalton Silva is one of the few upstanding men who can't be bought."

"Bullshit," Joe said as he sank back in his chair. "Everyone has a price."

"Not Silva. At least, not according to the people who felt him out to see if he would be interested."

"Do you think someone told Dalton what we planned?"

Orso drew in a deep breath and slowly released it as he crossed his arms over his chest. "I don't. I think he got lucky. Unfortunately for us, that means he has Emmy and is in the wind."

"Won't he have to call in and let someone in the marshals' office know?"

"Not if he thinks there's a leak in the department."

Joe flattened his lips. "Which there is. Damn. I hate smart men like Silva. Unless, of course, they're working for me. Do you think you can find them?"

"It's going to take some time. They could be anywhere."

"I'll give you anything you need."

Orso dropped his arms to his sides. Then, with a nod, he turned and walked out of the office, softly shutting the door behind him.

Joe closed his eyes and dropped his head back against his chair. His infatuation with Emmy had gotten him into this situation. Had he not tried to impress her, he wouldn't have wanted her around after hours. And she never would've seen who he really was.

The door to his office suddenly opened. Tony, Joe's best friend since grade school, worked as his *consigliere* or advisor. Tony helped mediate on occasion, but more than that, he represented the family in all business dealings—both criminal and legitimate. Joe knew that Tony had his back. Always.

"She's coming," Tony stated with a flat look.

Joe steeled himself for his wife's entrance. Stella had once been a beautiful woman. Coming from a crime family in New Jersey, she was well acquainted with the lifestyle. It hadn't been a love match. Their union was born of a joint venture that'd helped both his family and hers.

While they hadn't been in love, they *had* been civil. They'd even had a few somewhat happy years in the marriage. That all ended when they learned that she couldn't bear children. Joe wanted to pass on the business to his kids, but others in his family could take up the reins. He'd been disappointed in the news, but he had accepted it.

Stella hadn't been able to handle it.

First, she'd immersed herself in finding other ways to have children. No matter how many doctors told her that it wasn't possible, she simply went to another one, hoping someone would tell her what she wanted to hear. From one end of the country to the other, she spent mountains of money trying to find an operation or some form of fertility drug that would allow her to carry a child.

She came back heartbroken.

Joe suggested they adopt, but she wouldn't hear of it. Instead, she locked herself in their room and didn't come out for weeks. He could've broken down the door—and had he loved her, he might have—but he had a business to run. He couldn't hold her hand as she dealt with her grief.

Weeks turned to months. Stella sank deeper and deeper into depression. Doctors put her on all kinds of medication to help, but nothing stirred her. When she finally emerged, she drank. Heavily. She imbibed until she passed out and then started it all over the next day. It got to be so bad that Joe stopped having any social events at the house because she had embarrassed him on several occasions.

That's when Joe bought another house. One he could conduct business and entertain in without having to worry about his wife making an ass of herself. He allowed her access to a large bank account to get whatever she wanted—be it jewels or booze. So long as she left him alone.

The arrangement had worked great. Until the few times she decided to get sober. Then, she demanded that he return home. He always refused, and they had loud arguments where she accused him of cheating, and he called her a drunk. Within a week, she would be hitting the booze again.

The cycle had been ongoing for the last two years, and Joe was tired of it. He was past tired of it. He had cheated. He'd never denied that. What was he supposed to do? Wait for her to sober up? Because he didn't particularly care to have sex with someone who had passed out. He had needs.

He was a man, after all.

The door flew open as Stella strode in. The years of heavy drinking had taken a toll on her beauty. No longer did she glow with vitality. Her skin was pale and haggard. Her blond hair dull and brittle. She once carried herself well, but now she appeared frail and shrunken. Her clothes hung off her from drinking instead of eating proper meals.

"Joe," she said as she walked to the chair before his desk and sat.

Tony closed the door behind her, briefly meeting Joe's gaze. Joe eyed his wife. "This is a surprise."

"No, it isn't."

He didn't argue, just sat there waiting to see what she would say next.

Stella crossed her legs and set her Chanel purse on the floor. For the first time, he noticed that she wasn't wearing her wedding ring. The ten-carat diamond had cost him a fortune, but it had been worth it to have a union with her family.

"I'm not happy," she declared.

Joe didn't have time for this. "Neither am I. I haven't been for some time."

"Then we should do something about it."

"All right. Does that mean you'll check into a rehab facility and get yourself straight?"

She huffed, her gaze narrowing. "Actually, I am going to rehab."

"That's good to hear. I don't care what it costs. I'll send you anywhere you want to go," he said and reached for his pen to get back to work. It was his way of dismissing her.

"Yes, you are going to pay for it."

Something in her words stopped him cold. He raised his gaze to hers. "What is that supposed to mean?"

"It's been a month since I took my last drink. A month where I waited for you to check in on me. It didn't take long to learn that you haven't stepped foot in our house in over seven months. I knew you had another place, but I honestly believed you came home."

"Why would I?" he asked. "You were so drunk, you didn't know who I was. You ran your mouth constantly until you passed out. You picked fights and threw things. Why would anyone want to be around that?"

"I needed help."

"I tried to help you. Each time I did, you refused."

Stella quirked a brow. "I don't think you tried very hard."

"Probably not." He shrugged, glad that the debate was over. He looked down at the paper, wanting to get back to work. "At least, you've got yourself in order now. When you're sorted out, you can take your place by my side again."

"No."

Joe blew out a frustrated breath as he tossed his pen down and tilted his head to look at her. "No to getting yourself sorted out?"

"Oh, I'm going to do that. I said no to being by your side."

"Suit yourself. You haven't been with me in a while. No one will miss you."

Stella lifted her chin. "I'm leaving for New Jersey. A car is taking me to the airport the moment I walk from your office."

"A trip to your family sounds like a good idea. How long will you be gone?"

"Forever," she said as she grabbed her purse and got to her feet.

Joe frowned. "You're my wife, Stella. We can live in separate houses, but you have to be in Denver."

"I don't have to do a goddamn thing for you, Joseph Roma. Not for much longer, anyway. I've filed for divorce. My family knows everything. They're expecting me, and if I don't get on that plane, the entire family will descend upon Denver in a matter of hours."

"I see," Joe said softly. "I suppose the alliance our families had is over, as well?"

"That depends on the divorce," she said before turning and starting for the door. Just as she reached it, she paused and looked at him over her shoulder. "We might not have been in love, but we could've had a decent life together. You weren't there when I needed someone the most. I believe you get back in kind what you put out into the world. One of these days, you're going to need someone desperately, and no one will be there."

Joe watched her go, both relieved to have her out of his life and unsure how it would affect his future business dealings. He didn't have time to think about Stella, the divorce, or the repercussions when he had to focus on Emmy.

He and Tony exchanged a look. Tony nodded and followed Stella out. He would trail her, making sure she got on the plane to New Jersey as expected. Joe wouldn't have her family after him.

Chapter 9

Dwight stamped his feet on the porch steps to knock the snow from his boots. His breath billowed as he blew out. He was cold to his bones. The snowstorm had finally begun to let up about an hour ago.

Sam waited for him by the door, wanting the warmth of inside as much as Dwight did. He unlocked the door and walked inside the house. His gaze moved around the area, searching for Emmy as he hung his hat and did the same with his coat after removing it. Only the under-cabinet lights in the kitchen were on. Emmy had dimmed the living area lights, and the glow of a fire illuminated the rug and sofa.

Dwight started toward the fire. Sam rushed ahead of him, but it wasn't the heat from the fire the dog wanted. Instead, he went to the sofa. As Dwight neared, he spotted lean legs covered by a throw blanket. Emmy was curled on her side, fast asleep.

He looked at Sam, who rested his head on the couch near Emmy's arm. Dark eyes looked from Emmy to Dwight, silently asking for permission to curl up next to her. Dwight shook his head. With a sigh, Sam plopped down on the rug.

Dwight smiled to himself as he went to the fireplace and stretched out his hands to warm them. Damn, it had been a long afternoon. He was hungry and in need of a shower, but all he wanted to do was crawl into bed and sleep. He turned and sat on the hearth as he dropped his head into his hands and closed his eyes.

"Tough day?"

His head jerked up at the sound of Emmy's voice. His eyes locked with hers. "You could say that."

She pushed herself into a sitting position and swung her legs over the side of the sofa. After carefully folding the throw, she reached down to pet Sam, smiling as she whispered something to the dog. Then her gaze was back on Dwight. "Are you hungry?"

"Starving."

"I'm pretty good at heating things up. Or I can make you a sandwich," she offered.

He smiled. It had been a long time since anyone had offered such a thing to him. "It doesn't matter."

"You're covered in mud. Why don't you jump in the shower while I get your food ready?"

It was an offer he couldn't pass up. Dwight nodded and got to his feet. Without a word, he removed his boots to leave them there and walked to the master. The moment he got into the bathroom, he began tugging off his clothes. His cell phone dropped from his pants' pocket to the floor, and 11:42 popped up on the screen.

He retrieved the phone and put it on the counter next to the sink before turning on the shower. The instant steam began filling the room, he stepped beneath the spray. The water stung his skin because he was so cold, but he still didn't turn it down. Prickles of feeling from his toes ran up his legs as the water warmed him.

Dwight didn't know how long he stood there before he

finally reached for the soap and washed. He kept his eyes closed the entire time. Working on a ranch often left him exhausted at the end of the day, but today had been particularly difficult. He was drained—mentally, emotionally, and physically.

When he finished rinsing, he turned off the water and grabbed a towel to dry himself. His stomach rumbled, reminding him that he hadn't eaten since lunch. Dwight put on some underwear and a pair of sweatpants and a long-sleeved tee. He sat on the edge of the bed for just a moment.

The next thing he knew, his alarm was going off. Dwight groggily rolled over and stumbled his way to the bathroom, where he had left his phone. He turned off the alarm and braced his hands on the counter as he hung his head. Surely, it couldn't already be morning. He had just wanted a moment to close his eyes last night. But a check of his phone confirmed that it was indeed morning.

Dwight took a deep breath and straightened as he ran a hand down his face. Then he flipped on the light, blinking against the brightness. His eyes stung, letting him know that he hadn't gotten nearly enough sleep. After splashing his face with some water, Dwight removed the clothes from the previous night and dressed, not feeling up to shaving.

Only when he walked from his room did he realize that Sam wasn't with him. When he entered the kitchen, he remembered that Emmy had been getting food for him. He inwardly winced. Hopefully, she wasn't too upset about him falling asleep.

He got out some eggs to scramble. After heating a couple of slices of ham, he combined the egg and ham with some cheese, placed it all on a croissant, and devoured it. Dwight was still hungry, so he fixed another one.

By the time he finished the second one, Sam came down the stairs and sat by his bowl. Dwight scooped some kibble for Sam and then drank a tall glass of orange juice before brewing coffee. He stared out the kitchen window at the world of white before him. The sky was clear, the storm having pushed off sometime during the night. It would be a cold day, but at least they wouldn't be battling snowfall along with it.

Dwight rinsed his cup after he finished his coffee. He wiped out the pan and left it on the stove to wash later. He started to leave but paused to grab a piece of paper to write Emmy a quick note before putting on his coat and hat and walking from the house to start his day.

The brisk cold met him. He squared his shoulders, walked down the porch to the barn to let the horses out for the day, and began mucking stalls. When he reached the barn doors, he looked over his shoulder to the room Emmy had taken. He wasn't sure what made him look at the window. Not only were the blinds closed, but Emmy was still asleep.

"Lucky lady," Dwight murmured as he opened the barn door.

Emmy yawned as she walked downstairs after getting ready for the day. She was a little sad that Sam wasn't with her. When he followed her up to bed last night, she hadn't been able to wipe the smile from her face.

As she reached the kitchen, she listened to the sounds of the house. Without needing to look, she knew that Dwight and Sam were gone. She turned to get some coffee and saw the note on the table.

Sorry I fell asleep last night. I plan to try to get back for lunch but don't wait for me to eat.

Emmy thought about finding Dwight in his room last night. When he hadn't come out after his shower, she had warmed him some leftovers from the night before and carried the meal upstairs. That's when she'd found him asleep, dressed in fresh clothes, his hair still wet. She had lifted his legs one at a time to put them on the bed. She'd thought he might wake, but he simply rolled over. She turned off all the lights and took the plate back to the kitchen to put the food away.

She hated to admit that she had hoped Dwight would be there when she got up so they could continue their work in the office. But there were things he needed to do on the ranch. It was just that she didn't have anything to do.

"He did tell me to go outside if I wanted," she said aloud.

The more she looked at the snow, the more she realized that it wasn't feasible. For one, she didn't have the right clothes. She wouldn't be doing anyone any good if she went outside and froze. No, it was better she remained inside.

As she made some peanut butter toast, she realized that there wasn't anything else in the house for her to clean except the floors. The minute she finished her breakfast, she began looking for a vacuum and a mop. She located them and started cleaning the upstairs first.

Her mind wandered as she worked. She was thankful that Dwight didn't have a robot vacuum like she did because at least this gave her something to do. She took her time in the master. Not just because of the views. Something about the room calmed her. The entire house did, but the master even more so.

Emmy moved from room to room. With the downstairs vacuumed, she put it on the bottom stair and began cleaning the wooden floors as well as the tile in the master bath. She hummed to herself to fill the silence. Before she knew it, she was back at the stairs. She hauled the mop and vacuum upstairs and repeated the process all over again.

Her room was last. As she finished and moved out into the

hallway to finish the last little bit until the stairs, she thought she heard a noise. Emmy paused and listened, leaning to the side in an effort to look downstairs. But she didn't hear or see anything.

After several tense seconds, she went back to work, but she no longer hummed. Her ears strained to hear anything unusual. She finished the wood floor in the hallway and turned to start the stairs when she saw a woman standing at the bottom of the flight, wearing a big smile. Startled, Emmy screamed and jumped back, slamming her shoulder into the wall before plastering herself against it.

In an instant, she was back in the hotel room with the gun pointed at her head.

"I'm sorry. I didn't mean to scare you," the woman said, drawing Emmy's attention. The woman's lips twisted ruefully. "I should've announced myself."

Emmy's heart thudded painfully in her chest as she stared wide-eyed at the intruder.

The woman raised her hands and issued an apologetic smile. "I'm Vic. I mean Victoria. Dwight's sister."

Emmy slid down the wall. Could this really be Dwight's sister? If so, why hadn't he told Emmy that she was coming? Maybe he hadn't known. Or perhaps this wasn't her at all. And yet . . . she had the same piercing blue eyes as Dwight.

"You look quite pale," Victoria said as her frown grew. "I wanted to surprise you. I didn't want to give you a heart attack. Didn't Dwight tell you I was coming?"

Emmy shook her head, still unable to find words. With the initial shock over, she started trembling.

Victoria looked helplessly around. "How about some water? Would that help? And where the hell is my brother?" she finished, a note of irritation in her voice.

Emmy watched Victoria get a bottle of water from the fridge and bring it up to her. Emmy wasn't certain she could trust Victoria, but she didn't have many other options at the moment. She accepted the bottle and drank deeply.

Victoria sat on the top stair, facing Emmy. "That was real fear in your face when you saw me. Dwight told me you were here. Said he was doing a favor for a friend. I had a feeling that service was hiding you for a bit, but it's more than that, isn't it?"

There were so many things going through Emmy's head. After nearly being killed, she knew not to trust anyone. That meant this woman could, in fact, be an assassin. Emmy studied Victoria. She was trim with shoulder-length brown hair that had blond highlights. Her clothes were designer and fit her to perfection.

Just as Emmy was about to ask for some identification and think of a way to escape, Sam came through the doggie door and rushed up to greet Victoria with kisses, his tail wagging furiously. A heartbeat after, Dwight walked in. He took one look at Emmy and rushed up the stairs to her.

"What is it? Did you fall? Are you hurt?" he asked.

"I scared her," Victoria said.

Dwight cut his sister a dark look and turned back to Emmy. "I forgot all about her coming."

"It's fine." Emmy tried to hide how her hands still shook, but Dwight saw.

He flattened his lips. "Let's get you downstairs."

She wanted to tell him that she could walk, but her legs were like Jell-O. To her shock, Dwight lifted her and walked down the stairs to the sofa, carefully setting her down as if she might break apart at any moment—and perhaps she might.

"Damn," Victoria said as she followed them. "I feel horrible."

Emmy shook her head. "It's all right. Really. I'm just a bit jumpy."

Victoria ignored her and looked to Dwight. "She's still pale. Food, maybe?"

"I'll get it," he said and strode to the kitchen.

Emmy wasn't used to anyone fussing over her. It made her uncomfortable, but at the same time, it didn't feel as if she carried the weight of the world on her shoulders anymore. And that made her eyes sting with tears.

Sam jumped up beside her, resting his head on her lap once more. Emmy stroked the dog's soft fur, wondering if she could stay here forever. Something about the ranch and the people here made it feel almost like . . . home.

"Here," Dwight said as he brought her a sandwich on a plate with a large side of Cheetos.

She smiled at the mound of snacks and looked up at him. "Thank you."

He cleared his throat and motioned to his sister, who stood beside him. "Emmy, this is my sister, Victoria. Vic, this is Emmy."

"We've already met," Vic said with a roll of her eyes. Then she frowned. "Well. Kind of. It's nice to meet you, Emmy."

"Same," Emmy replied.

Dwight glanced behind him to move back and sit on the hearth. "I called Vic for help when I went to town to get the clothes for you. She told me to get the basics and said she'd get more."

"Which I have," Vic added. She looked pointedly at Dwight. "The bags are in the car."

It was Dwight's turn to roll his eyes. "Of course they are."

Once he had risen and walked from the house, Victoria turned to Emmy with a grin. "I kinda went a little crazy. I love to shop. It doesn't matter for who. If I didn't have my current job, I'd probably shop for anyone who would let me. What I'm trying to say is that I got a lot of clothes in all different styles. See what fits and what doesn't. You won't hurt my feelings. I can take it all back if I need to."

"You didn't have to go to so much trouble."

"Dwight said you didn't have any clothes. Sounds like you needed some."

Emmy shrugged and ate a Cheeto. "It's not like I'm going anywhere. I can make do with what I have. Thank you, though. I can't exactly get out."

"Like I said, I love to shop. It gave me an excuse."

"I'll pay you back for all of it."

Victoria made a sound and waved her hand. "I couldn't care less about that. What I really want is for you to go through everything and see what fits. I had to guess based on my brother's descriptions."

Emmy found herself smiling. Victoria was friendly and likeable. She went out of her way to make Emmy feel at ease. "I'm glad I got to meet you. Dwight's told me a little about you."

"Hmm," Vic said, frowning. "I'm not sure I'd believe any of what he said."

"It was all good things."

The door opened, and Dwight came in loaded down with bags. "What the hell, Vic? Did you buy out every store?"

Victoria gave him an innocent look.

Emmy stared at the packages, shocked at the number. Then Dwight went back out and came in with a *second* haul of bags.

"Hurry and eat," Victoria told her, bouncing up and down like a kid at Christmas. "I'm dying to see some of these clothes on you."

Chapter 10

Dwight stared down at all the bags and simply shook his head. Victoria had gone above and beyond, but that was just the kind of person she was. She had one of the biggest hearts of anyone he knew. Sometimes, people took advantage of that, and she had been hurt more times than he liked. But that was simply who his sister was. And he wouldn't change her for anything.

He looked over at Vic and Emmy. Emmy's face had color again as she smiled at whatever Vic had said. Though Emmy was fine now, she hadn't been when he returned for lunch. He could've kicked himself for not informing her of Vic's arrival. He couldn't believe he had forgotten.

The panicked look on Emmy's face would haunt him for months. He closed his eyes and tried to center himself. A mistake had happened on his watch, one that was his fault. It couldn't happen again. Emmy's safety was his responsibility, and he could never forget that.

He flexed his hands, recalling the feel of her in his arms.

His eyes flew open. No. No! He couldn't think like that. Whatever . . . emotions . . . dared to rise within him needed to stay dead and buried, no matter how appealing it was that they might flutter to life again.

"She's stunning," Vic whispered as she came to stand beside him. "Unbelievably so."

Dwight swallowed, not bothering to answer.

But Victoria was too shrewd not to pick up on that. She quirked a brow at him. "It's okay to admit she's possibly the most beautiful woman to walk this Earth."

"She's under my protection," Dwight said in a low voice as he met his sister's gaze.

"Don't play stupid with me. There are enough movies out there of this exact scenario where the couple gets together."

Dwight shook his head. "Don't, Vic."

"Fine," she said with a shrug. "Don't let us keep you. We've got girl stuff to do. I'll keep her busy."

"And the door locked."

Vic's brows snapped together. "Okay."

"There are people trying to kill her. If anyone shows up that you don't recognize, call me immediately."

A beat of silence passed before Victoria asked, "It's that serious?"

"It's that serious."

"Shit," she murmured and looked over her shoulder at Emmy. "No wonder she reacted so strongly to my arrival."

"She also has PTSD. Someone put out a hit on her. She's in witness protection, but someone leaked her location. Dalton, her handler, got to her right before the assassin pulled the trigger."

Victoria's lips parted in shock. "Holy shit."

"It's good you're here. At least, for a bit. Things went to hell last night, and it is keeping me farther from the house than I'd like."

She put her hand on his arm. "I got her. Go do what you need to do."

"You're the best."

"Damn right, I am. And I don't intend to let you forget it."

Dwight smiled and kissed her on the cheek. He then looked at Emmy and raised his voice so she could hear. "I'm grabbing a sandwich and heading out. You and Vic have a good time."

"Be careful," Emmy said with a smile and a wave.

Dwight hurried to fix a sandwich before leaving the house with Sam by his side. He felt better about leaving Emmy now that Vic was there. He had told Emmy how safe the ranch was, but he knew someone could find a way to get to her if they really wanted. And he had a suspicion that the people after Emmy wouldn't stop until they found her. That meant it was only a matter of time before they got to the ranch. But he would be prepared.

The missing calf from last night gave him a reason to upgrade his surveillance without causing a stir. Word spread quickly in their small town. By now, everyone would know that he had lost two calves last night. One that froze to death after falling through some ice in the river, and the other to wildlife.

Every ranch lost cattle throughout the year and budgeted for that, but losing too many meant you were out a lot of money come time to take them to sale. He'd had a decent year, but with the first significant snowfall bringing two deaths, he didn't want to take any chances.

Dwight ate his sandwich as he drove back out to where he and his men had been mending a fence. He'd already sent one of the younger guys into town with a list of things to get to upgrade the surveillance. They should be finished with the fence by the time he got back from town, and then they could get to work installing the new cameras.

He finished the last of his sandwich and put on his gloves before opening the door and getting out, Sam jumping into the snow right behind him. Dwight nodded to his men as he approached, and they got to work.

"I hope you can forgive me," Victoria said as she walked back to the sofa and sat after Dwight and Sam had left.

Emmy shook her head. "Don't think anything about it."

"I hope you don't mind, but Dwight just told me what happened to you. It's a big deal, and you have every right to be jumpy around people you don't know. I know I would be."

Emmy looked down at the plate. "I didn't want to come here, but Dalton had nowhere else to bring me. He told me Dwight's ranch was a safe place. I didn't believe him until I got here." She looked at Victoria. "I do feel safe here. I shouldn't because I know the people after me won't stop until they find me."

"Who are these people?"

"I work for a large bookkeeping firm in Denver. One of my clients was a successful Italian restaurant. I've worked on their books for nearly five years. A lot of communication passes back and forth between me, the restaurant manager, and the owner. Sometimes, it's easy to become friendly with those I work with. That's what happened with the Roma family. Joe Roma is well known and well liked in the community. He gives a lot to charity and helps those in need. He invited me to a Christmas event a few years back, and on a whim, I went. After that, he began inviting me to more parties. The more I went, the more I got to know not only Joe but also the rest of his large family."

Victoria nodded. "Makes sense."

"I should also add that Joe is a handsome man. He flirted, and I flirted back. I knew I couldn't get involved with him, so I didn't let it go any further on my end. But he did. He sent me small gifts. Nothing that would cause anyone at work to raise eyebrows, but enough to let me know that he was interested." Emmy shook her head. "Looking back now, I can see the last thing I should've done was continue attending the parties, but they were glamorous affairs. I don't really get out much. I work and go home. The parties gave me an excuse to get dressed up and meet new people. It got me out of the house to actually have something of a social life. It also helped that people would do just about anything for invites to these events."

Victoria smiled. "Oh, yes. I know the kind. I've been to a few. They're hard to resist."

"One dinner party I went to was smaller than usual. It was a more intimate affair. I realized then that these were the people Joe wanted in his life. Most I recognized from those he surrounded himself with at all times. There were maybe a handful of others like me, and I was very aware that by continuing to accept his invites, I was giving him the impression that I wanted to be with him. And part of me did. To have a powerful man like him showing interest in me? It was heady."

Victoria leaned over and put her hand over Emmy's. "We've all been lonely and wanting something like that. Don't beat yourself up about it."

"Had I stopped accepting his invitations, had I not toed the line of what was acceptable with a client, he wouldn't have asked me to stay after that dinner at the restaurant. And I wouldn't have agreed."

"But you did," Vic said in a soft voice as she straightened.

Emmy nodded. "I was in the kitchen with a wife of one of the men, helping to clear the dishes. She walked out first as I rinsed my hands. I started out of the kitchen when I heard voices coming from a room off the kitchen. I don't know why, but I followed the sound of the voices until I got to a door with a small window. That's when I saw Joe and his men staring at another man. The guy was shaking, he was so terrified. I couldn't hear what Joe said, but I saw him look at one of his men and nod. Joe's man took out a gun I hadn't known he had and shot the other man in the head. I covered my mouth to stop my scream. Then I hurried to the sink and turned on the water to begin rinsing off some of the dishes, hoping that no one would know what I had seen."

Victoria's eyes were wide. "What happened?"

"I stayed in there, washing and cleaning up until Joe came looking for me. He wore a smile like he hadn't just had someone killed. I was still shaking from the ordeal. He told me I was pale, and I told him that something from dinner hadn't set well. I could see that he wasn't buying my explanation, and I got scared. The closer he got to me, the more frightened I became until I rushed to the bathroom and vomited. Joe had one of the wives tend to me, and they took me back to my place. Days went by without a word from Joe. Then he invited me to another party."

Victoria shivered. "Oh, no."

"I hadn't turned one down in months and figured it would look odd if I said no to this one. So, I went. The entire time, different people from the restaurant asked me things, trying to trip me up to see if I had seen the murder. Somehow, I said all the right things. I went to the second party but declined the third. I was terrified that they would realize what I knew and kill me. I asked my boss to give Joe and his restaurant to someone else, but my boss declined. I had to keep up pretenses with Joe until I could find a way to get out from under him. It finally happened when I read that the Denver district attorney was looking into Joe."

"You went to the DA, didn't you?"

Emmy nodded. "I told her everything. And she told me that Joe was running the Roma mob again. I was utterly shocked. She called the US Marshals right then and put me into witness protection. I knew they had someone else in

WITSEC, as well. Two days later, that witness was killed. Dalton, who was in charge of my safety, began to suspect something. They had to move me three times because someone from Joe's organization discovered where I was. The last location was supposed to have been the safest place the marshals had." She hugged her arms around herself. "Had Dalton not arrived when he did, I would be dead."

Victoria blinked and shook her head. "I need a drink after hearing that. And you've lived it. No wonder you were as white as death when you saw me. You thought I had come for you."

"Yes."

"That settles it, then. It's time for something fun. Clothes," Victoria said with a bright smile.

Emmy was ready to change the subject. And she was looking forward to seeing what was in all the bags.

"This is going to be so much fun," Vic said as she rose and rushed to gather an armload of bags to take upstairs.

Chapter 11

It had been a long time since Dwight found himself anxious to get back home after a long day. Sometimes, the big house was too quiet. Other times, he enjoyed the solitude. More often than not lately, he hadn't been able to find the peace as he once had. Next thing he knew, Emmy was there.

Dwight paused before the house, looking through the large windows to the warm glow within. His sister was in the kitchen cooking and gesturing wildly with her hands as she always did. His gaze slid to Emmy as she moved around the table, setting it for dinner. She wore a burnt orange V-neck sweater and black jeans. Her caramel-colored locks were pulled back on the sides, giving him an unobstructed view of her beautiful face. She laughed at something Victoria said, and Dwight found himself smiling in response.

The difference in Emmy from when she first arrived was astounding, but he had seen firsthand that it would be a slow process for her. She had good days and bad ones. He had promised her a safe place, and if it was the last thing he did, he would ensure that.

He'd joined the military because he wanted to serve his

country. He'd joined the FBI for the same reason. When he moved to Homeland Security, it was because he'd wanted to protect the citizens of his country. The need to protect and shield against evil had risen like a tidal wave from the first moment he learned why Dalton was bringing Emmy to the ranch.

Dwight had been good at his job, but he had become disillusioned and unhappy. When his parents said they were thinking of handing over the ranch, he'd eagerly taken the opportunity for a change in lifestyle. He'd had no regrets. Still didn't.

Sam bumped into him as if reminding him that they were still outside. Dwight ignored the dog, his gaze locked on Emmy. Her smile was easy, but her eyes still held anxiousness and trepidation. Evil men had put that there—men who deserved to pay for their crimes. Dwight no longer worked in the law enforcement field, but that didn't mean he couldn't do his part to ensure that the men responsible were locked away.

Dwight walked to the porch and knocked the snow from his boots. Sam rushed through his door. Dwight heard the girls call Sam's name as he ran to them. Dwight opened the door and stepped inside, his eyes colliding with Emmy's as she squatted to pet Sam.

"Hi," Emmy said.

Dwight tipped his head to her as he shrugged out of his coat and hung it up with his hat. He forced himself to look at Victoria. "Smells good."

She gave him a knowing look. "It's Mom's famous stew."

"My favorite."

"I know." Vic gave him a wink and went back to stirring the pot.

Dwight took off his boots near the door. "I'm going to wash up."

"Please," Vic said without looking at him.

He strode to his room and closed the door behind him. Dwight stripped out of his work clothes and jumped into the shower to wash away the day. He was out in ten minutes and dressed in jeans and a shirt. When he returned to the kitchen, Victoria was just setting the stew on the table. Emmy filled three glasses with red wine before placing the bottle down.

"Emmy," Vic said as she motioned to the chair across from her.

Dwight glanced at his sister to find that she had put him at the head of the table. He took his seat as she dished out the stew and handed each of them their bowls. Silence stretched until Emmy had taken a bite.

"Wow. This is amazing," she told them before spooning more into her mouth.

Dwight smiled and took a bite. "Delicious, Vic. Thanks."

"I like to cook. Not sure why I don't do more of it at home," she said offhandedly as she ate. Then, Vic turned the attention on him. "How are things here?"

"Lost two calves yesterday."

Victoria shook her head. "And winter is just starting."

Dwight didn't want to talk about the ranch. He jerked his chin to Emmy. "I like the sweater. Is it new?"

The women shared a smile and a laugh.

"I take that to mean the afternoon was fun," he said with a smile.

Vic reached for her wine and sat back in the chair. "Oh. You could say that."

"I didn't even get through all the clothes," Emmy told him. "There are still about ten bags to go. You should've seen what all she bought."

"I carried them in," he said blandly. "I have an idea."

"You really don't," Emmy replied with a laugh.

Vic's eyes were wide when they looked at her. "What? I did warn you both that I love to shop."

Dwight listened with interest as the girls went through their afternoon of trying on clothes and shoes. But he knew there had been more to it. Victoria's arrival had been a blessing in disguise for Emmy. It had given her someone to bond with and let her forget, at least for a little while, what had brought her to Montana to begin with.

After dinner, the three cleaned the kitchen together before making their way outside to sit beneath the heaters and stare at the mountain. Dwight had a glass of bourbon while the girls had another glass of wine.

"I always forget how quiet it is here," Vic said into the silence.

Emmy nodded. "There are times during the day when I'm alone that I swear I can hear my heart beating. I never thought I was caught up in the rat race in Denver, but this proves that I was."

"Oh, I know I get caught up. Too easily, in fact. I should come back more." Victoria met Dwight's gaze and gave him a sad smile.

He reached over and placed his hand atop hers. "You have a life in Billings. A job. You do what you have to do. The ranch and I will always be here whenever you want to come and relax."

Victoria made a sound in the back of her throat. "As if you let me relax. You put me to work."

"Which relaxes you," he replied with a grin.

She rolled her eyes. "I hate when you're right."

Dwight looked over to find Emmy smiling at them. "We're on our best behavior in front of you."

"I don't believe that. I think this is how you are all the time."

Vic raised her brows as she looked at Dwight. "She sees past your bullshit. One of the reasons I've come to adore her."

"I've done nothing," Emmy said. "Look at what you did for me. A stranger, no less. I've never known anyone with such a big heart."

"I got to shop. That's all it was."

Dwight shook his head. "Now who's dishing the bullshit."

Emmy laughed and pointed at Vic. "See? I told you. You've got a huge heart. Seriously, though. You'll never know how much I appreciate what you've done for me."

"They're just clothes," Vic said with a shrug.

Dwight knew his sister was getting uncomfortable with the praise, but she needed to hear it. "It was more than clothes. Take the compliment, Vic. You deserve it."

"And much more than that," Emmy added.

Vic raised her eyes and twisted her lips. "All right. If you both insist."

Silence returned as the three turned back to their thoughts. It was a comfortable quiet, though.

After a few moments, Dwight said, "This is nice."

"The very best," Emmy said in a soft voice.

Dwight looked at her, wondering what she was thinking. He felt his sister's gaze and turned his head to her.

Vic gave him another knowing look. Then she said, "Being away from people is nice, but it can become isolating, especially if you're alone."

She was not so subtly telling him that he needed to start dating to find someone to spend his life with. It wasn't as if he hadn't tried. Though, in truth, he hadn't tried all that hard. It was easy to put dating on the back burner when the ranch had plenty to keep him busy. On nights when he got lonely, he buried himself in a book or work. Before he knew it, years had passed since he had come to the ranch. Years of being alone, except for the men who worked for him and Vic's occasional visits.

Then, out of the blue, Emmy had arrived. A beautiful woman who was undoubtedly appealing. If the timing were different, he might have let his attraction be known. But Emmy didn't need a lover. She needed someone who could watch her back and ensure that those after her never found her. What kind of ass would he be if he put her in a position where she felt as if she had to be his lover to be protected?

The thought made him sick to his stomach.

"I think I'm going to turn in," Emmy said as she got to her feet. "Good night."

Vic smiled. "I'll see you in the morning."

"'Night," Dwight replied and forced himself not to watch her walk away.

After the door had shut behind Emmy, Dwight figured he had to the count of five before Vic started talking.

He only got to two before she said, "I see the way you look at her."

"Oh? How is that?"

"The wanting way."

He shrugged without looking at Vic. "It's been a while since I've had a woman."

"Ewww. I didn't want to know that."

"Then you shouldn't have pressed."

"You know what I meant."

Dwight blew out a breath before meeting Vic's gaze. "Is she gorgeous? Without a doubt. But she isn't here on vacation. She's running for her life."

"I know. That doesn't mean there can't be something between the two of you."

"Of course there could be. Anything is possible. But I'm not going to put her in a position where she thinks she has to be with me."

Victoria rolled her eyes. "She has a mind of her own."

"She's also been traumatized. What you saw when you frightened her is just the tip of the iceberg. She had a gun to her head, Vic. The guy was about to pull the trigger when Dalton arrived."

"Emmy told me the whole story."

Dwight frowned briefly. Even he didn't know all of it. Dalton had told him the basics, which was really all he needed to know to do his duty.

"There's no doubt that she's scared and wary and wondering if each second might be her last. The thing is, big brother, chances don't come around very often. You are isolated here. Mostly by choice, I know. But it's a fact. Now you have an amazing woman in your home. She may not feel anything toward you. But what if she does? What if something develops?"

"And what if I'm too busy trying to determine that to know whether the people after her have arrived?"

Vic flattened her lips. "You don't give yourself enough credit. It's just the two of you in the house once I leave. It's a great way to grow closer to someone. And, who knows? Something might develop between the two of you. Personally, I think she's marvelous. Think on what I said, okay?"

Dwight nodded slowly.

Vic rose and kissed his cheek. "You're a good man, Dwight. You deserve happiness. Good night."

"'Night," he replied and returned his gaze to the distant mountains, barely visible in the darkness.

Chapter 12

"Promise you'll call," Victoria said as she hugged Emmy.

The morning was cold, the sky bright as they stood on the porch. "I will."

"I mean it."

Emmy chuckled. "I know you do."

Victoria leaned back and met her gaze. "Once I'm in your life, it's impossible to get rid of me."

"She isn't kidding," Dwight teased from beside them.

Vic rolled her eyes at her brother before returning her attention to Emmy and squeezing her hands. "You're doing the right thing in testifying. As scary as all of this is right now, you'll come out ahead. You do have my brother acting as your bodyguard."

Emmy glanced at Dwight. "Be careful going back."

Victoria winked at her before turning to her brother. Dwight wrapped his arms around her and lifted her feet off the floor, squeezing before setting her back down. "I expect more phone calls from you, as well."

"Yes, ma'am."

She playfully slapped him on the arm. Then the frown transformed into a smile. "I love you."

"Love you, too," he replied.

Victoria gave them a wave before walking down the steps to her car and driving away.

Emmy sighed, feeling as if the air had deflated inside her somehow. "She's a force."

"You don't know the half of it."

"You're lucky to have her."

He gave her a lopsided grin. "I agree. She also reminds me of that often."

They returned inside. Emmy shivered and poured herself another cup of coffee to warm up. She offered one to Dwight, but he shook his head.

"I need to get to work."

Emmy tried not to be disappointed. She wasn't looking forward to being in the house alone again. Not because she was scared but because there wasn't anything to do.

Dwight adjusted his cowboy hat. "You've cleaned every surface in the house. I understand that you need something to do. If you want, there are some things you can do in the office."

"Yes, please," she hurriedly replied.

He chuckled and motioned for her to follow him. Once inside, he sat in the chair and began telling her what needed to be sorted, filed, and shredded.

"I might be overstepping, but I could do some bookkeeping," she offered.

Dwight hesitated, his gaze darting to the computer.

That's when Emmy realized that Vic might not have shared her story with Dwight. "I've been a bookkeeper with a well-known firm in Denver for over eight years. It-it's just a suggestion."

"I'll think on it," he said and rose to walk to the door. There, he paused. "I should be back for lunch."

She met his blue eyes and smiled. "Sounds good."

Dwight walked out with Sam on his heels. A heartbeat later, she was alone. Emmy didn't want a repeat of when Vic had arrived, so she rose and checked all the doors. Dwight had locked the back door behind him, but she double-checked anyway. Then she felt the knife in her sock that she always kept with her. The gun wasn't so easy to carry around the house, but she wanted it with her while she was alone.

She retrieved it from her room and brought it down to the office. Then, she sighed and sank into the chair before reaching for the first stack of papers. It felt good to get lost in work that she knew and understood.

Before she knew it, Sam was beside her. Emmy checked the time on the laptop to see that it was, indeed, lunch. She rose and stretched her back and neck before walking into the kitchen just as Dwight came into the house.

"I'd ask how your morning has been, but I have a feeling you enjoyed it."

She laughed, nodding. "I did, actually."

They began gathering the items needed for sandwiches. They each made one, standing side by side.

It wasn't until they sat down that Dwight said, "I've been thinking about your offer from this morning."

She held up a hand to stop him as she finished chewing and swallowed. "I never should have put you in that kind of position. You don't know me. I would certainly never hand over my bank account information to a complete stranger."

"Nor would I," he told her as he popped a Cheeto into his mouth. "However, the ranch runs off a business account so the bookkeepers and CPAs can access everything. I can set it up so you can't withdraw funds or write checks—or transfer money somewhere I've not approved. In other words, I'd like to take you up on the offer."

Elation filled her. "Are you serious?"

"I'm behind on admin work. There are probably ten checks that need to be deposited, not to mention invoices that need to be sent. I have a handful of employees, and I need to work out there with them. It's difficult to do it all. I would never ask you to do this, but you offered. And, frankly, I'd be a fool not to take advantage of such a kind offer."

"It will benefit you, but as selfish as this sounds, I offered because it's something I want to do."

"It's a win-win for both of us then."

Emmy barely tasted her sandwich. She ate most of it but gave the rest to Sam. The one thing Emmy didn't waste was her Cheetos. After they were gone and her plate had been put away, she not-so-patiently waited for Dwight to finish. He took pity on her and paused in his eating to get the account set up for her.

"Have fun," he said as he gave his desk over to her.

She rubbed her hands together in glee, eager to dive into the account. "Oh, I will."

He chuckled and walked out, though Emmy barely noticed. She submerged herself in everything having to do with the ranch. The first thing she did was deposit all the checks, making sure to match them to outstanding invoices and mark them as paid.

Then she spent time going through the most recent part of the books, learning how the ranch operated. She was pleasantly surprised to find that Dwight had done a good job of staying on top of things. She could show him how to improve in a few ways, but it wasn't nearly as bad as she'd thought it might be.

The sound of someone clearing their throat made her look up from the computer. She jerked her head to the doorway to find Dwight leaning against it, wearing a smile.

"There you are."

She frowned. "What's that supposed to mean?"

"I called your name twice. Even poor Sam couldn't get your attention."

At the mention of his name, the dog whined.

Emmy smiled and gave Sam a good rub. Then she shot Dwight an apologetic look. "Sorry. I get absorbed."

"You aren't kidding. Have you gotten up at all?"

She rubbed her temples as she felt a dehydration headache coming on. "No. Usually, I keep water with me so I'll drink, which in turn forces me to get up and go to the bathroom."

"Moving around is good," Dwight teased.

She laughed and rolled her neck. "Yes, it is."

"Can you call it a day?"

"I think I will." She pushed back in the chair and rose.

They walked to the kitchen together, where she found an open bottle of wine and two filled glasses. Before she reached for the wine, she downed two glasses of water. All the while, Dwight took the pot of stew out of the fridge.

"Leftovers good with you?"

"It's perfect."

"We might be eating this for a few days. Vic made enough for an army."

With the stew heating on the stove, they moved to the living room. Emmy curled up on one side of the sofa while Dwight lit the fire. Once he was done, he put his back to it and remained there with his wine.

Emmy licked her lips as she watched Sam curl up by Dwight's feet. "Did your sister share my story with you?"

"She did not. Vic keeps things to herself."

"An admirable quality. However, I wouldn't have been upset had she told you. Or did you already know from Dalton?"

Dwight shook his head. "Dalton only told me that you were testifying against a powerful man in Denver, that there was a leak in the marshals, and that you were almost killed."

"That is succinct."

"He had to be."

She waved away his words. "Oh, I know. I was just commenting. Those are facts, things that he could share quickly and easily."

"You don't need to tell me anything more."

Emmy glanced at her wine before meeting his gaze. "I know. But I want to."

Dwight took the seat at the opposite end of the sofa. Sam jumped between them and put his head on Emmy's lap.

She slid her fingers into Sam's soft fur. After a deep breath, she told Dwight the same story she had shared with Victoria the day before. He kept his face impassive as he listened, showing very little—until she finished.

"Dalton was right to get you out of town," Dwight said.

Emmy waited for more, but he merely rose to stir the stew as he checked the heat. Then he got the bottle of wine and brought it back to refill their glasses. He set the empty bottle on the table next to the couch and slid his gaze to her.

"I knew someone had put out a hit on you. That was obvious to piece together. I wasn't expecting the mob. I had a minor run-in with some on the east coast," he said.

"Does knowing my story change things?"

He gave her a wry look. "Not at all. It lets me know what kind of people we're up against. Dalton would've filled me in had he been able. He likely counted on me getting the information from you."

Emmy felt lighter having told Dwight her story. She wasn't

sure how much it changed for her, at least not until it came time for the trial—if she made it that long. All she could hope for was that if anyone did find her, that Dwight and his men wouldn't be harmed. She couldn't stand it if Dwight got hurt—or worse, killed—because of her.

Chapter 13

For the next two weeks, Dwight and Emmy fell into a routine. He would make coffee for both of them, and while she didn't rise as early as he did, she didn't sleep late. At noon, he always returned to the house to find her diligently working in the office. He made sure she had water with her at all times.

After lunch, he returned to his duties, and she returned to the office, where she stayed until he came in for the day. She sat in the kitchen with him as he cooked, helping out when she could. They talked about anything and everything before and during dinner.

Once the kitchen had been cleaned every night, they either sat on the porch or remained inside. Sometimes, she turned on the TV. Other times, they read. Occasionally, they kept talking until it was time for bed.

Before Dwight knew it, it was Thanksgiving week. Since he and Vic didn't see each other for Thanksgiving, Dwight never thought too much about it other than the fact that his employees had the day off. But now he had a houseguest—one he wanted to spend the holiday with.

"You're quiet," she said that evening after dinner.

"Thanksgiving is coming up fast."

She raised her brows in surprise. "Is it really? I've not been looking at the dates."

"That's probably a good thing."

"It's been three weeks since I arrived."

He smiled at her surprise. "Yes, it has."

"Have you seen anyone suspicious?"

Dwight shook his head. "But we're not in the clear. We still have weeks to go."

"True, but I wasn't certain I'd make it this long."

He didn't want to tell her that he worried the mob was more likely to locate her the closer they got to the first of the year. With unlimited resources, it was simply a matter of time. But Dwight was prepared for that.

"Do you celebrate Thanksgiving?" he asked.

Her lips twisted as she thought about it. "When I was younger with my parents, we did. My mother always invited anyone who didn't have family or was alone. We always had a very big turnout."

"What a nice gesture."

"It was," Emmy said with a soft smile. "Once my parents were gone, I didn't have family. I spent a few Thanksgivings with some friends, but in the end, it's only been me."

"I'm the same. I was wondering if we should do something. I can cook a turkey and everything if you'd like."

She thought about that for a moment and then shook her head. "Don't go to that kind of trouble. But I think a nice dinner is in order. This could be my last Thanksgiving, after all."

"Don't think like that. Be positive."

"I'm being realistic."

He bowed his head in acceptance. "Any suggestions for our special dinner, then?"

"You're an amazing cook. I've loved everything you put in front of me. Well, except for that meatloaf."

Dwight nearly spat out his wine. "I admit, that was horrible. I never liked it, but I thought I'd give it a try."

"Please, don't ever cook that again."

"Deal," he agreed with a smile.

Emmy looked around the house. "Do you decorate for Christmas?"

"My mom used to go all out. I don't really have the time to get things set up with running the ranch."

"Are there still decorations?"

He glanced at a closet door. "Right there."

"Do you mind if I put them up?"

"Knock yourself out."

Her smile was blinding. "My mother always put up the Christmas decorations Thanksgiving week. I've always done it, as well."

"Then we must do it here."

"We?" she asked in shock.

Dwight smiled and shrugged. "I figured I could help. If you want, that is."

"Definitely. I can't wait to see what all decorations there are."

And he couldn't wait to decorate with her. The thought shocked him. As did the fact that he was excited to share the holidays with Emmy. Or maybe he shouldn't be so surprised. The fact was that he liked her there. They meshed well. They had a lot in common, and yet they could have meaningful conversations about the subjects that differed. He'd never had this kind of relationship with anyone in his life.

He looked forward to coming home for lunch and dinner. No longer did the house feel so big and quiet. It was filled with Emmy.

"You okay?" she asked.

He blinked and nodded. "Yeah. Why?"

"You looked deep in thought."

Dwight shrugged and set his empty glass of bourbon aside. "What do you think about getting out with me tomorrow?"

Her head swiveled to look outside at the falling snow. "In this?"

"It's supposed to stop overnight. I thought we could take a sleigh ride."

Her eyes widened. "Are you serious?"

"Why not? It'll get you out of the house so I can show you more of my beautiful state."

"I have been itching to get out," she confessed with a twist of her lips. Then she smiled. "All right. I'm game."

"Perfect."

Dwight was so excited, he barely slept that night. He woke before his alarm, anxious to have everything in order for Emmy's outing. He rose and quickly finished the things he needed to get done in the barn. After he returned to the house, Sam went upstairs to jump into Emmy's bed as he cooked breakfast. The smell of bacon soon got Emmy up and downstairs.

He loved the slippers she wore with the fur over the arch. She rubbed her eyes, yawning as she poured some coffee, but after a few sips, she was awake enough to eat.

"Bacon always seems to get me out of bed," she said with a chuckle after she finished off the last of her egg.

He had already checked the weather multiple times, but he did it once more. "It's a good day to get out."

"I'm really excited," she said, her light brown eyes shining. "When did you want to head out?"

"Whenever you get ready."

"Then let me go," she said after grabbing one more piece of bacon.

As soon as she left, Dwight made some hot chocolate and put it into a thermos. He grabbed the thick blankets they always used on the sleigh rides. Then he headed outside to hook up the horse, a smile on his face, his gait light. The idea of spending the day alone with Emmy was exhilarating. They both needed this break.

He walked from the barn to find Emmy bundled in earmuffs, a thick scarf, an insulated coat, and gloves, holding the blankets he had gotten out.

He rushed to her. "Here. Let me take those."

"Thanks. I'll get the thermos that was beside them."

It took him a minute to realize that the funny feeling in his stomach was nervousness. It had been so long since he'd felt anything like it. He led the horse out of the barn and stroked the animal's neck as he waited for Emmy and Sam to return.

"Wow," she said when she got a look at the sleigh.

He looked proudly at it. "It was my great-grandfather's."

"It's beautiful."

Dwight held out a hand to her. "Ready?"

"More than you know," she replied with a bright smile.

He helped her into the sleigh before climbing in beside her. After he'd situated the blankets over them, he whistled for Sam. The dog jumped in and circled the foot area where he usually stayed. He looked up at Dwight as if asking if he could get up on the seat like when it was just the two of them.

"It's fine," Emmy said and scooted to the side to make room for Sam.

Dwight shook his head. "The dog is spoiled."

"As he should be," she said and petted Sam.

Dwight gathered the reins, and with a flick of his wrist and a click of his tongue, set the horse into motion. Emmy's smile was huge as they set off. He turned the sleigh toward the mountains, the sky clear above them. He glanced over at Emmy and realized that he had needed this day as much as she did.

Though maybe for different reasons.

Ever since Victoria had left, he hadn't been able to get her words out of his head. Maybe he should let Emmy know of his feelings. Or at least see how she responded if he flirted. He didn't want to make her uncomfortable, but at the same time, he could no longer ignore the feelings within him.

He knew love existed. He'd seen it with his parents. He'd seen it with friends. Dwight just never expected to find it for himself. He had resigned himself to a life alone. Victoria would be the one to eventually have children, and he would pass the ranch to them—if they wanted it. He didn't want the family ranch to end with him, but he also didn't want to force it on anyone who wasn't interested in this way of life. It wasn't for everyone.

They rode closer to the mountains, alongside partly frozen streams and through wide-open pastures. Dwight could hardly take his eyes off Emmy the entire time. The pleasure on her face was priceless. He wished he would've done this sooner. For both of them.

Her head turned, and their eyes clashed. "This is amazing."

"We're not even at the best part."

She hugged Sam. "I'm so excited, I don't even feel the cold."

Another thirty minutes passed before he got them to the spot. He pulled back on the reins and told the horse, "Whoa."

"Oh, Dwight," Emmy said in a soft voice.

He smiled as he looked from the half-frozen waterfall to Emmy. Amazement filled her face as her gaze moved from high above them where the water flowed down the mountainside into the small pool and then into a stream.

"I've looked at this waterfall every day from my window," she said.

He inwardly patted himself on the back. "It is picturesque. My parents came out here all through the year. During the summer, they swam. Usually, they brought food, but it was always to spend some time alone together."

"That sounds special. How many girls did you bring out here?" she asked with a knowing grin.

Dwight laughed, caught. "A few. It never seemed as special as my parents made it out to be. Though they got the idea from my grandparents, who got it from my great-grandparents."

"A family tradition." Emmy nodded and returned her gaze to the waterfall. "I love the idea."

"It's much prettier in the summer."

"I don't know about that. This waterfall was one of the first things I saw when I walked into the bedroom. It's the first thing I look at each morning when I wake." She turned her head to him. "It has become special. And now, you've brought me to see it."

The urge to lean over and kiss her was so great, Dwight had to fight the impulse. All the possibilities Victoria had put into his head nudged him to take a chance.

Chapter 14

She wanted him to kiss her. Emmy was drowning in his eyes, making the moment slow and stretch endlessly. She leaned toward him slightly. Her heart jumped into her throat when his gaze dropped to her mouth, and he moved closer.

With her blood drumming in her ears and her stomach fluttering, she closed her eyes, ready to press her lips to his. At that moment, Sam stood, knocking Emmy back. The dog barked and leapt from the sleigh as he took off running in the snow.

Emmy pressed her lips together, irritated that the opportunity for the kiss she had been about to get had passed. She glanced at Dwight to find him looking at his hands. "Should we go after Sam?"

"What?" Dwight asked as he looked up at her. "Oh. No. Sam is fine. It's probably a rabbit. He won't go far."

"Okay," she murmured and went back to watching the waterfall.

The heat that had filled her just a few moments prior was gone, leaving her chilled. She rubbed her hands together as her mind went over what had happened. Well, she knew what *hadn't* happened—the kiss. Had Sam not stood, she would've kissed Dwight. She hadn't been mistaken, had she? He had been leaning toward her, as well.

Now she was second-guessing herself. Maybe she had wanted it so badly that she had only thought she saw what she wanted. It was as if she expected to be attracted to Dwight. His rugged handsomeness had been something she'd noticed right off, but she'd been too terrified after what'd happened in Denver to give much thought to it. However, as the days passed and they settled into a routine, she hadn't been able to think of much else.

Dwight was always there, steady and unruffled. He pushed her to think of new ideas, and he listened when she did the same. They talked, debated, and shared beliefs and opinions. Her favorite time of the day was evening, when the work stopped for both of them, and they spent time together.

The routine had helped her battle the PTSD, but she knew she still had a long road ahead of her. With her mind occupied during the day, the only time an attack came on was at night. Sam always seemed to know when she needed him. After she woke from a nightmare, he was beside her. His gentle encouragement unfroze her limbs and allowed her to eventually relax once more.

"You're cold," Dwight said and tucked the blankets tighter around her.

She laughed nervously. There hadn't been any awkwardness between them before, but there was now. Or was it just her?

He leaned down and grabbed the thermos. "Do you like hot chocolate? It should help warm you."

"That sounds delicious," she admitted.

He poured some into the top of the thermos that doubled as a mug and handed it to her. Emmy took a sip and sighed as the warm liquid ran down her throat into her stomach, radiating heat as it did.

"Better?" Dwight asked.

She looked at him and nodded before taking another drink. Then she held it out to him. "Want some?"

When he took it from her, their fingers touched, though she couldn't feel anything through their heavy gloves. Emmy didn't know why she was getting all twisted up about Dwight. He might be gorgeous with a no-nonsense air that she liked, but it wasn't as if she were going to live at the ranch for the rest of her life. This was only a temporary arrangement. She would be back in Denver soon.

If she lived through the trial.

Thought made all the hazy musings clear so she could see the truth of everything. All the doubt, all the uncertainty and reservations vanished.

Still, the nerves kicked in because she had never done anything like this before. Her breathing quickened, her heart pounding erratically. But she had to get the words out. "I need to say something."

"All right," he said as he poured more hot chocolate and handed the top to her.

"We both know there is a really good chance that I won't live to testify."

"Now—"

She held up a hand, stopping him. "Please. Let me finish."

Dwight released a long breath. "Of course."

Emmy looked down at the swirls of heat coming from the hot chocolate. She lifted the cup to her lips and drank. "Dalton was right. This ranch and you give me the best chance of staying hidden until the trial. I didn't think I would live this long, but I have. That gives me hope that I might stay hidden long enough to testify. But there's still the problem of getting from here to Denver and then to the courthouse for the trial."

She paused and glanced to find Dwight staring at her, his brows drawn together. Emmy swallowed and took the chance that had somehow fallen in her lap. "Unlike most people, I've been given a timeline of when my life might end. I know there's a chance I could live, but we both know the odds are not in my favor. Because of that, I want to live my life to the fullest. I want to do the things most people are afraid to do because they aren't sure of the outcome. What I'm trying to say, badly, is that this time with you has been the most incredible of my life. I . . . I'm attracted to you. I could ignore it and pretend that it doesn't exist and always wonder if something might have happened between us if I had just let you know. I don't want to do that, though. I want to put this out there. You won't hurt my feelings if you aren't interested. We'll never ha—"

She didn't get to finish her sentence as Dwight reached over and cupped her face in his hands before pressing his lips to hers. After a heartbeat, he leaned his forehead against hers as they breathed deeply.

"You have no idea how long I've wanted to do that," he confessed.

A laugh bubbled up within her. "It doesn't matter. Kiss me again."

Dwight scooted closer. Emmy went to grab him and forgot all about the hot chocolate she held, which ended up spilling on the blankets. Neither cared as they gave in to the passion each felt.

After a few kisses, they were both breathless when he pulled back and met her gaze. "Are you sure?" he asked.

"I've never been surer of anything. Knowing these could be my last weeks makes everything crystal-clear."

Dwight let out a shrill whistle as Emmy gathered up the

top of the thermos and screwed it back on. It wasn't long before Sam came bounding through the snow toward them, his tongue lolling. He jumped into the sleigh without fuss, and Dwight turned the horse around and headed home.

"Hope you don't mind, but I'm cutting the ride short," he told her with a grin.

She laughed. "I was hoping you'd do just that."

When they reached the barn, she helped him get the horse unhitched and brushed down. While he put the sleigh away, she rushed to the house, tore off her winter gear, and put the blankets in the washer to get the chocolate stains out. As she came out of the laundry room, Dwight stood in her path.

They stared at each other for a long moment before Dwight walked to her and took her hand, spinning her to follow him to the master. Once there, he faced her and gently tucked her hair behind her ear.

"You're the most beautiful being I've ever laid eyes on," he told her.

Tears pricked her eyes because she saw the truth of his words on his face, heard it in his voice. It had been a comment casually given, but one born of sincerity. Emmy placed a hand on his chest as she moved closer. She wanted this more than she had ever wanted anything before. It didn't just feel right, it felt as if it were meant to happen.

As if they were destined to be together.

She closed her eyes as his fingers slowly traced her jawline, moving down her neck and around to cup the back of her head.

"Look at me," he demanded.

Her lids fluttered open to find his blue eyes blazing with desire. Her heart skipped a beat at the sight of it. Her mouth went dry. She needed his kiss, and she wasn't going to wait for him to give it. Emmy lifted her face and pressed her lips to his.

A low moan tore from his throat as he wrapped his free arm around her, holding her tightly. She wound her arms around his neck and sighed. They exchanged long, lingering kisses full of yearning and need before he tilted his head and slipped his tongue inside her mouth.

Then it was her turn to moan. He tasted so good. And his kisses left her breathless, wanting more. So much more. Her fingers sank into the long hairs at the back of his neck. But it wasn't enough. She needed to feel all of him, had to *see* all of him.

Emmy began unbuttoning Dwight's shirt. He didn't stop kissing her as he jerked his arms free of the garment and tossed it aside. She slipped her hands under his thermal and met warm skin. She pushed her hands upward, moving his clothing until he had no choice but to tear his lips from hers until the shirt was gone.

He tried to kiss her again, but Emmy stopped him. Only because she wanted a good look at his upper body. Corded muscles covered every inch of him from his broad shoulders and thick chest that narrowed to a slim waist. His arms were defined with muscles, proving that he worked hard—and it wasn't with weights.

She flattened her hands on his chest and marveled at the man before her. Her fingers slid through curly, dark hair sprinkled across his chest.

Finally, she looked up at him. "Wow."

He gave her a crooked smile and murmured, "My turn."

Excitement pooled in her belly as he reached for her sweater and tugged it over her head. Emmy absently discarded the garment and already had her thermal shirt in hand when he grabbed it. With both tops gone, she stood before him in a pale pink bra.

Dwight blinked, staring at her breasts for a moment with his hands not quite touching her. The look of awe he wore left her speechless. She was the one who reached around and unhooked the garment to let the straps fall down her arms before tossing it away to join her other clothes.

"Damn," he whispered and cupped her breasts while running his thumbs over her already hard nipples.

She pulled his head down for another kiss. Their tongues tangled as he massaged her breasts and teased her nipples until she could barely remain standing. His hands moved to the waistband of her pants and opened her jeans. She liked how he thought and quickly followed suit with his.

Together, they yanked down each other's pants as well as their own until they were both free. Dwight pressed her against the wall and dropped to his knees. She watched, excitement building, as he hooked his fingers into her pale pink panties and slowly pulled them down her legs. Then he lifted one of her thighs and hooked her knee over his shoulder, gently licking her sex.

Emmy gasped with pleasure and flattened her hands against the wall, hoping to find something to keep her standing. All thought left her when his tongue swirled around her clit, sending her spiraling into a chasm of unending pleasure.

Chapter 15

If this was a dream, Dwight never wanted to wake.

He had Emmy in his arms, had sampled her kiss. And now, he was tasting her. Her soft moans drove him wild. He desperately wanted inside her, but he needed to bring her pleasure first.

Dwight looked at Emmy to see her eyes closed, her mouth open, and her chest heaving as she struggled for breath. Her hands gripped the wall. He continued teasing her swollen clit with his tongue while running his hands up and down her long, lean legs. The moment he felt her begin to shake, he intensified his efforts.

Her soft scream of pleasure that rushed through her made his cock jump in anticipation. He fought not to bury himself deep inside her right then.

When the last of her tremors subsided, he gave her a final lick and placed a kiss on each thigh before slowly straightening. Then he kissed her, letting her taste herself. Dwight turned her and maneuvered her to the bed.

Gently, he leaned her back, placing a hand on the mattress

to stop her from falling. He followed her down, never breaking the kiss. Her hands moved over his back, feeling the scars from his rough-and-tumble world. She slid her foot up his leg in a seductive move that made him groan with need.

She slipped a finger into the waistband of his boxer briefs and moved the band down over one of his ass cheeks. Dwight ended the kiss and got to his feet so he could remove them. When he looked up, Emmy was on her elbows, watching him.

"I could look at you all day," she said.

He ran his eyes over her curvy body from her full breasts with their dusky-tipped nipples, to the indent of her waist and the flare of her hips, then down those gorgeous legs of hers. "I know how you feel."

She smiled in response and then motioned him forward by crooking her finger. "There's a part of you I've not gotten to touch yet."

"I'm not so sure that's a good idea right now."

"Oh?" she asked with a quirk of a brow.

Dwight grinned sheepishly. "It's been a while for me."

"Me, too."

He put a knee on the bed and climbed over her with his hands on either side of her head. Then, slowly, he lowered himself atop her. Her lips parted as she let out a shaky breath. Her hands came up to touch his back. Slowly, she caressed her fingers down to his waist and then to his butt. All the while, they stared into each other's eyes.

The wanting he felt wasn't only because he hadn't had a woman in a while. It was something much more, something deeper. Something . . . unfathomable.

He couldn't catch his breath. His heart pounded with anticipation and exhilaration. And his body burned. For Emmy. All for Emmy. He wanted to put every second of this moment to memory.

Dwight ran a hand down her side to her waist. Then he

ground his arousal against her belly. Her breath hitched, her fingers sinking into his back.

"Don't stop," she begged.

With two words, he was utterly lost. He lowered his head, brushing his lips against hers before deepening the kiss. Flames of desire exploded again the moment their tongues touched. He gripped her hip, his hunger demanding that he claim her body.

He shifted, the head of his cock meeting her sex. To his surprise, she reached between them and wrapped her fingers around his arousal. Her breathing was ragged as she stroked his length. His hips moved in time with her hands. He stilled from the force of the pleasure the instant her thumb swirled over the sensitive head of his rod.

As if realizing that he was on the edge, Emmy guided him to her entrance. Dwight hissed in a breath and tore his mouth from hers at the feel of her hot, wet flesh surrounding him. He lost himself in the feel of her.

Their bodies moved together, the rhythm building faster and faster. Dwight looked into Emmy's eyes and saw the same yearning he felt within himself. As their bodies moved in a dance as old as time, he realized that he had been slowly falling in love with Emmy. Desire swelled even more as he felt himself tumbling toward his climax.

"Dwight," Emmy said as she stiffened, pleasure washing over her face.

The instant he felt her body clamping around his cock, he was lost. He gave one final thrust, sinking deep as he gave in to the orgasm. They clung to each other as ecstasy swept them away. It wasn't until long moments later when their breathing finally returned to normal that he pulled out of her and rolled to his back.

They looked at each other, sharing a smile. He motioned her to him with his head. Emmy rolled to her side and snuggled against him as he wrapped an arm around her, their legs tangled.

"This isn't how I saw the day going," he said with a smile.

She chuckled and glanced up at him. "I can't say I did either."

"I'm glad you spoke from your heart earlier."

"Life is too short not to take chances. My mother used to tell me that, and I've tried to live my life like that. I didn't do a very good job of it. I played it safe and rarely took chances. I preferred to stay in my comfort zone because it was easier. I never did anything spontaneous."

"I'd say going to that first party with Joe was impulsive."

She snorted softly. "Loneliness pushed me to do that."

"There's no shame in that."

"I had grand plans for my life and the things I wanted to do and try. I haven't done any of those things."

He tightened his arm around her briefly. "Your life isn't over yet."

"It's because I'm in this position that I said what I did this morning. The me before never would've had the courage."

"I'm glad you did."

He felt her smile against him. "Me, too. It was . . . freeing. I knew the worst that could happen was that you wouldn't be interested. I've always looked at the worst-case scenario in any situation, but it didn't matter how many times I knew the odds were in my favor, I could never take the leap and just try."

"Sounds like you discovered something about yourself."

"I did. I'm going to stop being scared that someone will say no. I'm going to go for it. I wonder how many opportunities passed me by while I was scared."

He kissed the top of her head, smiling. "It doesn't do any good to think of the past. Let it go and live for this current moment."

"Now that's great advice." She rose onto an elbow to look at him.

Her hair was mussed, her skin glowed, and her lips were still swollen from his kisses. He'd never seen anyone look so amazing before. He smoothed a strand of hair from her face and decided to take a page from her book.

"I have to tell you something."

She grinned, her eyes crinkling at the corners. "Okay."

"These last few weeks have been some of the best of my life."

"Mine, too," she said in a soft voice.

Dwight glanced down and took her hand in his. "The thing is, I'm falling in love with you."

She blinked, shock filling her face.

It wasn't what he wanted to see, but he had to tell her the truth. "I love you, Emmy. I don't want to just safeguard you until the first of the year. I want to spend my life protecting you, loving you."

"I-I," she stammered.

He smiled and put a finger to her lips. "You don't need to say anything."

She returned to her position on his chest as he stared through the windows out to the snow-covered valley and the mountains. He didn't regret sharing his feelings. Like Emmy had said, life was too short to let chances pass by. Whether she ever returned his feelings or not, he had told her his.

They lay in silence, their hearts beating in time. Her lashes fluttered against his chest as she blinked. There was so much he wanted to say to her, but he kept silent. She had a lot on her mind with the trial looming closer and closer.

"I want to come with you to Denver," he said into the room.

A beat of silence passed before she said, "I'd like that."

He sighed, a band loosening around his heart that he hadn't

known was there. "Dalton is more than capable, but both of you need someone you can trust."

"I trust you." She absently drew on his chest with her finger, then lifted her head a fraction to place a kiss on his skin.

"I'll do everything in my power to protect you."

He felt her smile again. "I know you will." She released a breath and then asked, "How did you and Dalton meet?"

"We went to college together. We hung out with the same people but weren't really close. After graduation, we went our separate ways. It wasn't until a joint venture between Homeland Security, the FBI, DEA, and the US Marshals that we ran into each other again. They had a team of four from each of the divisions to build relationships for future task forces. It was only supposed to be a training exercise, but it turned into much more than that."

She shifted her head to look up at him. "What happened?"

"They, meaning the heads of the four divisions, each wanted the training to be on their home turf. No one wanted to give an inch, so someone ranking far above them decided to send us out of the country to a place where no one had the upper hand."

Emmy raised her brows. "Where was that?"

"Britain. Word got leaked about our training, and a terrorist group attacked. I was shot in the leg and pinned down. Dalton managed to get to me and helped stanch the bleeding. Somehow, he got us back to the base, but during that five-hour stretch, a brotherhood formed. He saved my life. I told him I would always be there if he ever needed anything. After I left Homeland Security to come here, I made sure that he knew the offer still stood and always would."

"Now I understand why he trusts you."

"And why I didn't hesitate when he called."

Emmy released a breath and smiled. "I'm glad Dalton was there for you."

"We might not talk often, but the one thing we know above all else is that we'll be there for each other."

"So, was the joint training venture a success?"

He twisted his lips as he wrinkled his nose. "Yes, and no. It was a start. Not much headway had been made by the time I left."

"But out of that came a friendship that has kept me safe."

Dwight shifted her so that she lay between his legs on her stomach. He leaned down and placed his lips on hers for a lingering kiss. "That it has."

Chapter 16

Emmy met Dwight's blue eyes. "That story about you and Dalton ended well."

"It did," Dwight said with a shrug.

"You left out a lot."

He held her gaze before glancing away.

Emmy leaned forward and kissed him. "The attack and you being hurt was a lot worse than you make it out to be, wasn't it?"

"Yeah," he said with a slow nod.

"The other two on your team? Did they make it out?"

Dwight swallowed, his nostrils flaring. "Someone threw a grenade at us. Killed them instantly. In a blink, I felt like I was back in my military days. Instinct took over, but training can only do so much when you're wounded and pinned down."

"But you got out. You came home."

"I don't regret serving my country in any of the three capacities I did. But it takes a toll on a person's body."

"Not to mention their mind," she added.

Dwight pulled a face. "That's the truth. A lot of my friends didn't want to see anyone about their PTSD."

"Did you?"

"Absolutely. I didn't want to go through the rest of my life with all of that in my head. I mean, I still do. It'll always be there, but I've learned how to handle things. I'm not embarrassed to say that I took medication for a few months, but opening up to a therapist worked the best. They're trained to treat combat veterans."

She leaned her head to the side, loving how he reached over to play with the ends of her hair. "And after the training exercise with Dalton?"

"I went back to therapy. I knew that situation would trigger things, and I was right. I got a jump on it, but there were still some very rough months. Even now, years later, little things can elicit a memory of those traumatic times. Stress is a trigger in itself."

Emmy frowned and began sitting back, but Dwight held her in place. "My being here is stressful. I don't want to cause you any harm."

"You aren't," he told her pointedly.

"But I am."

He held her firmly. "Have I added extra security? Yep. Do I double-check things more than usual? Sure. Do I like protecting you? Absolutely. Is it a stressor? It's nothing I can't handle."

"And what if Joe and his men come? What if they find me?"

"I'll deal with it." He pulled her up and kissed her slowly, seductively. Then he whispered, "Having you here has been good. I knew the risks with what Dalton asked, and I readily accepted them. I still do."

She briefly closed her eyes. "I'll never forgive myself if you're injured. Or worse."

"Don't think like that. Keep positive."

"Easier said than done."

He grinned. "I've got something that will help."

That sexy smile always made her stomach flutter. "What's that?"

"Start a bath. I'll be right back," he said with a wink.

She moved so he could rise and walk out of the room with Sam on his heels. Emmy shook her head, still smiling. Despite her worry, she didn't want to ruin a perfectly good day with morbid thoughts. She took Dwight's advice and put them out of her mind, focusing on positive things instead. Like how great her body felt after sex with Dwight.

Emmy rose from the bed and started a bath. She tested the water to get it just right as she sat on the edge of the tub. The thought of sinking into it made her sigh in expectation. As the tub filled, she rose and caught a glimpse of herself in the mirror. She blinked, not recognizing the woman who stared back at her.

She put her hands in her mussed hair that looked as if master hands had artfully crafted it. Her skin was flushed, her pupils dilated. Her body didn't just look different, it *felt* it, as well. She slowly ran her hands from her breasts down over her hips. Images of her and Dwight tangled together filled her thoughts.

When her eyes refocused, she saw Dwight standing behind her in the mirror. His gaze blazed with desire. Emmy turned to him as he started toward her. His arm snaked out to wrap around her waist and bring her against him.

"Damn, woman. You drive me crazy with wanting," he murmured against her lips.

She threaded her fingers into his hair and pulled back to look at him. "Not nearly as much as I want you."

"That's debatable." He kissed her tenderly.

That's when she noticed that he held something in his right hand.

He grinned and jerked his chin to the tub. "Check the water."

She turned and noticed that it was getting near the top, so she shut it off. When she straightened, Dwight held out his hand. She accepted it as he helped her into the tub. "I hope you plan on joining me."

"I certainly do," he said.

She watched as he pulled a small stool close to the tub. There, he set two glasses and filled them with wine. He handed her one and said, "I'll be right back."

Emmy sipped the white wine and leaned against the back of the tub, making sure to flip her hair out so it didn't get wet. Dwight was back shortly, Sam sniffing the air after him. She learned why when Dwight set down a plate of cut cheese, olives, and crackers.

"I've never been so pampered," she confessed as she reached for an olive.

His smile widened. "Can I join you?"

"Please." She scooted forward so he had room to climb in behind her.

The tub was wide enough that they could sit comfortably back to front. He stretched out his legs as far as they could go but still had to bend his knees. She leaned back against him, the water lapping around them.

"This is perfect," she told him.

He kissed her temple. "It certainly is."

Emmy lifted her head enough to take a drink of wine. Her eyes grew heavy, and she let them close. She couldn't remember the last time she had been this relaxed.

"How do you feel?" Dwight asked.

She smiled and rolled her head to the side. "Happy and safe."

"Exactly my plan."

Emmy heard the smile in his voice. She sighed, wishing they could stay like this forever.

"Don't," he said, breaking into her thoughts.

She frowned. "Don't what?"

"You're starting to think about the future. That will shatter the positivity we've created. It's better not to think of that."

"You're right. I don't want anything to destroy this perfect day. But I'm going to have to think about the future eventually. Some things need to be addressed."

"Understood. Just not right now."

She took another drink of wine. "I can agree to that."

"What would you like to do after this?"

"After?" she asked with a chuckle. "I'm not sure you'll ever get me out of this tub. You brought food and wine."

His breath brushed her ear as he laughed. "It is a nice tub. I don't enjoy it as much as I should."

"You take baths?"

"Is that surprise I hear in your voice?" he playfully admonished.

Emmy shifted to lean her head back so she could see him. "I'm not saying it isn't done. It's just that women usually enjoy the baths."

"It's true I'm not like most men."

She nodded and returned to face forward. "I like that about you."

"Oh?"

The happiness in his voice made her smile. She hadn't forgotten that he had confessed his love, and while she had been surprised by it, she was both elated and saddened that he felt such feelings for her. Mostly because she feared what having her in his life could do to him. It was a conversation she knew better than to try and have with him. Dwight would only tell her that he was a grown man who could make his own decisions. While that was true, she also knew that had she not needed help, Dalton never would've brought her here. And her and Dwight's paths never would've crossed.

She wouldn't have known to watch the stars at night in Montana, how much more beautiful a waterfall could be, how much she loved sleigh rides, or . . . how much she had come to love living with him.

Sam sighed as he moved onto his side and stretched out on the tile floor to sleep. Both she and Dwight looked at the dog. Sam was another part of life on the ranch that Emmy had adapted to quite easily. Actually, there wasn't much about the ranch she *hadn't* come to love and admire.

"You're thinking again," Dwight said.

She finished her wine and leaned forward to set it on the stool by the tub. After popping a slice of cheese into her mouth, she returned to her reclining position and took Dwight's empty hand in hers. She threaded her fingers with his.

"I confess, I am."

He was silent for a moment. "I could take your mind off things."

She smiled. "You could."

"Or we could talk about whatever is on your mind."

She closed her eyes and let herself be in the moment. "I think I'd like to just sit here and listen to you."

"I'm not talking."

"You could recite the alphabet, and I'd be happy. I love your voice. You have the greatest voice."

He chuckled. "The alphabet, huh? That would get old pretty quick."

"Tell me what made you join the bureau."

He drank the last of his wine, then reached out of the tub to pour more into both of their glasses. "I had already decided that I was leaving the military once my tour was up. I toyed with the idea of joining the Secret Service, but I had a friend who had gone that route and wasn't exactly happy. Another friend had joined the FBI. He let me know that they were interested in me."

"Did you apply?"

"Not right away. I wanted more information, so I set up an appointment when I got back to the States. They accommodated my schedule, and I had meetings with them over a three-day period."

She wasn't at all surprised by his words. From what she had come to know about Dwight, he was thoughtful and methodical in his decision-making process. He took his time and weighed his options carefully. "How many people did you meet with?"

"About ten. Each higher up in the organization than the last. By the end of the third day, I knew I wanted to join them. As soon as I let them know, the official offer came in."

"What did you do with them?"

"I was a special agent. The guys in the black suits? That was me."

She nodded as she opened her eyes to look around. "I can see that. Especially with your training in the military. Where were you stationed?"

"Wherever we were needed. It was both demanding and rewarding. I liked my time there."

"If you don't mind me asking, what made you leave?"

He shrugged, causing the water to move. "I was offered a great opportunity at Homeland Security outside of the Secret Service. It wasn't an easy decision, but in the end, it was the best one."

"Would you have stayed at Homeland Security had your parents not wanted to hand the ranch over?"

"Hmm. I don't know. I was pretty burned out when my parents told me the news. That's why I didn't hesitate to resign and return to the ranch immediately. My father always told me to do whatever I wanted with my life. He never put the weight of the ranch on my shoulders, but in the back of my mind, I always knew I'd end up here. It's where I was born to be."

Emmy lifted his hand to her lips and kissed it. "You always seem to make the right decisions."

"I'm merely pointing out the good ones. I could bore you for weeks listing all the bad ones," he said with a laugh.

"But you've always followed your heart."

He set aside his wine glass and wrapped his arms around her to give her a little squeeze. "You haven't?"

"No."

"There is still time to change that."

She turned in the tub to face him. "I intend to do just that."

Chapter 17

Joe drummed his fingers on his desk. How could his life have gone so fucking wrong so quickly? He'd had everything.

He could pinpoint exactly where things started to go sideways—Emmy. His infatuation with her had blinded him to everything else. Because of his inability to control his desire, he had lost his wife and now faced a trial that had the potential to put him away for life.

A knock on the door sounded before it opened. Tony stuck his head in. Joe smiled at his best friend.

"Got a minute?" Tony asked.

Joe motioned him inside. Tony closed the door behind him and walked to the chairs before Joe's desk, sinking into one. Joe noted the tight lines around his friend's mouth. "What is it?"

"I heard from Orso."

"It's about time. The bastard is taking too damn long," Joe snapped.

Tony drew in a breath and slowly released it. "He lost the trail again."

Joe slammed his hands on the desk and got to his feet as he bellowed, "Again?"

"That marshal was smart," Tony said.

Joe straightened and stalked to the bar cart where he had the best liquors at his disposal. He poured himself a drink and downed it before pouring a second. He lifted the crystal decanter to Tony, who shook his head. Joe shrugged and put it away before downing his second drink.

He set the glass down with purpose and faced his best friend. "How many times now has Orso lost Emmy's trail?"

"Too many."

"And our friends in the marshals can't help?"

Tony twisted his lips ruefully. "They've been unable to get ahold of Dalton. Apparently, he doesn't trust anyone enough to do more than let them know that Emmy is safe."

"Fuck," Joe said with a long sigh as he stuffed his hands into his pants' pockets. "We've already lost weeks."

"We still have time," Tony said. "The longer Emmy thinks she's safe, the laxer she'll become and make it easier for us to find her. And you know Orso is good at what he does. He might continue losing her trail, but he'll eventually find it again."

Joe cut a look to his friend. "Will it be in time to stop me from going to jail?"

"She's their only witness. Without her, they have no case against you, and they know it."

Joe ran a hand over his mouth and returned to his chair. "Any word from Stella or her family?"

"Not since we were alerted that Stella arrived in New Jersey with her family."

Joe puffed his cheeks as he blew out a breath. "They've not answered your email about keeping the partnership?"

"No."

"That's not good for us."

Tony shrugged nonchalantly. "I never liked that arrangement to begin with. I know you thought being connected to the family would elevate you, but you don't need them. You've continued to build on what *your* family began. You have an empire here. You've also gotten the attention of some of the families from Vegas and California."

Joe sat back in his chair and steepled his fingers. Tony always did know how to stroke his ego to calm him down. Unfortunately, it wasn't working this time. "Part of that interest was my affiliation with New Jersey. That's gone now."

"Then prove you never needed them to begin with."

"I can't do anything until Emmy is dealt with. As long as the trial looms, I'm hindered. Every cop in the area is looking at us with a microscope. Even the ones on our payroll aren't doing what they used to."

Tony half-heartedly lifted a shoulder. "They've got to look out for themselves. Everyone does in instances like this."

"Including you?"

"I'm with you, Joe. I always have been. You know that."

Joe nodded, watching his friend closely. He hated that he was beginning to doubt everyone's loyalty. "Just wanted to test you out. What about the others?"

"No one is teetering. They're all yours. They know you, and they know the trial will never happen."

"I want to know the minute anyone starts to doubt that," Joe said, pointing his finger at Tony.

His friend bowed his head in acceptance. "I always do."

At that instant, Tony's cell phone vibrated. He took it out of the inside pocket of his suit jacket and raised a brow. His gaze clashed with Joe's. "It's Orso."

"Put it on speaker."

Tony set the phone on the desk and answered it, putting it on speaker. "Orso. I'm here with Joe."

"Good," Orso said. "I want to tell you personally, boss,

that I found the woman's trail again. The marshal is good, but I'm learning his habits. It's getting easier to find them."

Joe scooted forward in his chair. "I needed good news, Orso. Good work. You will find them."

"I gave you my word. I'll call you when it's done."

"Actually," Joe said, "I want to be there."

Tony's eyes widened in surprise. "I don't think that's a good idea."

Joe ignored his friend. "Did you hear me, Orso?"

"I did. When I find her, I'll give you a call so you can meet us."

"Good." Joe ended the call and looked expectantly at Tony. "Say what you want to say."

"Have you lost your goddamn mind?" Tony asked in shock and anger.

Joe quirked a brow. "I run this family."

"I know. I've been by your side through it all. Even before you took over. You've always been smart, but this is a bad move."

"How so?"

"For one, because everyone is watching you."

Joe waved away his words. "You and I both know I could get out of town without anyone being the wiser."

"You want Emmy gone so she can't testify against you. Why would you go anywhere near her murder? Do you want to implicate yourself?"

"I'm having her killed. I'm pretty sure that tells you I'll do anything not to go to prison."

Tony threw up his hands in defeat. "Then why do you want to go to her?"

"I want to see her face when she realizes that she's lost."

Tony blew out a harsh breath as he got to his feet. He tucked his phone back into the pocket and buttoned his jacket. Then he met Joe's gaze. "You aren't thinking clearly. I hope you come to your senses before Orso finds Emmy."

"And if I don't? You going to stop me from going?" Joe challenged.

Tony shook his head. "Of coursc, not. I just won't be with you."

Of all the things Tony could've said, that was the one that left Joe reeling. There hadn't been a single instance when his best friend hadn't supported his decisions or been by his side. Maybe he was being rash. Perhaps he did need to rethink watching Orso take Emmy's life.

Then he remembered how Emmy had taken *his* life. No one did that to Joe Roma and got away with it. He had to set a precedent. That way, no one in the future would dare to go up against him for anything.

Chapter 18

Dwight checked the sweet potato halves in the oven before going back outside to the grilling steaks. Emmy was curled up on the outdoor sofa, wrapped in a blanket with Sam after spending the day decorating the house for Christmas.

They shared a smile. Each day since the sleigh ride had been the best of his life.

He hadn't spoken of his feelings again, nor was he upset that she hadn't said she loved him. She had slept in his bed every night. They made love often, shared smiles, cuddled, and thoroughly enjoyed each other's company.

"Thanks for your help," Emmy said. "There's no way I could've gotten everything done."

Dwight chuckled and checked the steaks. "I didn't realize how much Christmas Mom had."

"You also didn't bother to tell me the tree was twenty feet tall."

"It's only twelve," he said with a laugh.

Emmy pulled a face. "I still needed a ladder. And even then, you're the one who had to put the star at the top." She smiled and looked through the windows inside. "It looks amazing, though."

Dwight followed her gaze to see the tree lit and the ornaments sparkling. Green wreaths decorated with red bows hung on the windows. The front door had garland draped around it as well as a wreath and three small Christmas trees of varying heights. Inside, there was garland along the staircase. Along with more greenery on the mantel. Emmy had also found their old stockings and hung those, as well.

But that wasn't all. Little bits of Christmas were scattered throughout. Whether it was a glass vase with colored ornaments sitting on his desk, Christmas towels in the bathrooms, or the four-foot tree she'd decorated for his bedroom, the season was in every corner of the house. And he absolutely loved it.

When the steaks finished, they went back inside, where he got the sweet potatoes and dressing finished. Emmy readied the wine and put the final touches on the table. Then they sat to eat.

"You said to cook whatever I wanted," he told her as he put a steak on her plate.

She flashed him a smile. "I meant it. Thanksgiving isn't about what we eat. It's about the people we spend it with. It's about the very reason for the holiday."

He covered her hand with his. "I'm glad you're here. Happy Thanksgiving."

"Happy Thanksgiving."

As they began to eat, Emmy said, "I thought that I might help you out on the ranch tomorrow."

He looked up in surprise. "I'd love that."

"I'm not sure what all you do, but I'm sure I can figure things out."

Dwight grinned. "We'll stick close to the house. I'll make sure my ranch hands aren't anywhere near."

"I keep forgetting about them," she said, her nose wrinkling.

"I trust them, but I think it's better if they don't know you're here."

She nodded quickly. "Oh, I agree. It's just that I've finally started to feel safe. I forget you have people working for you that don't know about me."

"It's because I talk about them. You feel like you know them, which makes you believe you've met them, and they you."

She swallowed her bite. "I suppose. I'm just so ready for this trial to be over."

Dwight hoped she didn't mean that she was ready to leave him. He tried not to let his mind go down that road, but he couldn't stop it.

"There are days when I can almost forget, you know?" Emmy continued. "Then there are some when it's all I can think about."

He glanced at her. "I'm sorry."

"You've done so much to help. Without you, I wouldn't be here now. You've helped me feel safe, but not so much that I'm not taking precautions."

Dwight nodded with a smile. "I understand."

"Have you heard anything from Dalton?"

"Nothing. Though, I didn't expect to. At least not until it gets closer to the trial."

Emmy tucked her hair behind her ear. "I'm sorry. I shouldn't be talking about this now."

"It's obviously on your mind. Talk if you need to."

She set her fork on her plate and looked at him. "It's because of you."

"Me?" he asked with a frown.

Emmy smiled, a little sadness in her eyes. "The time we've spent together has been . . ." She shrugged. "I can't even put it into words. It's Thanksgiving, a holiday I've spent alone the last couple of years. And now, I'm with you. We put up Christmas decorations."

"Was it too much?"

"It was perfect. That's what has me thinking about the trial. I'm tired of it hanging over my head."

He reached for her hand again and covered it with his. "I know. Not long now."

"I don't know if I can make it."

"You will," he told her. "I'll be right by your side."

That seemed to fortify her as her smile widened, and she returned to eating. But all Dwight could think about was how little time he had left with Emmy before Dalton came for her. Even though he'd said he would go with them to Denver, they'd said nothing about what happened after the trial.

That was primarily due to Emmy not wanting to think about the possibility that she might not live. Just because she made it to Denver, and even the courthouse, didn't mean she would live long enough to take the stand.

Dwight wanted to say so many things to her. He wanted her to come back to Montana when everything was done, but he also knew putting that kind of pressure on her right now would be disastrous. She needed to focus on remaining calm. She felt safe right now, and he didn't want that to change.

When the trial was behind them, he would talk to her. Hopefully, by then, she could tell him her feelings. He knew she cared about him. It was in the way she touched him, how she smiled at him and held him.

But he still needed the words.

Having her in his life, being a couple as they were now, he knew that she was the only one for him. However, they hadn't spoken of their current arrangement. After he had confessed that he was falling in love with her and she hadn't responded, Dwight had thought it best not to go down that path again just yet.

She hadn't brought up anything either. They had simply fallen into things that most couples did, including sleeping in the same bed together.

After the meal, they moved to the living room. To his surprise, Emmy turned out all the lights except for the ones on the tree and the various garlands. He stoked the fire and added another log. When he turned around, she held out a glass of bourbon for him.

"To the best Thanksgiving I've ever had," she said and lifted her glass.

He touched his glass to hers, smiling. "To the best Thanksgiving."

They each took a drink to seal the toast. Dwight then took her hand and brought her to the sofa so they could curl up together. Once they were settled, Sam jumped up to lie next to Emmy.

"Too early for Christmas music?" he asked.

She smiled up at him. "Not at all."

"Unless you want to watch something."

"I think I'd like to just sit and enjoy the evening."

"I can give you that." He took out his phone and found his Christmas playlist, then sent it through the speaker.

Perry Como's "It's Beginning to Look a Lot Like Christmas" filled the silence.

"I love the old Christmas songs," Emmy said as she began singing along.

Dwight took in the moment. The atmosphere, the amazing woman by his side, the love he felt for her, and the contentment he'd found. His heart clutched because the longer she was with him, the deeper in love he fell. He feared he would never recover from Emmy.

His dad used to talk about people finding soul mates. Several of Dwight's friends had divorced parents. His mom and dad were only one of a handful of couples that had not only stayed married but also remained deeply committed to each other. He'd known it was a rare thing, even as a child. As he got older, it became more and more apparent that finding that special someone who fit with you was like finding a needle in a haystack.

He had reconciled himself to living alone because he wasn't going to settle for anything less than what his parents had. The problem with that was that he actually had to get out and meet women to find his soul mate, which he hadn't done. He'd given himself all kinds of excuses for why he hadn't dated over the years, but they were all lies. The truth was, he feared that he would never find his other half. He couldn't be disappointed if he never looked.

Then Emmy came into his life.

He wrapped an arm around her, bringing her closer. She rested her head on his chest and hummed along with the music. He watched the firelight dancing on the fur rug, his thoughts lingering on Emmy and how he might keep her safe on the way to Denver and then to the trial.

"What are you thinking so hard about?" she asked.

Dwight's thoughts halted. He kissed her head. "A lot of things. Mostly about how happy I am right now."

She sat up to look at him. "I'm glad to be a part of today."

"Me, too."

"This ranch is incredible. I know it's hard work, but this life suits you."

He took a drink. "The really hard work is in the spring and summer. But this ranch is home. I can't imagine doing anything else now. For better or worse, I'll work it until I can pass it on or die."

"Do you want children?"

"It's a natural progression, I think. Graduate, get a job, find love, have kids."

She quirked a brow. "That wasn't an answer."

"I've never been against them. I've just never stopped to really think about it."

"What *do* you think about?"

He looked at the flames in the hearth. "My parents were deeply in love. The kind of love that people sing and write about, but few rarely find."

"That's wonderful."

"It was even more so to watch them. They told Vic and me to never settle for less than the real thing. Vic would always ask how we would know."

"What did your parents tell her?" Emmy asked.

Dwight glanced at her with a grin. "Mom said that Vic would know. We would both know without a doubt. And until then, we should wait."

"Is that what you've been doing? Waiting?"

"Hiding," he admitted as he turned his head to her.

Her eyebrows shot up on her forehead. "Hiding? Why?"

"I saw too many of my friends find love and then divorce. They wanted so badly to find *The One* that they mistook lust for love. Which is why the relationships fell apart. Both parties believed they were in love because they wanted it so desperately."

Emmy's face grew thoughtful. "It's something within all of us—that need to find love. To have someone with you through your life that you can depend on and who depends on you."

"We're born with that need. It's why there are so many songs and books written about love. We're all searching."

"Sometimes, we might be searching too hard."

He set aside his drink and took her free hand in his. "Have you ever been in love?"

"What I thought was love," she told him. "In both high school and college. I thought the guy I was with in college was the one. So many people seemed to get married in college because it was the thing to do."

"What happened to him?"

She shrugged and looked away. "He found someone else. I was heartbroken. It took a long time before I could step back and realize that he had done us both a favor. We weren't compatible. We wanted different things. One of us would've had to compromise, and that isn't fair."

"And now, here you are."

Her pale brown eyes met his. "And now, here I am."

Chapter 19

Emmy had never felt so twisted in all her life. She wished she could call the Denver district attorney and tell her that she had changed her mind about testifying. Emmy didn't want to leave the ranch—or Dwight—ever.

But that was out of her hands.

Worse, she knew that if she managed to stay hidden until the first of the year, then getting to the courthouse in Denver and testifying was where Joe and his people would come for her. She had such a short time left with Dwight.

That wasn't to say she didn't have faith in Dalton's and Dwight's attempts to keep her safe. But she knew the extremes Joe would go to in order to stay out of prison. He had the money and resources to ensure that his will was done. Emmy would end up in a grave, while Joe walked free to commit more crimes.

It was the reason she'd decided to testify against him. However, that was before she met Dwight, and her heart got mixed up in things.

She had never been happier. But at the same time, she only

had a short time to get in a lifetime's worth of enjoyment. It was also why she hadn't dared to allow herself to think about how deeply her feelings for Dwight went. Because if she discovered that she loved him, she wouldn't have the strength to leave and face death.

Dwight turned the conversation, telling her stories about his and Vic's childhood Christmases on the ranch. It helped Emmy pull herself out of the quagmire of dark thoughts. At least, for the time being.

When they went to bed, Dwight pulled her against him and held her tightly as if sensing her troubled thoughts. He didn't pry, and she didn't offer up anything. It was better that she kept such things to herself. Dwight had enough to worry about.

Long into the night after Dwight had drifted off to sleep still holding her, Emmy looked out the windows to the landscape, hearing Dwight's voice over and over in her head telling her that he loved her. Those words still hung between them. He deserved better than what she was able to give him.

If things were different, she'd give him everything she had. She knew in her heart that they could have a great life together. She *knew* it. That's when the tears came. She didn't stop them as they coursed down her face. Each one was a silent scream of unfairness, of lost hope, the theft of a bright future with a good man beside her.

Because she could no longer deny what her heart had known almost from the very beginning—Dwight was her soul mate, her other half. The man she had been searching for her entire life.

Suddenly, Dwight stirred, his arms going around her to hold her against him. "Shh. It's all right. I've got you."

But it wouldn't be all right ever again. Emmy had no choice but to continue down the road she had chosen. Even if she backed out, Joe and his people would continue hunting her. It was only a matter of time before they found her.

Emmy clung to Dwight, putting her face in the crook of his shoulder as she released the tears. He stroked her back, holding her gently but securely until her tears finally dried. They remained locked in each other's arms long after. Neither spoke. Emmy wouldn't know what to say even if she wanted to speak.

They watched the dark sky turn gray, then the palest shade of blue before the sun peeked over the mountains, bringing a new day. Dwight's alarm went off. He reached over with one arm and silenced it. Emmy released him, thinking he needed to rise, but he held her tighter.

"Not yet," he whispered.

She sniffed and snuggled against him. "I didn't mean to wake you."

"I don't care about that. Is there anything I can do?"

"Just hold me."

He kissed her temple. "There's nothing else I'd rather do."

Emmy didn't want to get out of bed, but Dwight needed to see to some things around the ranch. She had given in to a low moment. Now, it was time for her to square her shoulders and carry on.

She leaned back to look at him and placed a kiss upon his lips. "Thank you."

"We can stay longer."

She smiled, her heart near to bursting with how much she loved him. "We can pick this up later."

"I'm going to hold you to that." He searched her face. He must have been satisfied with whatever he found because he kissed the tip of her nose and released her.

The absence of his arms was like being doused in cold water. Emmy rose and gave Sam a rub on the head before changing clothes.

"Why don't you bring the rest of your clothes down here?" Dwight said as he tugged on his jeans.

Her head snapped up. "What?"

"I've made my feelings clear with you. I want you. With me. In this room. In all ways. I know it's only been a short time, but I know you enjoy being with me."

She nodded slowly. "I do."

"Then let's see where this goes."

"I know exactly where it's headed."

He raised a brow. "Do you? Because I don't."

"Dw—"

He held up a hand to silence her. "I know what you're going to say, and I understand. I don't want to live in the future. I want to live now. If you don't want to move your things, that's fine. I won't be angry. The invitation to share my room fully will always be open."

She watched as he went into the bathroom and finished readying himself for the day. Emmy was slow in putting on the clothes she had brought down the day before. Dwight walked past her and gave her a peck on the cheek before leaving the room to start breakfast.

Emmy made the bed, then went to the bathroom to tie her hair back and brush her teeth. She put on face and eye cream, then her boots—along with the knife—and joined him in the kitchen. He finished scrambling eggs as she poured them coffee. Their breakfast was quick, and before she knew it, she was getting bundled up for the day.

"Ready?" Dwight asked with a bright smile.

She loved how his eyes lit up when he was excited. They shone with an inner light she had never seen before. "Show me the way."

"Lead on."

He opened the door, letting in a blast of cold air. The ground had several inches of snow now with more forecasted over the next few days. Their feet crunched on the snow as they walked from the porch to the nearest barn.

"Good morning," Dwight called to the horses as he opened the doors wide.

Emmy laughed when the animals all poked their heads over their stall doors, waiting for him. A few even nickered.

Dwight glanced at her as he opened the door to the tack room. "Have you been around horses much?"

"Not really. I'm not afraid of them, though."

He emerged with a rope in hand. "That's good." Then he held up the rope, showing a latch on the end. "This is a lead. It clicks beneath the horse's head on their halter, allowing you to walk them out to the field. Once you get there, remove it and let them go."

"That sounds easy."

"It is. Come on, I'll show you."

Emmy was freezing but also happy to be learning more about the ranch other than the finances. She followed Dwight as he went to the first stall and rubbed his gloved hand up and down a white horse's forehead.

"This is Cloud," he said. "She's our oldest mare. She was my mom's."

Emmy held out her hand and let Cloud sniff her. "She's beautiful."

"She's very gentle. Though she does rule the herd here."

Emmy laughed. "Does she now? Good for you, Cloud."

The mare bobbed her head up and down as if in agreement. Dwight held up the lead in his hand and showed the latch end to Emmy again. She nodded and took note of how he attached it to the bottom of the halter. He then unbolted the stall and slid the door back on its rollers. Cloud walked out beside him. Emmy followed, smiling as she heard Dwight talking to the horse all the while. When he reached the pasture gate, he opened it and walked in with Cloud. The mare stilled as she waited for him to remove the lead. He gave her a gentle pat on her shoulder, and she trotted off as he closed the gate behind him.

"That seems easy," she said when Dwight returned.

"Want to try one?" he asked.

She licked her lips and nodded. "If you'll be with me."

"I'll be right beside you. This is routine for the horses, so they know exactly what's going on."

That helped to bolster her confidence. Emmy approached the next stall. The horse had a white blaze from its forehead down to its nose.

"This is Fireball," Dwight said.

Emmy let the horse sniff her before she stroked his forehead as Dwight had done with Cloud. "Hello, Fireball."

"He's a three-year-old gelding I bought last year."

"Did he get his name from his orangey color?"

Dwight chuckled. "No. Because he's faster than the wind and spirited."

Emmy kept petting him. "Spirited, huh?"

"Don't worry. He's a sweetheart."

"If you say so."

Emmy took the lead from Dwight and latched it to Fireball's halter. Before she opened the stall door, Dwight put his hand atop hers.

"Loop the lead a couple of times in your left hand to give it some slack. You don't want the rope dangling on the ground for you or the horse to step on. Also, if the horse tried to jerk away or rear, you've got slack still in hand to hold on and get things back under control."

She glanced nervously at Dwight. "There's a lot that goes into horses."

"This is only the beginning," he told her with a wink.

Emmy looped the lead rope as Dwight had instructed. Then she looked his way. He nodded in approval. She took a deep breath and looked into Fireball's big, dark eyes. "This is my first time doing this, so be gentle with me."

"I'll be with you," Dwight told her.

She slid the bolt free and pushed the stall door aside. Unlike Cloud, Fireball didn't move.

"Click your tongue," Dwight urged her.

Emmy did, but the horse still didn't move.

"Do it again but also tug a little on the lead to let him know what you want," Dwight instructed.

She did as Dwight told her, and to her shock, Fireball walked out of his stall. "It worked," she said.

Dwight laughed from beside her. "You're doing great. Just go at a steady pace to the pasture."

"I heard you talking to Cloud."

"Horses respond to calm, even tones. Raised voices and shouting will scare and startle them."

Emmy glanced at Fireball, her smile growing with every step. "Makes sense to me."

At the pasture, Dwight opened the gate for her as she led Fireball in and then unhooked the lead.

"Have a good day," she told him.

He slowly walked away, completely disinterested in her. But Emmy was so happy, she felt as if she were floating.

It didn't take long for her and Dwight to get the rest of the horses out to pasture. Then she learned all about cleaning the stalls. While it didn't exactly smell nice, she had to admit she enjoyed working alongside Dwight. Even if it was mucking stalls.

Next, they moved on to check the horse feed and see what needed to be reordered. She was shocked to learn that the horses didn't eat the same things. Each required a certain diet, and it was imperative that they got exactly what they needed.

"Dwight!"

The sound of the male voice caused Emmy to freeze. Dwight handed her the clipboard and put his finger to his lips as he met her gaze.

"It's okay. Stay here," he whispered.

He walked from the feed room, sliding the door shut behind him. Emmy backed up, her gaze locked on the door.

"What's up, Carlos?" Dwight said from the other side of the wall.

Emmy's heart pounded as she waited for the answer. She couldn't make out Carlos's words. The only thing that kept her semi-calm was the fact that Dwight seemed to know Carlos. Otherwise . . .

She stopped. Otherwise, what? What would she do? Run? The only place for her *to* run was the mountains, which would be tantamount to suicide since she knew nothing about surviving out in the wild. A wilderness that included bears, wolves, and mountain lions.

Emmy jerked when the door opened, and Dwight's form filled the entrance. She breathed a sigh of relief. Without a word, he walked to her and enveloped her in his arms.

"It's all right. It was one of my hands," Dwight said.

"I was so scared."

"You're still shaking."

Emmy pulled back to look up at him. "Is he gone?"

"Yes. Do you want to stay out here, or would you rather go back inside?"

"Inside."

"I'll take you," he said and linked his hand with hers.

Chapter 20

Orso smiled as he put his gun back into the holster. He didn't give the dead body at his feet another thought as he walked out of the office and got into his car. He opened his glove box and pulled out the Montana map.

After finding his current location, he scanned the area, looking east—the direction the owner of the storage facility had said he saw Emmy and the marshal head right after Orso had promised not to kill him. Orso pulled the small notebook he used to write notes out of his coat pocket. The marshal drove anywhere from three to six hours before exchanging vehicles.

Orso turned his attention to the map once more and calculated how far that would be on the map. After drawing a circle with a compass to accurately depict a radius, Orso realized the territory he would need to search was massive and included many mountains.

He had to start somewhere, however. Luckily, much of Montana was uninhabited. Towns were small and set far apart. It would mean a lot of driving time for Orso, but he wouldn't be searching huge cities like Denver.

The map showed a few small towns within the three-hour radius heading east. He'd begin there. If he didn't locate Emmy, he'd expand his search. He started his car and backed out of the parking space. He looked both ways to make sure traffic was clear before pulling out onto the road.

Once he set the cruise control to ensure that he didn't go over the speed limit, Orso called Tony. The phone barely rang twice before someone answered, the voice coming through the car speakers.

"Tell me you have good news."

"I'm heading east."

Tony's voice held a bite when he said, "That isn't good news."

"I located where the marshal picked up his next vehicle and got a direction. I'd say that's good news."

"If you haven't found her yet, then it's bad news."

Orso tightened his hands on the steering wheel. "They crossed state lines. Four times. For all I know, they drove through Montana and headed south. I'm doing my job."

"Not fast enough," Tony snapped. "Do you have any idea what the date it is?"

"Of course I know."

"We barely have any time left before the trial."

Orso clenched his teeth. "I know very well the time."

"Then you need to work faster. The woman should've been dealt with already."

"And she would've been had Joe sent me the first time instead of his cousin."

Tony snorted. "I happen to agree with you, but I'm not going to tell Joe that. Are you?"

Orso remained silent.

"Look, Joe isn't in a good way here. Other things are going on. We all assumed at least this would be over by now."

"I'm out here working alone, Tony. I can only do so much. But the one thing I can assure you is that I *will* find her."

"Before or after the trial?"

Orso slowly released a breath, bringing his rage under control.

"If it's after, don't bother coming home," Tony said.

"Is that a threat?"

"It is. Joe has paid you well for your services in the past."

Orso bared his teeth as his fury intensified. "And I've been loyal to him, just as I was with his uncle."

"Then do your fucking job because if Joe goes to prison because you failed to do what was required, you won't have a home to come back to."

The call disconnected.

"Bold threat from someone who won't be running the family," Orso said to himself.

He didn't take threats of any kind lightly. If Emmy eluded him until the trial for some reason, he would still finish his job and take her life. Then, he would find Tony and let him know what he thought of his threats.

Chapter 21

Dwight glanced at the house as he walked around to the barn. Emmy had told him repeatedly that she was fine, but he had felt her shaking. He knew how upset she had gotten when Carlos showed up. They had been having such a good time until then. He hoped it didn't spoil things for Emmy getting out of the house again.

Though, he wouldn't blame her if it did.

He'd been in tough situations before, but he had never had someone hunting him. People had shot at him, but he had never stared down the barrel of a gun—not like Emmy had. The government had trained him for tactical situations, conditions that were stressful and demanding. Emmy had none of that training—not emotionally, mentally, or physically.

The fact that she had been able to get on with her life in what little capacity she had while at the ranch was phenomenal in his opinion. It was a testament to her mental fortitude and inner strength. But a person could only withstand so much before they broke.

And Dwight feared that Emmy was nearing her breaking point.

Unfortunately, she had a ways to go before it was over. Getting from Montana to Denver and the courthouse would be the most stressful of any of the situations, which was why Dwight had begun to form some plans of his own to help both Emmy and Dalton.

They were rough schemes that had begun when he woke last night to Emmy crying. It'd killed him not to know the reason for her tears, but he could guess. She was frightened and worried. The kinds of emotions that couldn't be dealt with or answered and tended to get heavier and heavier as the days wore on. The only thing he could do was continue to make her feel safe at the ranch while ensuring that she was. Aside from that, he would do whatever he could to fill her days with laughter and fun.

His phone vibrated in his coat pocket. Dwight unzipped his jacket and pulled out his cell, seeing the same number Dalton had used when he'd called about bringing Emmy.

"Hello?" Dwight answered.

A beat passed before Dalton said, "Hey, man."

"Hey. How are you?"

"I'm good."

Which meant he was exhausted. Dwight could hear it in his voice. He glanced at the house and then headed inside the barn. "Anything I can do?"

"No. How is she?"

Dwight knew Dalton was purposefully not mentioning names in case anyone was listening to their call. "As well as can be expected. Making progress, but it's slow. She has good days and bad."

"Anything I should be worried about?"

"Normal stuff."

Dalton grunted through the phone. "Have you gone hunting lately?"

Dwight halted instantly. "Hasn't been a need."

"If you're going to have that big celebration for Christmas, you might want to get ahead of things and start bagging some game early."

Fuck. Dwight placed a hand against the edge of a stall and hung his head. Dalton was telling him that men were closing in. But Dwight needed to know how close they were. "I've still got time. I was thinking of holding off."

"The sooner, the better, I think."

"You're probably right."

"I'm going to miss hunting with you. I know you're good, but it's always better if you've got a companion to help bring home dinner."

Dwight pushed away from the wall. Dwight was warning him not to go alone. He wasn't sure if that meant more than one person was coming, or if the one headed their way was that dangerous. Either way, it didn't matter. "I know just the person to help."

"Be careful out there, though I don't need to tell you that since you know those mountains better than anyone."

A smile pulled at Dwight's lips. "That's for certain."

"I'll check in when I can."

Dwight put his phone away when the call ended. He stood in the barn for several moments, thinking. His options were few, but the one thing he knew was that he wouldn't let anyone near Emmy. There hadn't been urgency in Dalton's voice, which told Dwight that the hitmen weren't right at their doorstep. But they *were* getting close.

He blew out a breath and called Carlos, who had worked for his family since Dwight was in college. As soon as Carlos picked up, Dwight said, "I got a tip about possible trespassers coming. You interested in some overtime?"

"Tell me where and when, and I'm there," Carlos replied.

Dwight had known that he could count on Carlos, but hearing the words made him feel better. "I just got word. I've not even set up a plan yet."

"You know you can count on me, boss."

"I appreciate it."

"You need more people? My nephew is a hell of a hunter. He can track anything."

Dwight thought about that for a moment. "I'd be interested, but this is a private matter. Nothing that happens here can ever be spoken about."

"I'll make sure of it."

"You still on the south range fixing the fence?"

"I am. Junior's here with me."

Dwight glanced out the barn doors to the house. "How much longer will it take you?"

"About another two hours."

"I'd like to meet in the barn before lunch."

Carlos's voice was muffled as he yelled something to Junior. Then he said into the phone, "I'll be there."

Dwight disconnected and debated whether to tell Emmy about Dalton's call. She was already strung so tight. He didn't want her to worry more. But not telling her could make matters worse. Dwight decided that he would keep things to himself until he came up with a solid plan and put it into motion.

He walked to the small office near the tack room. It was where his great-grandfather and grandfather had conducted business. His dad had remodeled part of the downstairs to add the addition of the master bedroom. When he did that, he transformed the master into an office so he could have filing cabinets and warmth on those cold winter days. However, the space would be perfect for Dwight to talk privately with Carlos.

Dwight had just opened the door to the office when Sam barked. Dwight's head snapped up, and he turned. He glanced at his watch and realized that the farrier was scheduled to arrive. Dwight strode out of the barn at the same time Sven pulled to a stop.

Sam stood beside Dwight with his tail wagging, waiting for Sven to get out of his truck. Dwight shook his head with a laugh. Sven never came to the ranch without a treat for Sam. Sven unfolded his long, lean frame from the truck and pulled his beanie low over his ears as he smiled in greeting. He was in his mid-fifties, but he looked years younger. Dwight had never figured out his secret. Was it the food, the fact that Sven always seemed to be laughing at something, or was it Sven's wife? Whatever it was, it sure seemed to be working.

"Hey!"

Dwight nodded. "How was the drive?"

"Not too bad. More snow on the way."

That caused Dwight to frown. "You want to reschedule? I'd hate to have you on the roads during the storm."

Sven shook his head as he opened the toolbox in the back of his truck and pulled out a wooden box that had been handed down through the generations of his family, who'd emigrated from Scandinavia in the early 1800s to settle in this part of Montana. Sven's family contained the best farriers in hundreds of miles.

"I'll be fine," Sven said as he shut the lid to the toolbox and walked around the truck, holding out his hand.

After he clasped Dwight's hand and shook it, he pulled a treat from his pocket for Sam, who eagerly waited for Sven to toss it. Sam jumped up and expertly caught it, as usual.

Sven said, "I don't want to keep my beauties waiting."

Dwight looked down at Sam. "Round 'em up, boy."

Sam took off through the snow, jumping through the wooden slats of the fence to begin rounding up the horses.

"I'll get them brought in. I forgot you were coming," Dwight explained.

Sven's dark eyes watched him with humor. "I can't remember the last time you forgot an appointment. Who is she?"

"What?" Dwight asked in shock.

Sven laughed. "So, there *is* a woman."

"I didn't say that."

Sven's smile widened. "You didn't have to. Your expression said it all."

Dwight ran a hand down his chest as he glanced at the house. "There isn't a woman here."

Sven's smile vanished instantly. He stared at Dwight for a moment before nodding. "All right. Everything okay?"

No, everything wasn't okay, but Dwight couldn't tell Sven that. He started to open his mouth and give some lie, but that didn't seem right either. Instead, Dwight turned on his heel and went to bring the horses back to the barn. Sven was busy setting up his area and didn't say more when Dwight returned with the first horse.

By the time Dwight got them back into their stalls, he felt bad about not answering Sven. He walked over to the farrier as he bent at the waist, holding one of Cloud's bent legs between his as he started to file down the hoof.

"I'm sorry about not answering you. I've got a lot on my plate right now," Dwight said.

Sven nodded without looking up. "I can see that."

Dwight rubbed the back of his neck, unsure what to say next. Worry about impending visitors and how he could keep them away from Emmy filled his mind. The ranch had some decent hiding places, but nowhere Emmy could stay for days or weeks. Especially alone. Leaving was an option.

Dwight knew that Carlos and the others would keep the ranch going for as long as needed, but he wasn't sure that was the way to go. If he and Emmy remained at the ranch, they could set up a defense. Whereas if they went on the run, they would be at the mercy of wherever they happened to be.

"There's a heaviness around you I've not seen before," Sven said.

Dwight's gaze slid to the farrier, who still had his head down, working. "Oh?"

"Whatever's going on, you know you have friends who can help."

"There are some things that it's better not to involve others."

Sven released Cloud's back hoof and straightened. He met Dwight's gaze. "That's true when it comes to money and danger."

Dwight waited for Sven to say more, but the farrier walked around to Cloud's other side and leaned against her to shift her weight so he could pick up her back fetlock and examine her hoof.

"I've found that money and friendship never go well," Sven said. "I also knew how well your father managed this ranch. You've kept to the ideals he taught while also bringing the ranch into modern times. Its success tells me that money isn't your problem."

Dwight crossed his arms over his chest and waited for whatever else Sven had to say.

"Danger is another animal, altogether. Some think they're better doing things on their own." He straightened and looked at Dwight over Cloud's back. "That kind of thinking is perilous. It can make a man forget that he has friends. That this community is tight because we rely on each other in times of need."

Dwight shook his head. "This isn't a hay barn burning. It's something else entirely."

Sven's lips twisted as he went back to work. "Your father and I used to talk about your jobs. He never got into specifics, but he didn't need to. I heard the pride in his voice when he mentioned you. But I also heard the fear. He knew you put your life on the line more often than not. Some might think people like you simply like the adrenaline that kind of lifestyle brings. Then again, they don't know you like I do. They've not seen you find peace out here."

Dwight's gaze moved to the house as he thought of Emmy. He'd found more than peace on the ranch. He'd found love, the kind he hadn't thought could ever be his. The kind his parents had told him to wait for.

"Then again," Sven said, breaking into his thoughts, "it takes a certain type of man to do the jobs you've undertaken. Men like that came out west and built this country." Sven released Cloud's leg and stood tall as he leaned an arm on the mare's back. "It's men like you who don't go looking for danger but stand in the face of it. Men like you also realize that their strength doesn't only come from within or because of training—it's because of the people they surround themselves with."

"You make me sound like a saint."

Sven chuckled. "A saint you are not, my friend. What you are is a good man. One I'm glad to know."

"Thank you."

The farrier smoothed his hand down Cloud's back. "When you were in the military, you had a team, right?"

"I did."

"Same when you were in the FBI and with Homeland Security."

Dwight pressed his lips together, knowing what Sven was getting at. "I didn't work alone, if that's your meaning."

"Exactly. Chew on that for a bit before you make any hasty decisions."

"I don't have any decisions to make."

Sven smiled and shrugged. "Whatever you say. Just know that I'm here if you ever need anything. And I'm a hell of a shot—though you know that."

Dwight couldn't help but smile as he shook his head. "Everyone in the county knows about your aim."

"Good." Sven said no more as he went to work on Cloud's front hooves.

Chapter 22

Emmy rotated her neck as she took a break from the computer. She stretched her back and yawned before checking the time. Another week had passed since she had freaked out about Carlos coming to the barn when she was there. The ranch hand hadn't seen her, but she couldn't seem to tell her mind that.

She hadn't gone back out to help Dwight since. He hadn't pushed her to come outside, and she couldn't decide if that was a good thing or not. More times than not, he was there for lunch. But he never missed dinner.

The evenings were magical. No matter what they did, they did it together. The way Dwight looked at her made her think all things were possible. The way he held her made her yearn for a future with him. It was so easy to love him that it was getting harder and harder not to tell him how she felt.

She pulled up the calendar on the computer to mentally check off another day. A part of her wanted to do something grand and adventurous every day since these might be her last. The other part of her liked the routine, the normalcy that she had with Dwight. It was a glimpse into what life would have been like if they had met under different circumstances. The life they could've had if she hadn't been witness to a crime.

Emmy pushed back the rolling chair and got to her feet. She walked out of the office, clicking off the light as she did. As she made her way to the kitchen, she looked out the windows to the barn to see the illumination within. With the end of the year creeping closer, the days were getting shorter and the nights longer. She hesitated to turn on lights in the house so others might see her, but she needed to be able to see. Odd that she never thought about it when Dwight was with her. Probably because she assumed that the workers had gone home by the time he came in.

There were no blinds on the windows to shut and thwart prying eyes. She would either need to make do in the growing darkness of the house or turn on some lights. Emmy decided to leave the lamps off. Her eyes grew accustomed to the darkness so she could make her way easily enough to the kitchen.

She used the light from the microwave over the stove to heat some water for tea. The electric teapot soon had the water boiling. She poured the water into her mug over the tea bag and set a timer.

Emmy rubbed her hands up and down her arms. She had been chilled all day. No matter what she did, she couldn't seem to stay warm for long. After so many cups of coffee, she became too jittery, so she'd switched to herbal tea. Snow had fallen steadily for almost the entire day. She couldn't wait to snuggle beneath the blankets with Dwight tonight. She always slept well when it was cold out and blankets weighed her down.

When the timer went off, she added some honey to her

mug then took it to the sofa to sit beneath a blanket. Not turning on the television or the lights to read left her with her thoughts. Dalton would return soon to bring her to Denver.

She had to admit, she was glad that Dwight wanted to come with them. It wasn't that she didn't think Dalton was capable. He certainly was, and he'd proven his worth by getting her out of Denver and to the ranch. But Dalton needed someone he could trust—someone who could help him. Dwight was that man.

Emmy would feel a lot safer knowing that both men were there. But would it be enough? She had known of Joe Roma's connections when he first became a client. She always liked to know a little about those she worked with to help her better understand how they did business and if there were ways she could help them save money.

Joe was known for his lavish parties, where the upper crust of Denver society came out to play. Sometimes, celebrities were there, as well. However, everyone coveted an invitation to his intimate dinner parties. Only those that Joe liked the best, the ones he brought into his inner circle, got invited to those.

Emmy had been to both. She had liked the lavish parties, where she could sit back and watch everyone with a bit of awe. The booze flowed freely, and there was never-ending food. Women dressed in decadent formalwear while dripping with jewels. Emmy had been one of those little girls who had loved playing dress-up, and those kinds of parties let her do just that. Not to mention getting to meet people she never would've had the opportunity to mingle with.

During one of the lavish parties, Joe had introduced her to two businessmen that he knew. Within a month, both had moved their accounts not just to the company she worked for but had also specifically asked for her. That had gotten her noticed by the top brass at the business. Six months later, after another two of Joe's acquaintances moved to her, they gave her a promotion and a nice pay raise that included a corner office.

She had thought her life was finally moving in the direction she wanted. It wasn't the money, either. She had never overspent. There were occasional splurges, but she had never been a big spender. Probably because as a bookkeeper she'd seen so many people do just that. She even rented the gowns she wore to Joe's lavish parties because she couldn't justify spending the money for a dress she would likely only wear once.

While the big social gatherings were fun, she truly loved the dinner events. Sometimes, there were as few as six at the table. Other times, there were as many as twenty. Emmy had never known who would be there—the mayor, a senator, professional athletes, celebrities. Every dinner was different in the atmosphere, the food, and the conversation.

Joe was a born entertainer. He knew how to make sure all his guests were well taken care of. And he spared no expense. For Emmy, who had never been to anything close to such events, it had been like being granted access to a whole other world.

She had gotten caught up in the glitz and the glamour, in the attention Joe and others paid her. Because of that, she hadn't seen what was really going on. Or maybe she had and just hadn't wanted to admit it. It didn't matter now. The past was the past. She could only move forward.

Emmy drank her tea and looked out the windows, hoping to get a glimpse of Dwight. Her gaze moved to the Christmas tree. It was beautiful. Tall and coated in lights with ornaments in a vast array of colors and dating back over a hundred years. The only thing missing was presents.

Without hesitation, Emmy took out the phone Dalton had given her and dialed Victoria's number that she had added in for Emmy.

"Hey, you," Vic said when she answered, a smile in her voice.

Emmy smiled in return. "I'm not interrupting anything, am I?"

"Only me watching Ted make a mess in the kitchen. He said he knew how to bake. I told him he didn't. Now, he's trying to prove he can."

"I can," Ted's voice hollered in the background.

"He can't," Victoria whispered.

Emmy laughed.

"What's up? Everything good?" Vic asked.

"Yeah. We're fine. It's been quiet."

"That's good, right?"

"Definitely."

There was a beat of silence before Victoria asked, "Then why do I hear something in your voice?"

"I don't know. Just a feeling I've had for a few days."

"Well, the first is approaching. Maybe you're caught up in that."

Emmy shrugged, even though Vic couldn't see her. "I hope that's it."

"If something was going on, Dwight would tell you."

"Would he, though?"

Victoria made a sound through the phone. "Now that you ask that, I'm not sure. Dwight is a protector. He's always felt like it's his duty to protect others. I've also seen how he looks at you. It's different with you. And because of that, he might try to keep things from you so you don't worry."

"Hmm."

"Do you really want to know? You're already worried."

Emmy wrinkled her nose. "I don't know. I think having the information is vital for making decisions, but if it's something I can't change, maybe not knowing is better."

"That's what I think. And it might be nothing. What I do know is that Dwight will do everything he can to keep you safe."

"You haven't told Ted anything, have you?"

"No," Vic answered immediately. "I promised you and Dwight I wouldn't."

Emmy released a breath. "Thank you. There's one more thing."

"Sure. What is it?"

"I want to give Dwight something for Christmas. That's a little difficult since I can't get out to shop, and I can't shop online either."

"Sure, you can," Vic said. "Use my credit card. Everything will be under my name, so no one will be the wiser."

Emmy hesitated. "Eh, I don't feel comfortable with that. You've already spent so much, and I can't pay you back until after the trial."

"It's just money."

"Says the woman who has enough to spare."

Victoria laughed. "Point taken. Then you've got a couple of options. You could make him something."

"I'm not handy or crafty at all. Unless it's with numbers," Emmy said in disappointment.

"Or . . . you can tell me what you'd like to get him, and I'll have it sent to the ranch."

Emmy sank onto the sofa to lay her head on the arm. "That's the same as you giving me your credit card."

"Not really. I'll be doing the buying."

"I don't know," Emmy said with a sigh.

"Think about it and let me know. By the way, Dwight sent me pictures of the house. You did an amazing job decorating."

Emmy grinned at the compliment. "Thank you. Dwight helped."

"Did he really decorate, or did he stand around and hand things to you?"

"I'd call that decorating."

Victoria snorted loudly. "I'm just glad you got him to help. Ted likes to sit on the sofa and watch."

"I'm adding in my two cents," he hollered from the background again.

Emmy laughed at the two of them. "I wish I could meet Ted."

"You will."

Emmy didn't correct Vic because she really hoped she *did* get to meet him. "I won't keep you. Thanks for the advice."

"Anytime. Talk soon."

The line went dead. Emmy lowered the phone and set aside her now-cold tea. She had no idea what to get Dwight for Christmas. He'd never mentioned anything that he wanted. The last thing she wanted was to give him something he didn't like. She'd been the recipient of bad gifts before and knew how disastrous they could be.

She snuggled under the blanket, her mind drifting as she waited for Dwight. In an instant, she was dreaming. She knew it was a dream because she didn't have a care in the world as she and Dwight curled up on the couch before the fire with Sam. Half-drunk glasses of wine and dirty plates sat on the table beside them from dinner. Snow fell outside as the fire popped.

"Merry Christmas," Dwight said.

She met his gaze. "Merry Christmas."

"This is the first of many together."

"I don't want to dare hope."

He cupped her face in his hands. "You don't have to hope.

It's going to be so. I promised. Nothing will happen to you. I don't break vows."

"I love you, Dwight. I'm sorry I didn't tell you sooner."

He put his finger to her lips. "I don't care how long it took. I'm just glad you said it. Say it again."

She smiled brightly. "I love you."

Emmy waited for him to say it back, but he seemed frozen. Then blood welled at the corner of his lips and ran down his chin.

"Dwight?" she asked, fear making her heart beat double-time. "Dwight."

His head slumped forward before he fell to the floor. Emmy's mouth opened on a silent scream when she saw Sam covered in blood, lying unmoving next to Dwight. A shadow moved, drawing her attention. She swung her head around and saw a faceless man pointing a gun at her head.

"Time's up."

Emmy woke with a scream, fighting against whatever tried to keep her arms and legs contained.

"Emmy! Emmy, it's me. It's me!"

It took her a moment to recognize Dwight's voice. Her vision cleared, and his face came into view. She realized that lights were on all through the house now. But she didn't move. She couldn't. The dream clung to her like talons digging into her soul. She couldn't breathe, couldn't think.

"You got tangled in the blanket," he said calmly while moving it away. Then his gaze met hers. "It's me."

Her gaze lowered to his mouth where she had seen the blood. Tears welled.

"It was just a dream," he said softly. "It wasn't real."

The first tear fell down her cheek. "It felt real."

He pulled her against him. The instant she felt his arms around her, she clung to him.

"Shh," he said as he ran his hands soothingly up and down her back. "You're safe."

"You would tell me if I wasn't, right?" He hesitated, and she pulled back to look at him. "I've had a bad feeling for a few days now. Tell me it's my imagination. Tell me I'm crazy."

Dwight sighed. "You're not crazy."

Chapter 23

Dwight hated the fear he saw in Emmy's eyes. He'd kept the truth from her for good reason, but now it was time she knew everything. He dreaded it, but it was time. Hearing her scream, seeing the terror in her eyes when she woke from the nightmare was like a knife to his heart.

Emmy had suffered enough for doing the right thing. He wanted her to be happy, to be content and wear the smile he had gotten used to seeing. The only way that could happen was if she testified and put Joe Roma away.

"Tell me," Emmy demanded.

Dwight ran a hand down his face before meeting her gaze. "I wanted to get the facts before I said anything. I want you to know that I always planned to tell you tonight. I need you to know that I didn't keep it from you because I didn't think you could handle it. I wanted to present the problem as well as a plan."

She nodded. "Okay."

"Dalton called the other day. We spoke, making it sound like chitchat, but it was code. He asked about you, about how things were. Then he let me know that someone was getting close."

"Oh, God," she murmured.

Dwight took her hand, gripping it firmly as he caught her gaze. "They're not here yet. Just close enough that Dalton wanted to give me a heads-up."

"Should I leave?"

"I thought about taking you somewhere, but in the end, both Dalton and I think the best thing is to remain right here."

Her pale brown eyes widened. "Here? So you, Sam, and anyone else here can be killed?"

"Not only is this my ranch, but I know this land inside and out. Not to mention my tactical training. Dalton's suggestion was that I hunt those coming."

"You're leaving."

It wasn't a question. His heart ached at the resignation he saw on her face. "No. Like I said, I've taken the last few days to form a plan and implement it."

"I don't understand."

"I'm using the cameras I already have, repositioning them to pick up any movement coming close to the property. I have four men out there ready to move at a moment's notice and capture whoever it is. There will be rotating teams for round-the-clock surveillance."

Emmy squeezed her eyes shut. When she looked at him again, she shook her head. "I didn't like the idea of you being involved. Now, there are more?"

"No one knows specifics. These are my employees and friends—people who know this land as well as I do. People I trust. No one is saying anything to anyone. They know bad people are coming, but they don't know why or for who. Nor will they."

"We have some time until the first of the year. It's not right to have these people out there that long."

"I have a feeling whoever is getting close to us will come sooner rather than later."

"Once they find us, all they'll do is send another if the first one is killed."

Dwight shrugged. "This isn't Denver. It's Montana."

"It isn't the Wild West, either."

He gave her a smile. "Trespassing on private property isn't something we take lightly. Those men out there know nothing about you. They simply think they're helping me out with a situation that has gotten out of control—which is the truth. They willingly offered their services. Well, all but Carlos. I asked him to help. He told me about his nephew, who is an expert tracker. Billy prefers animals to humans. He spends most of his time in the mountains by himself anyway. Carlos sent him a message, and Billy is going to stay around the ranch."

"Is that a good idea?" she asked with a frown.

"Whoever is coming is from the city. I doubt they'll have much experience out here. Besides, Billy will blend in so well with the landscape, I doubt many people will be able to find him."

She studied him for a moment. "I don't want to die, but I don't like anyone putting their lives in danger. Especially without knowing the real reason."

"Every man taking turns patrolling knows this land inside and out."

"And the men coming after me are killers for hire. They won't hesitate to take someone's life. Including yours."

Dwight glanced down at their joined hands. "Whoever comes for you, however many there are, they won't get close to the house."

"Unless they come up the drive."

He blinked at her statement. From the very beginning, he'd assumed that whoever they sent would try to come in undetected for the element of surprise. He hadn't stopped to think the hitmen would drive up to the house. Had Emmy not said something, he would've overlooked that.

"That would take some balls," Dwight said.

Emmy shrugged. "The marshals at the hotel were gone, leaving me unprotected. That allowed the assassin to get into my room easily. Joe Roma has connections everywhere and money to spare. People can be bought."

"Not everyone. Dalton wasn't."

"I'll be forever thankful for that. Because if he had been, I'd be dead."

And Dwight never would've had Emmy in his life. Now that she was here, he didn't want to lose her. Not to hitmen. Not to anything.

She licked her lips and released a sigh. "Thank you for telling me all of this. I don't like it. Then again, I don't like any part of what's happened to me since I went to the DA. I could deal with things when it was only my life in jeopardy. But it's more than that now. There's you and Sam, and then there are these other people I don't even know."

"Trust me, Emmy. Please," Dwight pleaded.

"I do. Completely. It's just . . . if someone gets hurt, especially you, I'll never forgive myself."

"I won't get hurt."

She looked away irritably. "You can't promise that."

He put a finger on her chin and gently turned her head to him. Cupping her cheek, he smiled. "I survived two tours overseas in the military, not to mention my four years in the FBI. My training through all three jobs has given me knowledge few have. Couple that with the fact that we're on my territory, and the odds are in our favor."

"I hope you're right."

"I am," he said softly before leaning in to kiss her.

She returned his kiss with fervor. "Just keep me updated on everything, please."

"I can do that. I just don't want you to worry."

"I'll worry regardless. I can't help it, even though I know nothing can come of my worrying."

Dwight held her close. "We'll get through this."

He just hoped it was a promise he could keep.

With every day that passed without a sign of anyone, Dwight found it harder and harder to keep sending his friends and employees out to keep watch. Yet, he knew without a doubt that someone would come for Emmy.

There had been no further word from Dalton. Dwight had tried to call him three times, but Dalton never answered. That left Dwight with a bad taste in his mouth. As he'd promised, he told Emmy everything. Sometimes, she took it in stride. Other times, she sat quietly with her thoughts.

He made sure they kept a routine for Emmy's sake. It had taken him a while, but he finally got her to leave the house again. Over the last several days, Emmy had gone out with him to care for the horses in the mornings. Then, she'd return to the house. He was happy that she felt safe enough to leave the house. It was a small step, and he knew it cost her a great deal every day.

While she enjoyed the horses, she was a ball of nerves until he walked her back to the house. Only then did she relax somewhat again.

Dwight looked at the clear sky. A storm had come through in the early-morning hours, blanketing the ground with three inches of snow on top of the foot they already had. In the distance, he saw more clouds coming in, bringing in another storm and more snow. The temperatures would plummet overnight. He rubbed his hands together and swung his gaze to the house.

Beside him, Sam let out a low growl. Dwight looked at the dog before following Sam's gaze to the driveway. That's when Dwight heard the crunch of tires on the snow. The black BMW sedan that came into view wasn't a vehicle he recognized.

"Sam, go to the porch," he told the dog.

Sam let out another rumbling growl as he trotted up the steps, his gaze never leaving the sedan. Once the dog got into position, Dwight moved away from the barn. He had only taken two steps when both the driver and passenger doors opened. A middle-aged couple got out of the car, smiles on their faces.

"How can I help you folks?" Dwight asked as he eyed them suspiciously.

They were dressed nicely, matching the car they drove. He didn't trust them. He wouldn't have even if Emmy hadn't been there. There were just some things you didn't see in this part of the country.

"Hello," the man said as he closed the door to the car and came around the front. He wore an expensive puffer jacket in an obnoxious, bright yellow. "Sorry to bother you, but we're lost."

Dwight watched as the woman came to stand with him. They wrapped their arms around each other as if wanting everyone to believe they were a loving couple. They might be, but Dwight wouldn't assume anything.

"This isn't the time of year to be getting lost in these mountains," Dwight said.

The man laughed nervously. "We're figuring that out."

"It's my fault," the woman offered with a glance at her husband. "I just wanted to get out and do something."

Dwight couldn't have cared less what story the couple gave. Be it truth or fiction, none of it mattered. He just wanted them off his property. "Where are you headed?"

"We're supposed to be staying at a B&B," the man said. "A place called the Hartsfield Ranch."

The more the couple spoke, the more uneasy Dwight became. "There's no ranch around here with that name."

"We must have taken the wrong exit," the woman said.

Dwight shifted his feet and nodded his head to the road. "Your best bet is to head back the way you came. You'll want to be off this mountain before the storm rolls in."

"We're used to snow," the man said.

The woman playfully slapped his chest. "Gordan, our Utah weather is nothing like this."

"Why Montana?" Dwight asked them.

The man was taken off guard. "Pardon?"

"Why are you in Montana? You could've gotten great scenery in Wyoming."

Without missing a beat, the woman said, "Our son and his wife live in Casper. We were visiting them for Thanksgiving. I've always wanted to see Montana, and since we were close, we decided to take a trip."

It sounded plausible, but Dwight wasn't taking any chances. "Cell phone reception is spotty in some parts of the mountain. You'd be better off using a traditional map rather than a GPS."

"You don't happen to have a map, do you?" the man asked.

Dwight shook his head. "Afraid I don't."

"Do you know how long it'll take to get back to the interstate?" the woman asked.

Dwight looked from her to her husband. "Depends on the weather you run into. I wouldn't chance waiting to get back on the road."

"Thanks for your help," the man said with a too-bright smile.

The woman waved. "Merry Christmas."

Dwight touched the brim of his hat, tipping his head to her, and watched as the couple got back into the car and drove away. He had no proof that they weren't who they said they were, other than that queasy feeling in his gut that told him they were scouts of some kind.

Did they want to see how many people were at the ranch? How friendly or welcoming he was?

"I didn't like the look of them," Carlos said as he walked from the barn to stand beside Dwight.

"Me, either."

"Are they the ones you're worried about?"

Dwight ran a gloved hand over his jaw and shook his head. "I have no idea. They fit the part they played, but anyone with the right training can play a part."

"What do you want to do?"

Dwight squeezed his eyes closed and looked at the mountains. "I want to do some hunting myself."

"Then go. I'll watch the ranch."

He met Carlos's hazel eyes, saw the salt and pepper hair peeking from beneath his Stetson. "I can't."

Carlos searched his face for a moment before nodding. "You've not been far from the house since the first of November. That's when all this started, didn't it?"

"It did." There was no harm in divulging that bit of news.

"That's right about the time the woman arrived."

Dwight blew out a breath as he crossed his arms over his chest. He didn't say anything, just waited for Carlos to continue.

"That was the day my horse lost his shoe, and I brought him to the barn. I saw the SUV in the drive as you spoke to the man. Then the woman got out and went inside the house."

"How do you know they didn't both leave? Just as this last couple did?"

Carlos's lips twisted ruefully. "I saw her out here with you a bit ago as you taught her how to take the horses to pasture."

"I didn't know you were around."

"Since you didn't tell me about your visitor, I decided it was best if I didn't ask questions. Your life, your business. At first, I thought she was someone new you were seeing, but it didn't take long for me to realize that something was up with you adjusting the cameras around the ranch. Not to mention buying new ones. You confirmed it when you asked if I would rotate keeping watch."

Dwight stared at the man who was not only his top hand but also someone he considered a friend.

"I'll do anything for you," Carlos continued. "I told your father that, and I'm telling you. My loyalty is to this family and the ranch."

"I couldn't run this ranch without you, you know that. I trust you with my life, but it isn't my life on the line."

Carlos glanced at the house. "It's hers. I saw the two of you together, you know. You make a good-looking couple."

Dwight couldn't help but smile at the thought of Emmy.

"So," Carlos said, "does she know you love her?"

Dwight laughed as he shook his head in wonder. "How the hell did you come up with that notion?"

"It's all over your face."

Dwight could only stare in shock at Carlos.

"It isn't exactly your fault. I was looking for signs of your feelings for the woman. Had I not seen the two of you smiling together, I wouldn't have thought twice about her."

"Stop," Dwight said and put his hands on his hips. "You deserve an explanation, but I can't give you one."

Carlos nodded in understanding. "Men are natural protectors. We were made to keep our families and those we care about safe. For you, that protective streak is even wider and deeper. Just know that when it comes to your friends, we're as protective of you."

Dwight dropped his chin to his chest and clenched his teeth. When he raised his head again, he looked Carlos in the eye and said, "The people coming are after the woman staying here. She's set to testify against a mob boss."

"I appreciate you sharing. I also want you to know that the story won't pass my lips."

"The thing is, everyone helping me needs to know what we're up against. Thinking it's poachers or cattle rustlers is doing a disservice."

Carlos looked over his shoulder toward the back of the ranch. "You don't have to tell anyone anything."

"I need to."

"Call them."

Dwight shook his head. "That's the one way I would never impart information like this."

Chapter 24

Emmy couldn't concentrate on work. She finally gave up and walked out of the office to stretch her legs and get some water. As she came into the kitchen, she saw Dwight staring out toward the driveway. She followed his gaze and spotted the car pull up. The instant she saw the sedan, she stumbled back a few steps.

The instinct to run pounded through her. Then she looked at Dwight. He didn't stand easily as he usually did. He was alert, his gaze locked on the couple. Dwight didn't order them off his property, but he also didn't say much. She wished she could hear the conversation, but she refused to go near the door.

It wasn't long before the couple drove away. But that didn't ease the knot in Emmy's stomach.

She wanted to rush out to talk to Dwight and discover who the couple was, but she couldn't make her feet move. Then a man came out of the barn. The way Dwight spoke to him, it was someone Dwight knew. Most likely someone who worked on the ranch.

Emmy dropped her head into her hands and sat there trying to get herself sorted. So many emotions ran through her, including fear and alarm. She had done everything she could not to look at the calendar and see the first of the year drawing closer and closer.

Christmas was her favorite time of the year. At least, it usually was. Joe Roma and his thugs had ruined even that for her.

She raised her head and dropped her arms to her sides. That's when she saw Sam sitting by the door. Emmy strode to him and dropped to her knees beside him. She wrapped her arms around him and buried her face in his cool fur.

"Oh, Sam," she murmured.

He stood still, allowing her the time she needed.

She took pity on him and straightened. He lifted his snout and gave her a little lick on her chin as if telling her that he understood. She rubbed the top of his head and got to her feet. When she looked out the windows, Dwight was still talking to the man. Emmy thought about calling Dalton. She wasn't sure what she would tell him other than she was scared. But she had been frightened for a while.

Actually, that wasn't true. She had resigned herself to death on the way from Denver to Montana. It wasn't until a few weeks into her stay at the ranch that she began to relax, realizing that she should enjoy whatever time she had. Then she had fallen head over heels for Dwight. It was so easy to feel safe with him that she forgot the looming deadline that awaited her at times.

She wanted to do what was right and put Joe behind bars. She should be able to do that without fearing for her life. Thanks to the laws that made the prosecutors turn over witness names, it made it easy for people like Joe to ensure that no one stayed alive long enough to testify against him.

Though she knew the law had been put there to protect the

innocent people being prosecuted, she couldn't help but feel that it was wrong. Especially for those in her predicament. What was done was done, though. She had decided her path, and she had been fine with the consequences.

"That was when I thought the marshals would protect me," she said to herself.

Emmy looked out the window again to see that both Dwight and the man were gone. She debated whether to go looking for Dwight. If the couple had raised a red flag, he would've told her. Right? She couldn't be sure. Trying to guess Dwight's motives and decisions only made her insane, so she stopped.

Or tried to.

She threw up her hands and let them fall to her legs. There was no way she could go back to the office and work now. She was too ramped up. Emmy paced the house, looking for something to do, anything to take her mind off things. But nothing caught her interest. All she wanted to do was talk to Dwight.

The desire to hear his voice, to know what he was thinking outweighed the danger of anyone on the ranch seeing her—as terrifying as that usually was for her. Because if she didn't get some answers, she wouldn't be able to calm down.

Emmy put on her jacket and boots and opened the door. Sam stayed beside her as she made her way down the stairs and across the snow-covered lawn to the barn. As she drew nearer to the barn entrance, she slowed, listening for voices. Dwight had told her that he would remain close to the house, so she knew he was around somewhere. She just wanted to make sure he wasn't with anyone.

She quietly walked through the barn but didn't see any sign of Dwight. When she came to the back entrance, she peeked around the corner. With no one in sight, she started to turn away when Sam trotted to the fence nearest her. That's when

Emmy saw Cloud. She waved at the horse, but the mare wasn't interested in her. Cloud stuck her head between the fence slats so she and Sam could touch noses.

It was such a sweet gesture that Emmy found herself smiling. Sam sat and looked at her. Emmy glanced around to make sure she didn't see anyone, then walked to the fence. The minute she was near, Cloud lifted her head and issued a soft whinny.

"It's good to see you, too, girl," Emmy said as she pulled her hands from the pockets of her coat and rubbed the horse's nose.

She didn't do it for long since her hands were freezing. She hadn't bothered to put on gloves since she didn't think she would be outside very long.

Emmy pressed her forehead against the mare's neck. "Thank you. You've made me feel better."

"Animals have a way of doing that. Especially horses."

She spun around in surprise at the deep voice. Emmy found herself staring at the man who had been talking to Dwight. He was of medium build with a face that had seen many summers. It was then that she recognized his voice from the first day she had helped Dwight in the barn. This was Carlos.

He held up his hands and smiled. "I didn't mean to frighten you."

She searched the area, hoping Dwight would come out.

"We've not had the pleasure of meeting," he continued. "My name is Carlos."

Emmy glanced at him but didn't say anything.

"Dwight had to leave for a few hours."

Her stomach dropped to her feet with those words.

Carlos's voice grew softer as he said, "He didn't expect you to come out of the house. Otherwise, he would've introduced us."

"He said he wouldn't leave."

"Some things have come up."

She was shaking. Emmy wasn't sure if it was the cold or the fear. Probably both. "Where is he?"

"There," Carlos pointed to the mountains.

The only reason Emmy had gotten through each day was because of Dwight. Without him, she didn't know what to do.

"Easy," Carlos said. "Take a breath. You need to breathe."

She looked at him as if he'd lost his mind. Then realized she *had* been holding her breath. Emmy gulped in air and leaned back against the fence.

"Emmy, I need you to listen to me carefully."

"You know my name," she said. Had Dwight told him everything?

A frown briefly marred Carlos's forehead. "I know Dwight cares about you. I know he'll do everything in his power to keep you and everyone on this ranch safe. I know he's trying to keep his promises to everyone, and he's having a hard time. It's why I finally stepped in."

She wanted to like Carlos, but she didn't know the man. "Why do you say that?"

"I've known Dwight and his family for over twenty years. I didn't tell him or anyone else that I saw your arrival. Nor did I say anything when I saw you and Dwight together with the horses that morning. I told him all of this, just as I'm telling you. I wanted Dwight to know that whether he told me what was going on or not, I would stand with him and fight. However, he came to the conclusion that everyone needed to know who they were up against."

"The couple," she said. "That set him off."

Carlos nodded once. "We both felt something wasn't right about them. It could be nothing, but I know Dwight. The way he's been taking extra precautions told me that something was going on. I trust his instincts."

"Why didn't he tell me this himself?"

"He wanted to get to the others and warn them."

Emmy put her hands in her pockets in an effort to warm them. "If he went off that quickly, it's because he's worried. He wouldn't be troubled if there wasn't a reason."

"He's taking precautions. There's a difference."

Emmy shook her head. "I don't want anyone to get hurt."

At this, Carlos chuckled. "You aren't from here, so you don't know. You should be worried about those coming. We know this land. We're not only avid hunters, but we're also expert marksmen. These people won't know what hit them."

"I wish I could believe everything you're saying, but you've not gone up against these people."

"Maybe not, but I don't need to in order to know what kind they are. They kill for money."

Her eyes widened. "Exactly."

"And we're defending a ranch and the occupants we call friends."

"These are assassins. They don't care about anyone or anything. Their job is to take lives."

Carlos merely smiled. "That is what will allow us to win."

She knew there was no way she could change his mind. Emmy blew out a breath, a white cloud forming in front of her face. "How long will Dwight be gone?"

"Not long. I'll be here until he returns. The best thing you can do is go back inside the house and wait."

"That's all I've been doing for weeks."

"Trust Dwight. He won't let you down."

Emmy knew that. She was just afraid that she would destroy everything Dwight held dear. Her worst fear was that he would be killed trying to keep her safe. He had given his word to Dalton, but now it was time for her to think about going out on her own. Dwight's entire life had been upended thanks to her.

She nodded and walked away from Carlos, her mind turning a thought over and over again. Once inside the house, she locked the door and removed her coat to hang it on the hook. Then she looked around the house with a heavy heart. Suddenly, she realized what she wanted to give Dwight for Christmas.

Chapter 25

Orso lowered his cell phone as he sat in the parked car at a rest stop. He drummed his fingers on the center console. This was only the second time in his career that he had called in outside help. There was just too much terrain for him to cover in the time allotted. He should've already finished with this job and moved on to another.

Yet, he was still in Montana, looking for a woman who seemed to have vanished into thin air.

His search hadn't uncovered any more places where the marshal had changed vehicles. After a call to a friend, Orso was able to determine Silva's last location based on CCTV footage. Emmy would stand out in the small town of Field Point. Unfortunately, Orso stood out, as well.

While parts of Montana were developing subdivisions, ranches made up most of the state. Going to each one and poking around was simply out of the question for one individual. Which was why Orso had brought in help. But even those now working for him had come up empty.

The ranchers weren't talking. Unless they searched all the houses and every outbuilding on the ranches, there was no telling where Emmy and the marshal could be. For all Orso knew, they were in a remote hunting cabin somewhere.

It seemed infeasible to him that he wouldn't finish an assignment. It would be the first time. And it didn't sit well with him at all.

He could still get Emmy. It would be easier if he could finish the job now, but Orso would make sure that she never took the stand against Joe. Whether Orso killed Emmy on the way to Colorado or at the courthouse in Denver, he would get the job done.

Orso turned the heat up in the car. "I fucking hate Montana," he grumbled.

He wanted to return to the town, but too many outsiders showing up at once raised suspicions. Instead of a hot meal, he would be stuck picking up something questionable at the local convenience store. It wouldn't be the first time he'd eaten such, but he was getting tired of it.

He'd considered retirement for a few years now. Perhaps Emmy would be his last job. He wouldn't go out with a big bang as he wanted, but then again, it was rare for men in his occupation to get to determine their retirement. Most were either killed by rival families or caught by the police. He considered himself lucky.

"That luck might be running out," he said as he put the car into drive. His stomach rumbled with hunger, causing his irritation to grow.

By the time he pulled into the convenience store's parking lot, he was in a foul mood. He glanced at the gray sky as he got out of his SUV and hurried into the store. Once inside, he was less than pleased by the meager offerings. He ignored the conversation between a customer and the cashier behind him.

A glance at the mirror in the corner showed the cashier to be a tall, portly man in his sixties. Orso decided on some cheese and crackers, a bag of Chex Mix, a bottle of unsweetened tea, and fried apple pie for dessert. His doctor would have a fit if he knew the bad food Orso had consumed since tracking Emmy.

But he'd make up for it with healthy meals during retirement. Orso was tired of the cold. He wanted to be somewhere warm. The thought of all the old people in Florida made him sick to his stomach. Never mind that he was getting up in age, as well. He wouldn't fit in with that crowd. No, he'd have better luck in California. There were so many eccentrics there that people wouldn't look twice at him.

Orso took his food to the register. Two other people milled about the store. One was a frazzled-looking young mother, a toddler in tow. The other was an older woman with a slight limp. Her face was red, and she wore a purple beanie over mousy brown hair in desperate need of a wash.

"Hey, Mike," the woman said as she passed.

The cashier raised his hand and smiled. "Hey, Irene."

Orso set his items on the counter and pulled out his wallet as Mike rang up everything.

"How are you today?" Mike asked him with a smile.

Orso shrugged. "Hungry and cold."

"If you have a long drive headed south, you best wait. There's a storm coming in a few hours."

"Thanks for the info," Orso said and paid with cash.

Mike began putting the items in a bag as Irene walked up. Orso wanted to snatch his food from Mike's grubby hands, but he made himself wait. The last thing he wanted was to do something that would make his stop memorable to the people here.

"Whew. What a day," Irene said as she set a jug of milk and a loaf of bread on the counter.

Orso glanced her way to find her smiling at him. He gave her a nod, fisting his hand when Mike paused.

"How's Jerry?" Mike asked Irene.

She laughed softly. "He's helping Dwight at the ranch. They're doing some hunting."

"Hunting?" Mike asked in shock. "For what?"

Orso suddenly found himself very interested in the conversation. And happy that Mike was taking his time.

"Yeah, I thought it odd, too," Irene said. "Jerry said it was a favor for Dwight. He didn't tell me what they were hunting. No other ranchers have said anything about a bear or cougar that I know of. Have you heard anything?"

Mike shook his balding head, his brow furrowed. "Not a word. I wonder what's going on at the ranch."

"What ranch would this be?" Orso asked.

Irene's head turned to him, but she clammed up. It was Mike who said, "Riverlands."

"I hope he finds whatever he's hunting," Orso said as he took the bag from Mike's grip and walked to his car.

The minute he was behind the wheel, he drove away. He returned to the rest stop since it had free Wi-Fi, which meant reception, something hard to come by in the mountains. Orso pulled out his phone and looked up the Riverlands ranch. He then compared it to the map of Montana he'd been using to dictate where to send the people helping him.

"I'll be damned," he murmured when he realized that it was close to the location where Dan and Nancy had stopped to ask for directions.

Orso quickly dialed the couple. Nancy answered on the second ring. "The ranch you stopped at," Orso said. "What was the name?"

"Riverlands," Nancy said.

Orso smiled. "You said the owner wasn't friendly."

"To be fair, not many are," Dan said.

Orso thought about that for a moment. "Are you sure you spoke with the owner?"

"Hard to say," Nancy said. "He was alone. We didn't see anyone else other than a dog on the porch. But the ranch was big."

"Did he introduce himself?"

"Never gave his name. Though he did ask why we came to Montana," Dan said.

"Thanks."

Nancy asked, "Do you need us for anything else?"

"No, head out," Orso told them. "I'll wire your money now."

He hung up and sent the money from his phone. Then he reached for his cheese and crackers as he mulled over the information he had gotten. Had he not stopped at the store, he never would've learned that Dwight at the Riverlands ranch was hunting something.

Chatty people said all sorts of things they shouldn't when they were familiar with their surroundings. It was how Orso got most of his information. If only people knew what others heard and picked up, they would never open their mouths without checking to see who was around.

He finished the cheese and crackers and opened the tea to take a long drink. He put the trash in the bag and reached for the Chex Mix. As he put each individual piece into his mouth, he considered the possibility of coincidences. From his experience, there was no such thing.

Which meant he needed to turn his attention to the Riverlands ranch and its owner, Dwight. It only took a little digging to discover that the owner of Riverlands was Dwight Reynolds. A quick background check uncovered that Dwight had worked for Homeland Security and the FBI, and had been in the military.

Without a doubt, Orso knew that Silva had gone to Dwight. Whether the marshal was on the ranch or Silva had dropped Emmy off, Orso didn't know. Yet. But he was sure that Emmy was there.

An hour earlier, Orso had worried that he would have to finish the job on the steps of the Denver courthouse. Now, he could notify Joe that Emmy would be taken care of before Christmas, ending the trial before it even began.

He started to dial Joe's number, then paused. Orso understood why Joe wanted to be there to witness Emmy's death, but this situation needed to be handled carefully. No other outsiders could be brought in.

Orso called Tony instead. The instant he answered, Orso said, "I've located her."

"About fucking time," Tony snapped in a low voice.

Orso heard Joe talking in the background. "The situation is fluid."

"What the hell does that mean?"

"It means that she's been dropped off with someone who can handle himself."

Tony grunted and mumbled, "Hold on." A few seconds later, he asked in a clear voice, "So?"

"Are you alone?"

"I am. Why?"

Orso blew out a breath. "She's hiding out on a ranch. One run by a man who is highly skilled. On top of that, he's got people looking for anyone trying to get onto the ranch other than through the usual ways."

"I see," Tony said after a moment.

"I don't think you do. This man is dangerous. Joe wants to be here when the job is about to be finished, but I don't think that's a good idea."

"Something we finally agree on." Tony sighed loudly. "You take care of the issue however you see fit. No doubt the situation will be fluid enough that you won't have time to put a call into Joe so he can fly up there."

Orso smiled. "Exactly."

"Don't fuck this up, Orso. We're all stressed about the impending trial."

Orso carefully folded the map. "I always finish my jobs. You don't need to worry about that."

"Good to hear."

The call ended. Orso set the cell phone in the cupholder and put the car into drive to head to his motel. He had some planning to do. He wasn't at all worried about Dwight's training. Orso had been trained, too. What he needed was the element of surprise.

His gaze lifted to the sky as a smile formed. The impending storm would likely give him just that. No one in their right mind would venture out into terrain they didn't know during such a storm—no one except for men like him.

Chapter 26

What a fucking long day. By the time he walked up the porch steps to the door, Dwight was exhausted. He couldn't wait to get inside and see Emmy. The entire time he'd made the trek out to those helping him, all he could think about was her. He'd hated leaving her, but it was necessary.

He opened the door and stepped into the warmth of the house. Sam rushed past him and ran to the back, where the office was. Dwight hung up his hat and coat before taking off his boots so he didn't track snow through the house. Then he followed Sam. Dwight found himself smiling when he heard Emmy talking to Sam.

As he leaned his shoulder against the door and watched the pair, he couldn't help thinking how grateful he was that Emmy had come into his life. She lifted her head, her light brown eyes meeting his. Her lips curved into a smile. She stood as he pushed away from the door and walked to her. Dwight wound his arms around her and held her, breathing in her clean scent. He closed his eyes to enjoy the moment to its fullest.

"Long day?" she asked.

He pulled back to look at her, searching her face. There was no anger there. "Very. How were things here?"

"Uneventful. Carlos is nice."

Dwight inwardly winced.

"Why didn't you just tell me you needed to go? I would've been fine."

He shrugged. "I had a hard time leaving after promising you I wouldn't."

"People are out there risking their lives for me, and they don't even know it. I understand why you did what you did. I just wish you would've told me."

"I'm sorry."

She grinned, shrugging as she glanced at his chest. "Everyone knows now?"

"They do."

Emmy backed out of his arms and licked her lips. "It was the right decision. I can't help but feel uneasy about it."

"A blizzard's moving up from Wyoming. No one in their right mind will be out in it. And if they are, then they're as good as dead. The storm will last through the night, so I sent everyone home."

"I would've, too."

But he saw the apprehension in the way her lips pursed. "They'll be back as soon as the storm passes. Like I said, no one will be out in the weather."

"I'm sure you're right."

"I am. How about some dinner?"

She looked him over. "You're exhausted. I'll make us some sandwiches."

"Sounds good," he said with a grin.

They walked together to the kitchen. When he tried to help her, she directed him to a chair with a stern look, followed by a soft smile. He sat, watching her, all the while wondering how he had gotten through life without her. She had only been with him a short while, but at the same time, it felt as if she had always been there.

Like she fit.

The missing puzzle piece to his soul.

He'd never thought of himself as particularly romantic, but he knew what he felt. He'd known quickly. His love for her had only grown as the days passed. He suddenly rose and walked to her, catching her hands in his.

"What?" she asked with a frown.

Without a word, he pulled her after him to the master bathroom. Once there, he turned on the shower then faced her and began removing her clothes.

She laughed playfully. "I left the food out."

"I don't care," he said, desire pumping through him at an alarming rate.

There must have been something in his eyes because she nodded and quickly started unbuttoning his shirt. In short order, their clothes were gone. Dwight couldn't wait. He had to taste her. He pulled Emmy into his arms and ravaged her lips.

No matter how much he kissed her, he could never get enough. He ran his hands over her back, holding her tightly and pressing her against his arousal. She moaned into his mouth. Everything Emmy did inflamed his blood and made him crave her even more.

He opened the shower door and maneuvered them into the stall without breaking the kiss. Hot water sprayed around them, soaking them instantly. He spun her so that her back was to the tile. Then he reached down and hooked his hands beneath her thighs, lifting her so her legs straddled his waist.

She tore her mouth from his and gripped his shoulders as her eyes darkened, her desire palpable. Her lips, swollen and wet from his kisses, parted as he slowly entered her. As his cock filled her, she bit her lip seductively. Dwight's balls tightened at the sight. He couldn't remember ever wanting someone like this, yearning for them as much as he did Emmy. She had seeped into his life like a mist, blanketing everything with her scent, her special *something* that he now knew he couldn't live without.

He began moving his hips. Slowly at first, then gradually increasing in speed. She moved in time with him. Their breathing was erratic, and their moans filled the room. Emmy locked her ankles together and gripped him tighter with her legs. He knew that she was close to climaxing by the way her body grew rigid.

Dwight pumped his hips faster, driving deep inside her. Her nails dug into his shoulders as she stiffened, a cry falling from her lips. He watched the pleasure cross her face, his heart expanding at her beauty. He didn't stop moving until she grew limp. Her eyes opened as she smiled. But he wasn't nearly finished with her yet.

He pulled out of her and lowered her feet to the floor. Then he turned her so that her back was to him. She put her hands on the tile in front of her and bent at the waist, pushing her fine ass toward him. Dwight guided himself into her again, pushing deep. He closed his eyes and sighed. She felt so damn good.

She moved against him with every thrust he made. He gripped her hips and slid in and out of her wet heat until he buried himself deep and let out a shout as he orgasmed. Dwight remained inside her until his breathing evened out. When he pulled out, she straightened and turned to him, wrapping her arms around him as she gave him a lingering kiss.

"I love you," he told her.

She looked up at him and smiled. Her lips parted, but he couldn't bear to hear her say what she had the last time. He kissed her to silence her. He'd known not to say the words again, but they had tumbled from his lips of their own accord. Now that they had been said—twice—he wasn't sure he could stop saying them.

He wanted her to know that he would move mountains for her. He wanted her to know that he would do absolutely anything to make her happy and keep her safe.

Dwight ended the kiss and reached for the soap as he lathered a sponge. She raised a brow when he smiled at her. He winked before slowly washing her from head to foot and back up again. He paid particular attention to her breasts and between her legs. When he finished, he moved her beneath the spray of the shower and let her rinse.

He watched as she leaned her head back and wet her hair. While she did, he put some shampoo in his hands and waited for her to look at him. He had never washed anyone else's hair before. As his fingers slid into her thick tresses, he found the act of massaging her scalp and running his hands through her strands relaxing. Her eyes had closed, showing that she enjoyed it as much as he did. They rinsed her hair together, then repeated everything again with the conditioner.

Just as he reached for the sponge and soap, she grabbed it. He laughed when she quirked a brow at him, giving him a daring look. The moment her hands moved over his body to wash him, all he could think about was taking her again and hearing her cries of pleasure.

All too soon, she finished. But to his delight, she wanted to wash his hair. He leaned his head back so she could reach him better. The bliss he felt at her hands on his scalp was indescribable. He was wondering how he could convince her to wash his hair every day when she finished.

After he was all rinsed off, he pulled her into his arms for another lingering kiss. He pressed his forehead against hers and stood beneath the spray.

"This was incredible," she said.

He nodded. "We should do it more often."

"That would be nice."

Dwight lifted his head and turned off the water so they could towel off. Sam lay in the doorway of the bathroom, watching them as they dressed and headed back to the kitchen. Dwight poured a glass of bourbon for himself and wine for Emmy just as she finished the sandwiches.

They had just sat when the roar of the wind reached them. Dwight looked outside and saw that the snowstorm had begun. "We'll be fine inside."

"That's good."

He took a bite of the sandwich and began chewing when his cell phone rang. Dwight jumped up and saw that it was his neighbor. "Hey, Bobby."

"I hate to be the bearer of bad news, but your herd is on my property. It looks like part of your fence is down," Bobby said, the sound of the wind coming through the phone.

Dwight looked outside again. He'd sent Carlos and the others home, and it would take him too long to get out to the fence and gather the cattle before the full force of the storm set in. "I'll come get them once the storm passes. You aren't out in this, are you?"

"I'm in my truck. Listen, I would've waited until morning about all of this, then I saw the heifer."

Worry settled into Dwight's gut. "My heifer?"

"She's tangled in barbed wire. I tried to get to her—"

"I'm glad you didn't," he said. Bobby was a seventy-five-year-old rancher who had no business being out in weather like this alone. "Get home to Myrtle before she has my head along with yours. I'll take care of the heifer."

Bobby hesitated. "Why don't I wait for you?"

"I'll be fine. Thanks for the heads-up."

"Be safe, son."

The call ended, and Dwight lowered the phone to the table before he met Emmy's gaze.

"You're going out there, aren't you?"

He nodded. "I've already lost two calves. That's five grand right there. I can't lose any more cattle, especially to something like this."

"It's one cow."

"It's a heifer. That young female will be ready to bear a calf come spring. I need her."

Emmy set her hands on the table and pushed to her feet. "Then I'll come with you."

"I've done this countless times before."

"I've got a bad feeling. I've had it for a few days now."

He reached over and took her hands. "No one in their right mind would try to come at you in this weather."

"You said anyone who gets out in this would die."

"Anyone who doesn't know what they're doing. I'm going to drive out there and walk the short distance to the fence. A few clips to free the heifer and make sure she doesn't need medical attention, and then I'm back in the truck headed here."

She lifted her chin. "Then it isn't a big deal for me to come with you."

Chapter 27

Emmy should have felt good that she'd convinced Dwight to let her come with him, but that wasn't the emotion swirling within her. Instead, apprehension sat at the forefront, followed closely by fear. And none of it had anything to do with the storm.

She couldn't say what made her feel such things, only that the emotions were there, and she was doing the best she could with them.

The truck bounced as it hit a hole hidden by the snow. She gripped the handle near her head and stared out through the thick falling snow. The truck's headlights did little to light the way. The heat was on full blast, but she couldn't stop shaking. Her breath locked in her chest when she spotted the rickety bridge. She didn't try to look out her window to see why there was a bridge. Sometimes, it was better not knowing.

Curiosity got the better of her, and she glanced down just as the front tires rolled off the bridge. She got a brief glimpse of a deep ravine. Emmy jerked her eyes up, wishing she hadn't seen that. The snow swirled outside, allowing her to get a quick look at a forked tree.

Sam nudged her with his nose as he put his paws on the console from his position in the back seat. Emmy glanced at him and rubbed his face, but she returned her attention to the road in an effort to help Dwight see through the ever-increasing snowfall.

"Shit," he murmured.

Emmy looked at him to see his lips pressed together. She had no idea if they were still on the road or not. Snow covered everything. All she could hope for was that Dwight knew where he was headed.

"We're almost there," Dwight said.

She nodded, her gaze returning to peer through the windshield. It seemed the storm's intensity grew with every second that passed. She wasn't sure how Dwight continued driving, much less how he would get out when they reached their destination to free the cow. She felt the force of the wind even inside the truck. Emmy had been in snowstorms before, but nothing had prepared her for this level of a blizzard.

Emmy couldn't wait to get back to the warmth and safety of the house. Neither she nor Dwight spoke as he concentrated on driving. Even Sam seemed uneasy with the storm as he continually moved around in the back seat. The one thing Emmy knew for sure was that Dwight had been right—no one would be out in this. That meant if they could make it back to the house, they would be safe until the storm passed. It was something she hadn't thought she'd be able to say, but the truth was right before her.

The truck slowed. She turned her head to Dwight to see him looking out his window. Sam barked. Dwight put the truck in park and blew out a breath before facing her. That's when she realized that they had reached their destination. The fact that she couldn't see a foot past the truck terrified her.

"I'll be quick," he said.

She reached over and grabbed his arm. "This is insane. How will you find your way back to the truck?"

"I'll tie a rope to the mirror and myself."

Of course he would have an answer. He'd lived most of his life in this climate. If only she could be as calm and collected. "You're going to need help."

"No," he stated firmly. "And that isn't debatable."

"I'm he—"

"No," he said over her. "I'm used to this weather. You aren't."

She licked her lips and glanced outside.

He blew out a breath. "I gave in to you coming, but that's as far as I'm willing to go. Please, stay inside so I can do what needs to be done."

Any arguments Emmy had died on her lips. "All right," she relented.

Dwight smiled and leaned over to give her a quick kiss. "Thank you."

Before she could say anything else, he opened the door. The wind howled, the cold slamming into her even as snow blew into the cab. Sam barked relentlessly until Dwight whistled as he put on his gloves. Sam jumped over the seat and out into the weather with his master. Then, the door closed with a sense of finality that Emmy couldn't shake.

She shuddered, thankful that Dwight had left the engine running and the heat on. She watched as he pulled something out of his pocket. That's when she realized it was rope. Thankfully, he had thought ahead. Once he had the rope tied to the side mirror, he wrapped it around his waist and formed a knot.

Emmy didn't take her eyes off him as he started walking away from the truck. Within seconds, the storm swallowed him. A chill ran down her spine, the same kind she'd gotten when the hitman had busted into her hotel room.

"We're safe," she said aloud. "At least, from the men trying to kill me."

She couldn't say the same about the storm. Minutes ticked by with aching slowness. Several times, she contemplated getting out and trying to help Dwight, but she quickly dismissed the thought. She had to trust him to do his job.

Despite her best efforts, Emmy couldn't sit still. She was agitated and anxious. Not a good combination. Her thoughts ran wild with dozens of horrific scenarios where both she and Dwight died from hypothermia. Her mind had always run to the worst-case scenarios, even before deciding to testify for the DA. Now, her imagination was even worse.

She looked out the driver's side window again, hoping to see Dwight. The only thing she saw was a sheet of white. Emmy crossed her arms over her chest and huddled deeper into her jacket. The heat didn't do much to warm her, and she couldn't imagine how cold she would be without it.

To calm her mind, she closed her eyes and took a couple of deep breaths. She thought about Dwight's smile and his way of making her feel secure and happy. She thought about the passion they had shared in the shower. Her stomach fluttered at the memory of his mouth and hands on her body.

She had wanted to tell him of her love, but he'd stopped her. Though she wasn't sure why, she'd decided to let it go because there had been something in his eyes. She had foolishly believed that if she kept the words to herself, they couldn't consume her. But she had been wrong.

It wasn't keeping the words in that did it, though. It was being around Dwight. Getting glimpses of what a life with him would be like. That was what made her love grow. He had been kind, patient, and gentle. Not once did she fear for her safety while at the ranch because she had seen the hardness in his eyes. He could tell her about all the jobs he had done, but it didn't mean the same as seeing the determination on his face, his desire to protect his property and those within. He was the kind of man every woman wished for. The kind who would die for the woman he loved. The kind of man that would stand beside his other half no matter what obstacles came their way.

He was, without a doubt, old-fashioned in many regards. Emmy hadn't realized until she met him that old-fashioned was exactly what she wanted. A man to hold the door for her and let her enter first—not because she wasn't strong enough to do it herself but out of respect.

The ranch meant hard work but being there had transported her back in time to when things had been simpler. And she hadn't missed the city once. That might be because she'd known she couldn't get out, but she thought it was more than that. She didn't miss the noise, the crush of people, the cars. The smells.

Sure, having things close was convenient, but she would rather have the quiet, the beauty, and the peace. Driving a little for things wasn't a big deal. Had she not been forced to the ranch, she never would've known the things she had been missing. Never would have realized the things her soul craved. Never appreciated the simple things in life.

Like a good man.

Something slammed against the truck. Emmy's eyes flew open, her heart thudding. She looked at Dwight's door but didn't see him. She unbuckled her seat belt and leaned over the console to put her hands on his seat so she could peer out the window in case he had fallen. Emmy listened for Sam's barks, for anything, but she only heard the howl of the wind.

Then what had hit the truck?

Her blood turned to ice as fear clawed at her. The only thing that kept her from coming completely unglued was the fact that humans wouldn't be out in this. The thought of an animal, a hungry one, going after the wounded heifer,

Dwight, and Sam made her crane her neck one way and then the other to see if she could catch a glimpse of anything.

Just as she was sitting back down, someone wrenched her door open, and she found herself staring down the barrel of a gun.

"Thanks for making it easy," the man said.

Chapter 28

"Dammit!" Dwight yelled as he struggled to clip the barbed wire to free the heifer.

The young cow was crying out in pain and looking for the herd. Sam stayed near without riling her. Dwight's fingers were going numb, and the wind cut right through him.

He paused, lifting his head. He could've sworn that he heard a scream. He looked over his shoulder toward the truck, but he couldn't even make out the vehicle's silhouette. Dwight remained perfectly still, listening intently to see if he could hear the noise again. The heifer kicking him pushed him back into action.

Finally, he got the last of the barbed wire cut. He pocketed the shears and let the heifer get to her feet. Once she was standing, he motioned to Sam, who stopped her from running off. Dwight saw blood, but with the storm, he couldn't determine how deep the wounds were. He could tie her to hold her but getting anything done with the wind would be nearly impossible. He would have to take his chances and see about the heifer come morning when the skies cleared.

"Sam!" he called.

Immediately, the dog rushed to his side, allowing the heifer to run to the waiting herd. Dwight lost sight of her before she crossed the stream. He blew out a breath, hoping that luck would be on his side, and the young cow would survive until the morning.

He rubbed his hands together. It was time to get back to Emmy. Dwight turned and grabbed the rope at his waist. Then he started pulling on it to drag himself toward the awaiting vehicle. Sam stayed in step with him the entire time. They had gone about ten steps when Sam let out a low growl. Dwight's head jerked to the dog. He knew that growl. That was a danger warning, an indication of something or someone suspicious.

They weren't that far from the truck. Dwight decided to pick up the pace and get to Emmy quicker. He tugged on the rope to tighten it again and make sure he was headed in the right direction when it suddenly went limp.

"What the fuck?" he murmured.

Dwight pulled on the rope, coiling it at his feet. He repeated the motion again and again until he reached the end. That's when he saw that it had been cut.

Years of training kicked in. He remained calm, assessing his options. He didn't have a gun or any other weapon, but he didn't need one. He knew enough to knock someone out—or take their lives, if necessary—with nothing but his body. And if someone were after Emmy, then it would be necessary.

Dwight squatted next to Sam, who had his ears pointed toward the truck. He let out another low growl.

"Easy," Dwight told the animal. "Let's not let him know you're here."

Sam never took his eyes from whatever he was staring at.

Dwight couldn't tell how close the truck was. He couldn't see the headlights through the dense snowfall, nor could he hear the engine over the wind. It took him two tries, but he finally got Sam's attention. Normally, the dog responded instantly, so whatever was out there was enough to make Sam nervous.

He gave Sam the same commands he would when he wanted the cattle contained. Without hesitation, Sam took off, bounding through the thick snow. Dwight slowly got to his feet and untied the rope at his waist. He looped it loosely in his hand, making a knot at the end. He wasn't sure what he would find when he reached the truck, but he would be prepared.

Dwight started forward in the same line he had been following before the rope loosened. The wind pushed him to the side, doing its best to shove him off course. He gritted his teeth and kept putting one foot in front of the other. Then, finally, he caught sight of the headlights.

There was no time for relief, though. Danger was out there. He gritted his teeth and carefully moved forward, wishing with everything he had that he would've refused Emmy's request to come out here with him. But he'd believed she was safe. She should've been. And that's where he'd gone wrong. He had underestimated the people after her, but he would make sure that didn't equate to her death.

Dwight moved to the right. A brief lull in the wind let him glimpse the truck. Unfortunately, that meant that someone could see him, as well. He spun the other way and tried to run when pain exploded through him.

"Noooooooo!" Emmy screamed. She didn't know if Dwight had been hit or not, but the assassin had shot at him.

She reached for the door handle to open it when the man was suddenly back in the truck with the gun pointed at her.

"You have no idea what I've gone through to find you," he told her.

She looked into his dark, dead eyes. He wasn't at all what she thought a hitman should look like. If she saw him on the street, she would think he worked at a library or something. He had an unassuming appearance—the kind that people forgot. Which, she supposed, was what made him so good at his job.

"I told you I'd go quietly if you left Dwight alone," she said, not hiding her fury.

He shrugged. "So?"

"You didn't have to shoot at him."

The man smiled, a cold, calculating grin that made a chill crawl down her back. "Consider it compensation for the killing of Joe's cousin and my time."

"Joe's cousin?" Emmy asked in confusion.

"The man at your hotel room. The one the marshal shot? That was Joe's cousin."

"How was I supposed to know that? And how is that even my fault? I didn't pull the trigger."

Stony dark eyes regarded her. "The minute you went to the DA, everything became your fault. Now, get your fucking hands off the door and onto the steering wheel. Your friend is dead. Just as you're about to be."

By the ice on his eyebrows and the hair sticking out of his beanie, she realized that he was cold and wanted an easy way back to his vehicle. His mistake had been putting her behind the wheel and killing Dwight. She had nothing to lose now. Nothing except getting to someone to notify them about Dwight. There was still the possibility that he was alive, a chance that someone could save him. But they had to know about his injury first.

"Then finish me now." She had no idea where the courage came from. That was a lie. She did. It was the fury at Dwight's possible death. She had feared this moment, but now that it was here, she didn't care. All she wanted was to make sure Dwight got medical attention if he was still alive.

The man chuckled. "Don't worry, sweetheart. Your time is coming. Right now, you're going to drive me."

She'd been contemplating whether she could put the truck in drive before he pulled the trigger. Now, he was giving her what she wanted. "Why?"

He raised the gun, his face going taciturn. "Drive, bitch."

She lifted her chin and faced forward before putting the truck in gear. Emmy knew snow, but she had never driven off-road before, and that's exactly what Dwight had done to bring them here. She also had no idea which way it was back to the ranch. On the one hand, that was bad for Dwight. On the other, it meant that the hitman might just freeze to death—if she made sure he couldn't drive the truck.

An idea began forming as she slowly pressed the accelerator to move the vehicle forward. She managed to turn the truck around without hitting anything. She saw a flash of dark fur in the headlights. She smiled because she knew it was Sam. A glance showed that her captor hadn't noticed. Sam would stay with Dwight until she could send help.

And she *would* send help.

The man she loved was out there, possibly shot. She wouldn't entertain the other option. No matter what the hitman told her. Until she saw Dwight's body, she would keep hope in her heart.

"Joe wanted to come see you die."

Emmy didn't bother to comment. Though, she wasn't surprised by the statement. Joe's ego was massive. The fact that someone he had brought into his inner circle had turned on him was too much. He wanted revenge. Having her killed wasn't enough. He needed to witness it.

"I've got to hand it to you and the marshal," the assassin continued. "This was a great place to hide out. The only problem was the small town. Everyone talks. It's just a matter of being at the right place at the right time to overhear the right bit of conversation."

So, that's how he'd found her. It didn't matter anymore. Her worst fear had arrived. She'd known all along that she would never make it to the trial. She mourned the loss of a life with Dwight, of being loved and of loving him. She also hated that Joe would get away with his crimes because no one else could testify against him.

But the fear that had sunk its claws into her for weeks was gone, replaced by determination and fortitude. Death no longer made her panic. Everyone died. It was how she would die that terrified her. At least, it used to. Knowing that death was upon her now, that she wouldn't live to see the next sunrise, made a calm settle over her.

It was the weirdest feeling. Somehow, she knew she wouldn't have such emotions if she hadn't fallen in love with Dwight. He was all that mattered now. If her last effort saved him, then she could die happy. Her only regret would be not telling him about her love.

"Do you know where you're going?"

Emmy barely held back the snort. It was something the asshole should've asked before he'd told her to drive. "Of course," she lied. "I've been out here with Dwight every day since I arrived. I never left his side."

"A fat lot of good that did you," the hitman stated with a spiteful grin.

She had never hated anyone more. He initially seemed harmless, but upon closer inspection, she could sense the evil in him. The malevolent soul within. She had never been this close to pure evil before, and it caused an uneasy sensation. She had always believed that people were never good or evil but a combination of both with some leaning more one way or the other. Not so with the man beside her. Without a doubt, she knew there wasn't a shred of good within him.

The tracks the truck made on their way to the heifer were long gone. Emmy wasn't sure if she was headed toward the house or not. She hoped so because there was that small ravine with the rickety bridge. It would be the perfect place to crash the truck and ensure it wasn't drivable.

It became easier to see as the storm slacked off some. Now, she could make out about ten feet in front of the truck instead of the three of before. It wasn't much, but she would take it. She tightened her hands on the steering wheel, her body tense, fear churning in her belly. Her sense of direction had always been shit. While she'd thought she should veer to the right, she instead veered to the left, hoping that by doing the opposite of what she would normally do, she would reach the ravine.

Please. Please. Pleasepleasepleasepleaseplease.

"Why did you turn on Joe?"

The last thing she wanted to do was talk. "Does it really matter?"

"Nope. Just curious."

"Then go fuck yourself."

The man chuckled. "Now I understand why Joe liked you so much. From what I heard, you could've been his mistress. Possibly even his wife, eventually. He would've done anything for you. Then you had to go to the DA."

"Just because he has money and power doesn't mean he gets to choose if someone lives or dies."

"Actually, that's exactly what it means."

She shook her head. "I could go into a lengthy conversation about why you're wrong, but your moral compass was clearly destroyed long ago—if you ever had one—so I won't bother."

"Sanctimonious bullshit."

She rolled her eyes as he made her point.

"If we had more time, I'd take you back to Denver and present you to Joe myself. Instead, we'll go back to that big house you've been hiding in so I can FaceTime Joe, and he can see your death for himself. If there had been a signal out here, I would've already done it."

Emmy's breath caught when she saw the forked pine. She had seen it after they crossed the ravine. Her heart rate quickened. This was her chance.

She pressed the accelerator, increasing the speed the minute the ravine came into view. She didn't want to telegraph her intentions too early, but it was difficult to keep her excitement at bay. As the bridge approached, she floored the gas pedal and jerked the wheel to miss the bridge.

Her breath caught in her lungs as they went over the side of the ravine, the engine revving. An instant of silence reigned before she heard the hitman yell. Emmy closed her eyes and raised her hands to shield her face.

Chapter 29

Dwight rolled onto his back, gritting his teeth in agony. Breathing was difficult, made worse by the frigid temperatures. He cracked open his eyes to see Sam pacing in front of him, whining softly.

He had to get up and get to Emmy. Dwight had no idea how long he had been lying in the snow or how much blood he had lost. The pain shooting from the wound in his back told him the bullet had found its mark. But that wouldn't stop him. He grunted as he carefully pushed himself up into a sitting position.

The wind had died down, allowing Dwight to hear the crunch of snow as someone neared. Was the bastard coming back to finish the job? He hoped to hell he was. Dwight prepared himself to strike. It would be clumsy and ugly, but his life and Emmy's depended on it. Sam was there to help, as well.

"Dwight!"

His head jerked toward the voice. Sam issued a short bark and rushed to the man.

Dalton lifted his goggles and lowered his mask to uncover the bottom portion of his face. "Shit. That's a lot of blood."

"What the fuck are you doing here?"

"I'll explain on the way," Dalton said as he hurried to Dwight and knelt behind him, shrugging off a backpack.

Dwight tried to turn his head and look over his right shoulder, but the pain stopped him. "On the way where?"

"After Emmy and Orso."

"Is Orso a hitman?"

"Yep," Dalton said.

Dwight didn't say more as Dalton packed the wound with ice. Dalton dug in his backpack and pulled out a bandage roll, quickly wrapping it around Dwight's chest and shoulder to hold the snow in place.

"This will have to do until we can get you medical attention," Dalton said.

Dwight tried to move his shoulder. "This is perfect. Let's get going."

Dalton tossed a beanie at Dwight since his cowboy hat was missing. Then Dalton closed his backpack and shrugged it on as he got to his feet. Dwight tugged the beanie on before accepting Dalton's hand to get up. Then they set out, following the fast-disappearing tire tracks with Sam trotting alongside them.

"I think it's time you tell me what you're doing here," Dwight said.

Dalton pulled his mask up and re-donned his goggles. "As soon as I left Emmy at the ranch, I knew it was only a matter of time before Roma sent someone after her. I figured my best bet would be to find out who it was and tail them as they tracked Emmy."

"Smart thinking. That way, you could stop them before they got to her."

"That was the plan." Dalton shrugged. "I staked out Roma's

place, watching everyone come and go. I knew the moment I saw Orso that he was the man going after Emmy. He was so intent on finding my trail that he never thought to see if anyone followed *him*. I was able to stay with him all this time without him knowing I was there."

Dwight was winded from his wound and trudging through the snow. "He's used to being the hunter, not the hunted. That gave you an advantage."

"That it did. He underestimated me."

"So that's how you knew to warn me that someone was close."

Dalton glanced at him and nodded. "Orso called in some help. He had several couples working for him, going from ranch to ranch, asking questions."

"I knew those people weren't legit."

"Others not trained like us wouldn't, though."

Dwight paused and looked around. "Did you see which way they went?"

"Back the way you came."

Dwight fisted his hands, trying to get feeling back into his fingers. "Why didn't Orso kill Emmy when he found her?"

"I don't know, but it's buying us some time. I never thought Orso would come out in this storm, but the minute I saw him gathering supplies earlier, I set things into motion myself."

Dwight looked at his friend. "He cut my fence, didn't he?"

"Yeah," Dalton said with a nod as they began walking again. "He also caught the cow and got her tangled in the wire, just to make sure you'd come out here."

"Orso may know the way back to the ranch, but I don't think Emmy does. Did you see who was driving?"

Dalton shook his head. "I was too far away. For an older guy, Orso moves quicker in the snow than I do. I lost track of him for a short period. That was enough time for him to shoot you and take Emmy."

"Don't beat yourself up about it. You were ahead of the game with him, giving us time to prepare for an attack."

"We're losing the tracks," Dalton said.

Dwight jerked his chin to Sam. "But we've got my dog."

Dalton chuckled softly. There was a brief stretch of silence before he said, "If we don't get to them soon, Emmy–"

"Don't say it," Dwight ordered, more harshly than intended.

Dalton's brown eyes met his. "You're in love with her."

"I am."

"I guess I should've seen that coming."

Dwight picked up the pace. He was out of breath, wounded, and scared that he might lose the woman he loved. If he found Emmy dead, he would tear Orso limb from limb. He would want justice immediately, and he'd deliver it to the assassin himself. There wouldn't be a lengthy trial or a jury that could be bought and swayed.

"I won't stop you," Dalton said suddenly.

Dwight glanced at his friend and frowned. "What?"

"I see that look on your face. I won't stop you from going after Orso. In fact, I'll be right beside you."

They walked for what felt like hours. The truck, even if driven as slowly as Dwight had when they'd headed out to the heifer, was still making better time than they were. He couldn't even be sure of the time that had passed since they left, and Dalton had found him. For all Dwight knew, Emmy and Orso had already made it back to the house.

But there was also a chance they were lost.

"There is no road to travel on," Dwight told Dalton. "It would be easy to get lost or turned around."

Dalton nodded, his breathing ragged. "I thought of that."

"That could give us time to find them."

"Possibly. It could also frustrate Orso, making him kill her right then before disappearing."

Dwight shook his head. "That bastard isn't leaving this ranch alive."

"Even if he does, I'll have evidence to convict him."

"How so?"

Dalton's eyes crinkled at the corners. "A buddy owed me a favor. A rather high-up-in-the-food-chain buddy who got me a warrant to bug Orso's phone. We're recording everything he says."

"Will that be enough for Roma's trial?"

"Everything helps at this point."

Dwight blinked the snow from his lashes. Sam halted, his body stiffening. Then he took off running. Without hesitation, Dwight followed the dog. He ignored the pain of his wound and tried to keep Sam in sight, but the dog was fast. Luckily, his prints were easy to follow for the moment. The rapid snowfall would eventually erase them, but for now, they could track Sam.

The instant Dwight saw the tree, he knew what was up ahead. Then he heard Sam's barking. Dwight ran faster, getting ahead of Dalton. They came to a halt when they spotted Sam at the edge of the ravine, barking incessantly.

"No," Dwight said as he rushed to the edge. As he looked over the side, he spotted his truck upside down in the water. "I've got to get down there."

"You're wounded."

Dwight glared at his friend. "I'm going down."

Dalton nodded and dropped his backpack to the ground. He opened it and pulled out some climbing rope. Dalton wrapped the rope around the tree and threw both ends over the edge of the twenty-foot ravine. Dwight gathered the two pieces of rope and stepped between them before wrapping them around his waist and then between his legs as a makeshift harness. As Dwight backed up to the edge, Dalton came to stand beside him.

"I'm coming with you."

Dwight gave him a nod. He then looked at Sam. The dog sat, watching him intently. "Stay," he ordered.

He rappelled down the ravine. The exposed dirt was icy and muddy, making things slippery, but he got to the bottom without incident. As soon as his feet touched the earth, Dwight released the ropes and rushed into the icy water to the truck. The front end was smashed to the point it was unrecognizable. The top of the vehicle had caved in from the landing, crumpling the sides and bowing the doors.

His heart thumped loudly as he prayed that Emmy was alive. He reached the driver's side first. The window was smashed to bits, and he spotted Emmy's caramel tresses hanging in the water just inches from her head. Her arms and hands dangled in the frigid water. Glass was all around her—in her hair, on her clothes.

Dwight tried to open the door, but it was stuck. His fingers ached and wouldn't move properly, but he managed to get them between a portion of the door that was bent outward. Then he lifted a foot from the water and braced it against the truck as he yanked.

The door didn't budge.

"Hang on!" Dalton shouted as he splashed into the water and came up alongside Dwight.

Together, they tugged on the door. There was a groan as the metal finally gave way, and the door opened a few inches. It took several more attempts before they got it open enough for Dwight to get to Emmy.

"Baby," he murmured as he gently moved her hair out of the way so he could see her better.

His heart clutched when he saw the blood that covered her face. His hand shook as he moved it to her nose to feel for breath. The rush of relief that went through him when he felt her exhale was so great, he nearly passed out.

"She's alive!" Dwight shouted.

"Thank goodness. What about Orso?"

Dwight leaned down to peer across Emmy. The sight of the older man with the motor crushed into his chest and his head underwater told Dwight that he was dead. Dwight glanced at Dalton. "Dead."

"Are you sure?"

"Absolutely." He then reached around Emmy and tried to unlatch her seat belt, which was the only thing holding her above the water. Dwight slammed his hand against the outside of the truck. "Dammit."

Dalton's voice was filled with concern. "What is it?"

"The seat belt is stuck."

"Let me try."

Dwight reluctantly moved out of the way so Dalton could attempt to free her. But Dalton didn't have any luck either.

"We need to cut the seat belt," Dalton said.

Dwight shoved his friend out of the way as he recalled Emmy always carrying a knife with her. He found her feet and lifted her jeans to find the blade stuck in her boot. He withdrew it and handed it to Dalton. "You cut while I catch her."

With one slice, he severed the seat belt. Emmy dropped into Dwight's arms. Dwight managed to keep her out of the water, but it was difficult to move her with his injury. Dalton helped him carry her out of the stream and onto dry land.

Once she was on the ground, Dalton rubbed her hands to warm them while Dwight inspected her face to see where the blood was coming from. She had tiny, jagged cuts all over her face. He found the largest near her hairline—the one responsible for the blood. Her head had hit the steering wheel, most likely.

"Wake up, Emmy. Come on, baby, open those pretty eyes for me," Dwight urged.

Dalton glanced up at him. "I'm worried about her hands. We have no idea how long they were submerged in the water. She needs medical attention immediately. Both of you do."

"Let's get her up the ravine."

"Boss!"

Dwight and Dalton looked up to see Carlos and several other men. Dwight didn't care how they were there, he was just happy to see them. "Emmy's unconscious and injured. We need to get her up."

"On it!" Carlos shouted.

Dwight wasn't sure how much longer he would last. The cold and blood loss were taking their toll on him. He stared at Emmy, silently willing her to wake up.

"Stay here," Dalton told him.

Dwight held Emmy to him, offering her as much of his warmth as he could. The wind had died down to only a few gusts, but the snowfall had yet to taper off. He could hear Sam barking from above. There were also voices, as well as the sound of vehicles. Dwight watched as a makeshift stretcher was lowered from the top of the ravine, along with Carlos. Dalton and Carlos walked to him and Emmy.

"What are you doing here?" Dwight asked.

Carlos adjusted his hat and glanced up at the others standing on the edge of the bluff. "Bobby was worried about you. He stayed out there in case you needed help with the heifer. When he heard the gunshot, he knew something was wrong and called me. I phoned a few others, and we came straight out here.

"And we're glad you did. I'm Deputy US Marshal Dalton Silva."

The two men shook hands. Carlos twisted his lips. "My nephew, Billy, remained on the mountain. He saw two men where they shouldn't be and tracked them. He thought you were with the other man at first. Once he realized you would get to Dwight, Billy followed Emmy in the truck. He was getting ready to shoot the man when Emmy sent the truck over the edge."

Dwight met Dalton's gaze before nodding at Carlos.

Carlos turned his attention to Dwight. "We need to get both you and Miss Emmy up the bluff. Let me take her."

Dwight released her and watched Carlos gently lift her into his arms, carrying her to the stretcher. Dalton helped Dwight get to his feet, and they moved slowly toward Carlos as he tied Emmy so she didn't slip out. By the time Dwight reached Carlos, they were already hoisting her up.

"You've lost a lot of blood," Dalton told him.

Dwight didn't take his eyes off Emmy until she had reached the top and was in the others' hands. The edges of his vision began to darken. He tried to remain conscious, but his body had had enough.

Chapter 30

"There she is."

Emmy felt as if she were clawing her way out of tar. She heard voices and lots of movement around her. She recognized one voice, but she couldn't quite place who it was. As she drew closer to consciousness, fear rode her. It was deeply rooted, something telling her that her life was in jeopardy.

"Easy, Emmy. You're safe. You're safe."

The instant she recognized Dalton's voice, she calmed. Then the memories came rushing back—including losing Dwight. She opened her eyes as tears welled and fell from the outer corners to run across her temples.

Dalton leaned over her, wearing a smile. "I was beginning to wonder if you'd ever wake."

"H—" she began, then cleared her throat. "How did you find me?"

"I tracked Orso. He was the guy who came for you. After I dropped you with Dwight, I headed straight back to Denver and waited. I knew Joe would send someone. When he did, I followed him."

Emmy sniffed, nodding as she looked around the sterile

room to realize that she was in a hospital. "You need to go back out there. Dwight was shot."

"I know," he said calmly.

More tears came. The hope she'd held onto that Dwight might have survived was dashed. "Oh."

"No, no," Dalton said with a grin. "He's alive. He helped me get you out of the truck."

Elation filled her. She raised her hands to her face and let the tears flow. Finally, she looked at Dalton. "Where is he? I want to see him."

"He's resting. He came out of surgery about an hour ago."

"Surgery?" she asked, her voice rising. "He *was* shot, then?"

Dalton nodded. "Orso shot him in the back. Thankfully, it missed his spine and went through and through, but there was a lot of damage. Still, he's going to make a full recovery."

Emmy closed her eyes and sighed, her heart bursting with joy.

"What happened?" Dalton asked as he handed her a glass of water with a straw in it. "How did you end up in the ravine?"

Emmy drank deeply before answering. "He wanted to take me back to the house, where there was cell reception. Apparently, Joe wanted to see my execution on FaceTime. It was a stroke of luck that he didn't kill me immediately. I recalled the ravine and prayed that I remembered how to get there. When I saw it, I floored the gas pedal and sent us over. Tell me you have him in custody."

"I don't, actually. But only because he's dead."

"That won't stop Joe from sending someone else."

Dalton twisted his lips. "No, unfortunately, it won't. Don't worry. You're here under an assumed name. I've been in contact with internal affairs, who is doing an investigation into the marshals after I presented evidence."

"That's great, but there's still time before the trial. Do I have to go through this again?"

"I turned over evidence to the DA from Orso's phone as he was hunting you. The conversations were enough to get Joe and his right hand, Tony, arrested for attempted murder. They're both being held without bail. And the trial has been moved up."

Her brows rose. "Really? When?"

"Two days' time."

"The judge granted this?"

Dalton nodded, a crooked smile on his lips. "He did when the DA presented all the evidence and proved that your life was in imminent danger."

Emmy gently touched her head, for the first time realizing there was a dull ache there. She winced when she met a tender spot.

"You sustained a concussion. But other than a few cuts from the glass, you're in good shape. We worried about your fingers because they were in the water for a bit, but the doctor said you should be fine."

"I need to see Dwight. Will you take me to him?" she begged.

Dalton winked at her. "Hang tight. I'll get a nurse to bring a wheelchair."

Emmy glanced down at her red fingers. She couldn't believe her gamble had paid off. Excitement and nervousness made her stomach flutter, and her heart beat erratically. It took forever and a day before the nurse arrived with the wheelchair. Once she was seated, Dalton pushed her out of the room and down the hall to an elevator. They went down two floors before the elevator doors opened with a ding. Dalton pushed her down an impossibly long hall and turned left before finally slowing in front of a room.

He stood to the side and opened it. Emmy couldn't wait

for him to push her through. She put her hands on the wheels and rolled herself in. When she saw Dwight lying in the bed asleep, fresh tears came. She didn't stop until she was by the bed. Then she reached over and took his hand in hers.

She took in the red, abraded patches of skin over his face. He had suffered greatly while in the storm, but he had managed to pull through. He was strong both physically and in spirit, and it showed.

His head turned toward her, and his eyes slowly opened. His chapped lips turned up at the corners when he saw her. "Hey," he said.

"Hey," she replied, blinking rapidly to stop more tears.

"Why are you crying?"

She licked her lips, her face crumpling as she cried harder. "Because I thought I'd lost you."

"I know the feeling."

They shared a long look. Emmy sniffed and wiped at her face with her free hand. "I realized when Orso shot you that I regretted something terribly."

"What's that?"

"Never telling you that I loved you."

Elation filled Dwight's face. He squeezed her hand tighter. "You stole my heart within days. I would've waited an eternity for you to say those words."

"I was such a fool. I thought I would soon be dead, so I tried to stop myself from loving you."

"None of that matters now."

She shook her head. "No, it doesn't. It looks like I'll be done with all this trial stuff soon. They moved the date up to two days from now."

"You won't be entering that courtroom alone," he stated.

Emmy smiled and leaned forward to place a kiss on his hand. "That's because you'll be beside me."

"You're damn right, I will," he said with a wink.

She looked around, just realizing that Dalton wasn't in the room. "Dalton has all the specifics. He brought me here, but I don't know where he is now."

"I don't care about Dalton. I'd rather have you. Come, climb in bed with me."

"Your wound—" she began.

He cut her off. "Is on the other side. I need to hold you."

Since she needed to hold him, as well, she didn't argue the point. Emmy moved slowly until she was beside him, curled against him. He wrapped an arm around her and sighed contentedly.

"I love you," he whispered as he closed his eyes.

She smiled, hers closing, as well. "I love you, too."

Epilogue

Later . . .

"How does it feel?" Dwight asked as he finished tending to the fire in the hearth and turned to face Emmy.

She hadn't stopped smiling since they returned home earlier in the day. "Fantastic."

Multiple armed guards from various agencies had escorted Emmy and surrounded the courthouse, inside and out. Dwight had sat in the courtroom and watched proudly as Emmy gave her testimony in front of the jury. Her voice never wavered, even when the DA asked her to point to Joe Roma.

Joe had hatred in his eyes, but Dwight knew he would spend the rest of his days behind bars. The FBI had arrested most of those in the Roma mob, and they awaited trial, as well. Dwight knew that just because Joe had been arrested and would no doubt be convicted, he still might seek revenge against Emmy. But she wouldn't be the only one he went after. Following her testimony, six other witnesses had come forward to give accounts of other crimes that Joe and his mob had committed.

Emmy patted the sofa with a smile. "Come sit."

Sam looked up at Emmy adoringly as she scratched his

belly after climbing up on her other side. Dwight couldn't blame him. He couldn't stop staring adoringly at Emmy, either.

"How are you feeling?" she asked once he sat.

He shrugged. "The painkillers are working great."

"I don't want you overdoing it."

Dwight slowly put his feet up on the coffee table and stared into the fire. "I know Christmas isn't for a little bit, but I'd like you to open a present early."

"Really? I'd rather wait."

"I don't think I can."

Emmy laughed. "Well, if I'm opening, then you have to, as well."

He frowned. "You didn't have to get me anything."

"It isn't much," she said as she got to her feet and walked to the tree. She lifted a few presents, then returned with one in her hand. "But I wanted to give you something."

He accepted it with a smile and an eagerness to know what was inside. He raised his brows. "Now?"

"Now," she said with another laugh.

Dwight removed the bow and tore off the paper to find a plain white box. He set it on his lap and took off the lid. After he pulled back the tissue paper, he saw a frame cushioned within, featuring two pictures of him and Vic. One when they were kids, and a more recent photo.

Emotion choked him as he lifted the frame from the box. "I've told myself many times that I'd get an updated picture of us, but I kept forgetting. This is perfect," he said as he met her gaze. "Thank you."

She beamed and leaned forward to kiss him. "I had a lot of fun looking through the old photos that Vic sent me."

"Oh, I can imagine," he replied with a chuckle. He set the picture on the table beside him before tossing aside the box. "Ready for yours?"

"Maybe," Emmy said with a wrinkle of her nose, her apprehension showing.

He had barely been able to wait this long to give it to her. Dwight shifted and pulled out the small box he'd stuffed between the cushion and the arm of the sofa.

"Oh," Emmy said in a soft voice, reaching for it.

He watched her intently as she slowly opened the velvet box and saw the ring within. Dwight slid awkwardly and slowly from the sofa to one knee. "I love you with every fiber of my being. I can't imagine a single minute without you. I want you in my life. Through the hard times, through the good, and everything in between. You've brought joy and happiness to my life that I hadn't known was missing. The only thing I want this Christmas, and all the holidays to come, is you. Will you be my wife, Emmy?"

A tear slipped down her cheek as she got on her knees before him. "I love you so much my heart could burst. Yes, Dwight Reynolds, I'll marry you."

He pulled her against him with his good arm and kissed her. Whatever the future held, he knew they would face it together.

Read on for a Bonus Short Story by Donna Grant!

WISH UPON A COWBOY

Chapter 1

December 23
Wyoming

"Turn around when possible," said the nasally female voice from the GPS.

Cady wanted to hit something. Hard. "There's no damn place to turn around!" she yelled at the voice.

"Turn around in two hundred yards."

"Turn around?" Cady asked in exasperation. "There's nothing but snow. For days!"

She was panicking. It was the last thing she should do, but Cady couldn't seem to stop the emotion now. It had overtaken her like a tsunami.

And swallowed her whole.

"It was that left turn ten miles back. I knew I should've taken it," she grumbled.

Cady shook her head and leaned forward as she gripped the steering wheel tightly, in hopes that another street would somehow materialize. Though, she wasn't even sure she was on a road. The GPS had been spotty, at best. It had gone in and out several times. During one of those instances, she had made a decision regarding which direction to go. Obviously, she'd chosen wrong.

"I just need to turn around. There has to be someplace to do that. Right?" she asked herself in a small voice. "A road? A driveway? A rest stop?"

The car crept along. Cady didn't want to miss her chance to turn around, and there was no way in hell she would attempt to back up—even in a straight line. She knew her limits. Backing up more than a few feet out of a parking space and parallel parking were no-nos.

And if she were honest, some drive-thrus. Whoever had designed the narrow drive-thrus that a Hot Wheels car could barely maneuver in should be shot. She had scraped her wheels too many times. Of course, the answer to that was to stop going to drive-thrus, but that was easier said than done when she led such a fast-paced life.

"I just want to go home," she whispered as emotion welled.

A second later, she let out a shriek as the steering wheel jerked to the left, and the back end of the car fishtailed. Cady took her foot off the accelerator and turned the wheel in the direction of the spin. That should've been enough for her to get control. Except she hit another patch of ice, causing the car to spin wildly. In the next instant, the seat belt jerked her back, and her head snapped forward as the car went nose-first into a snowbank.

Cady sat there for several minutes, trying to get her bearings. She gingerly touched her throbbing forehead. Luckily, there was no blood, but she would have a raging headache soon. She drew in a shaky breath and shivered. That was when she realized that the engine had stalled. Cady tried the ignition, but it wouldn't engage.

She reached for her cell phone she had put in the cupholder, but it was gone. Flustered and terrified, she hastily unbuckled the seat belt and began searching for it. Several panicked moments later, she found it lodged beneath the passenger seat. She had to contort herself just to get it out since it was wedged.

"Finally," she said with a sigh as she sank back into the driver's seat with her phone.

Now, all she had to do was call someone to come and get her. She glanced at the time on the phone. She was still way ahead of schedule for the airport. That meant she could still make her flight. That would be the only good thing to come out of the day.

She searched through her contacts for AAA and pressed call. Nothing happened. She jerked the phone away and looked at the bars to find none. Just as she was about to let her anxiety get the better of her, she remembered that 911 calls always go through. The smile on her face vanished when her phone went dead.

"Noooooooo," she said, tears threatening.

She couldn't charge her phone because the car was dead, and of course, she had to forget her portable charger at home. Cady rested her forehead on the steering wheel and released the tears she had been holding in for days. With the floodgates open, she couldn't *stop* crying.

When the tears finally subsided, she sat up. As she sniffed and wiped her eyes, she spotted a few flurries in the air.

"Perfect," she stated sarcastically.

She loathed snow. She detested the cold. This was the last place in the world she wanted to be, but she hadn't had a choice. Now, she was stuck in a snowbank, freezing her ass off. The irony wasn't lost on her.

"When I get back, I'm quitting. No more will I continue being David's whipping girl. I've proven myself over the last five years, but what does he do? He sends me to this godforsaken place right before Christmas just to get a signature because he's going to Tahiti. That's it. I'm done."

She crossed her arms over her chest and glared out the window to the piles and piles of never-ending snow. She used to like the color white, but the more she gazed at the landscape, the more she came to develop a distinct aversion to it.

The minutes ticked by with agonizing slowness. She felt each one—and the colder she became. She had been dressed for business, not a day in the frozen wilderness. The thin dress pants did nothing to keep her legs warm. Even the stiletto boots she wore felt like she had stuck her legs in a vat of ice water.

She dreamed of her house. Of sitting curled up on her sofa with a glass of wine and a movie, a fire in her gas fireplace, her couch overlooking the magnificent view of Austin. Her home was her refuge. A sanctuary from the hectic and chaotic legal world she had chosen as her profession.

Though she wasn't so sure her home would be a haven anymore. The tightness that had been in her chest for the past few weeks resurfaced. It had been her home for eight years, and she had shared three of those with Jared.

Cady closed her eyes as she tried not to think of him, but it was too late. She had always sworn never to date another lawyer because she knew the lifestyle. But he hadn't taken no for an answer and had pursued her until he finally won her over. They had been together ever since. She'd thought they were good. Then, she'd decided to surprise him at his office, only to find him and one of his female colleagues screwing on his couch.

It was the first time she had ever felt nauseated and furious at the same time. She hadn't known whether to hit him or vomit on him. She should've been sick all over him. It was what he deserved.

Cady blew out a breath, pulling her thoughts from the

whirlpool of self-pity she had desperately tried not to get sucked into. She had been grasping at the edges of control, and if she let herself think about Jared and what he had done to their relationship, she wouldn't be able to hold on any longer.

She rubbed her hands up and down her arms. Her expensive Burberry coat was supposed to keep her warm, but her teeth were chattering. How much longer could she stay out here before she froze to death?

Cady wasn't sure she wanted to know the answer. Getting out and walking was out of the question. First of all, she had no idea where she was. Second, she wasn't certain she was still facing the direction she had been going. Third, she wasn't dressed to survive such harsh conditions.

The road had looked important. As if it were used often. Surely, that meant someone would drive by soon and find her. She realized that she didn't have her hazards on and quickly pressed the button. That should get someone's attention.

Another hour crawled by, and though she hated to admit it, there was no way she would make her flight back to Austin. She had already paid a fortune to get the last seat on the flight—all because she had been determined to be home for Christmas.

"Why? I would be alone at home or here in a hotel. What difference would it have made?" she asked, rolling her eyes.

But she knew the answer. Celebrating the holiday in the comfort of her home was better than in a hotel—no matter where that hotel was, or how many stars it carried.

The sun was sinking quickly into the horizon. A terror she had never known before crept over her. She knew very little about freezing to death, but she didn't think it would happen quickly or painlessly. How long would it take someone to find her? A day? A week? Why did it even matter? She hated when her thoughts took her down such depressing roads.

A knock on the passenger window startled her enough that she let out a scream and put a hand to her throat, her head snapping to the side. She found herself looking into the most beautiful gold eyes she'd ever seen.

"Ma'am? You okay?" he asked.

A surge of relief poured through her, wiping away her fear in an instant. Cady smiled, happy that someone had found her, even as a part of her brain warned her that this could be a serial killer. Too many episodes of *Criminal Minds* made her think that everyone was a serial killer. Then again, it had kept her safe.

"Yes!" she hollered through the window. "No. I mean, no, I'm not okay. Please help."

"My name is Zane. I've got a house nearby where I can take you to get warm and get some help with your car."

"That would be great."

He dropped his chin to his chest so that his cowboy hat hid his face. Then he looked back at her. "It might help if you open the door."

She hesitated to unlock it. On the one hand, if she did, she could get out of the weather and somewhere warm with the possibility of getting home. On the other, she could end up as another victim if this was a serial killer.

"Ma'am?"

Cady was cold. So cold, her brain wasn't working right. She had to get warm. She decided to chance it. She unlocked the door. The minute she pressed the button, he opened the door and squatted beside her.

"Are you hurt?"

My God, his voice was as smooth as velvet. A deep timbre that made something in her go absolutely still. As she stared into his gold eyes, she saw flecks of green and bronze, the iris ringed in what she could only describe as copper. It took her a moment to comprehend that he had asked her a question.

"Uh . . . No, no. I'm fine. Just cold."

"How long have you been out here?" he asked, a frown forming.

She shrugged. "Three hours."

His lips twisted as he got to his feet and took a few steps back to look at the front of the vehicle. "The car is buried too deep in the snow. It's going to take a tow truck to get it out, and that isn't happening today." His gaze swung back to her. "I can't leave you out here any longer. You need to get indoors quickly."

Cady had to admit, if she had to be rescued, having a man as handsome as this one do it wasn't so bad. She let her gaze move over his strong jaw and chin. He had his hat pulled low, but she saw pale brown strands of hair peeking out near his collar.

"I don't live far," he said.

She nodded. He'd said that before. Maybe she hadn't responded the first time. "Thank you. I would greatly appreciate your help."

He held out his gloved hand. Cady blinked at the unexpected gesture. If she were lucky, she might encounter a man who held a door open for her in Austin, but none had ever helped her out of a car. She slid her hand into his. His grip was firm but gentle as his fingers closed over hers.

The moment she got to her feet, he was there to make sure she was steady. Which was a good thing because her legs were wobbly, and her feet were blocks of ice. She felt better and better about this man with each passing moment.

Right up until he turned them, and she saw the horse.

Instinct made Cady jerk back. Her knees gave out, causing her to slip, and she began falling backward until he caught her, pulling her against him before pressing her between him and the car. Concern filled his gaze.

"Are you sure you aren't hurt?" he asked.

She swallowed nervously and glanced at the huge beast staring at her with large, black eyes. "I-I'm not hurt."

He followed her gaze to the horse before returning his attention to her. "Then what is it?"

"I'm terrified of that," she said, pointing to the animal.

"Well, then. We have a problem. That's my transportation."

"Can you go home and get a vehicle? You said you were nearby."

He blew out a breath. "There are two issues with that. The first is that getting here by truck would take me twice as long since I'd have to stick to the roads."

"Okay," she said with a shrug. "I can wait."

"That brings me to the second problem. That," he said and pointed over his shoulder.

Cady looked around him to see into the distance. "What am I looking at?"

"A blizzard that will reach you before I can get back."

She watched in shock as he walked to the horse and picked up the reins.

He then looked at her. "Are you coming? Or would you prefer to freeze?"

So much for thinking that she was being saved by something right out of a book. She bit the retort on her lips and leaned inside the car for her purse and keys. She shut the door and walked carefully around to the back of the vehicle, using it to make sure she didn't fall.

"What are you doing?" he asked.

She was glad that she had her back to him because she couldn't contain her eyeroll. "Getting my suitcase."

"I'm not carrying that."

Cady spun around to glare at him. "Well, I'm not leaving my things."

"You are if you're coming with me."

She was really beginning to dislike . . . Her eyes narrowed as it dawned on her that she didn't know his name. Oh, wait. He did tell her what it was, but she couldn't remember. Maybe now would be a good time for a proper introduction. "I'm Cady Adams."

"We need to get a move on."

She stood where she was, refusing to go anywhere until he told her his name.

Finally, he blew out a long breath. "It's nice to meet you, Cady. I'm Zane. Now, can we leave? We're barely going to make it to the house as it is."

Yes! That was his name. She breathed a sigh. Cady looked longingly at the trunk with her luggage before walking to Zane.

He put his boot in the stirrup and swung his leg over the horse to mount. Then he held out his hand.

"I'll walk," she said and lifted her chin to show that she meant business.

"Lady, you won't make it half a mile in those shoes in this weather. The horse isn't going to hurt you."

"You don't know that."

"I do, actually. I raised him from a colt."

Cady eyed the animal. She was shaking just thinking about being near him. The last time she had been this close to a horse was when . . . She couldn't even think about that, it was so debilitating.

"Cady."

She looked up into Zane's eyes. His voice was warm, seductive even.

"I can get you somewhere safe and warm, but that means getting on Brego."

Cady couldn't help but smile when she heard the name. "Brego, as in Aragorn from *Lord of the Rings'* Brego?"

"That's right," he replied, his lips softening.

"The extended movies?"

He sighed. "The books."

Cady looped her purse handle over her shoulder and took a deep breath. She couldn't feel her toes. Her nose was numb, and her fingers were beginning to hurt. Remaining out in these conditions was no longer an option.

The last thing she wanted to do was climb atop her greatest fear, but it seemed that Fate was giving her no alternative.

"You can do it," Zane encouraged.

She faced irate boardrooms and furious judges without hesitation. She had always gone after what she wanted. *Driven*, people called her. She just liked to think of herself as someone who didn't give up on the things she wanted. And right now, she desperately wanted to get warm.

Cady's hand shook as she lifted it to Zane, who gripped it firmly.

"Good girl. Now, put your foot in the stirrup," he directed.

Now that he had a hold of her, she knew he wouldn't let go. Cady saw that his foot was out of the stirrup. She had to move closer to the horse to lift her leg high enough to get her foot into the loop. The instant she did, Zane pulled her up and turned her so that she sat across his lap.

She gasped to find herself within the confines of his arms. Very strong, very able arms. She glanced at him, but he didn't spare her a look as he clicked to the horse, and they set out. When Brego began walking, she tightened her arms on her purse that she had situated in her lap and tried not to think about being so high off the ground.

"Easy. She's adjusting."

Cady shot Zane a glare when she realized that he was soothing the horse and not her.

Chapter 2

City people. Zane couldn't stand them.

They came to Wyoming in droves, and it infuriated him. Companies were buying up huge swaths of land, cutting trees and putting up electrical grids and water plants. If anyone balked, these new players would say they were getting most of their electricity from wind turbines. Turbines that were eyesores in the once-stunning wilderness.

The woman was no different. Zane flattened his lips as he thought about Cady. Who came out to Wyoming in a pair of heels and dress pants? Her coat was laughable. She had no gloves, scarf, or anything to cover her head. It was like she was asking to die of hypothermia.

Zane knew the moment he saw the vehicle's flashers that he would find trouble. He just hadn't expected a petite blonde with blue eyes that reminded him of the summer sky. Though, he had to admit there had been real terror in her gaze when she saw Brego. He knew some people were afraid of horses, but he'd never encountered anyone until today.

He had pushed her hard to get on Brego. Probably too hard, if he were honest. But he didn't want to get caught in the storm. Had she not taken his hand, Zane had been prepared to haul her up regardless. She had been out in the weather too long already. If the storm caught them, he wasn't sure if she would make it or not, especially not wearing the right clothing.

The look she had given him when he calmed Brego made him want to smile. He'd had to bite his tongue to hold it in. She had spunk. He'd give her that.

Her breathing was ragged, her chest rising and falling rapidly as she gripped her purse as if her life depended on it. Zane glanced at her face, but she had it turned away from him.

"You're going off the road," she said in a tight voice.

"It's the quickest way to my place."

Her breath billowed past her lips in short bursts. "Th-the horse could step in a hole or off a mountain."

Zane didn't bother to mention that they were *on* a mountain, and there were no cliffs nearby. "Brego knows the way. So do I. We travel this often. Cady, you need to even your breathing. You're going to hyperventilate."

"I haven't . . . done that . . . since fourth grade."

He put a finger on her chin and turned her head to him. He hated that he enjoyed gazing into her eyes so much. They were such a unique blue. Not bright, not dark, but a fathomless color somewhere in between that sucked him in with one look.

"The cold is getting to you."

She closed her eyes. "I'm tired."

Zane pulled her tighter against him so she could share his body heat. "Try to stay awake."

"I just wanted to go home," she murmured. "It's Christmas. Home to an empty house. Bastard."

He frowned, unsure if she was calling him a bastard or if it was her confusion since her words were beginning to slur.

He needed to keep her awake. The best way to do that was to keep her talking. "Where is home?"

"Austin."

He should've known. Now that she said it, he recognized the Texas drawl. "What are you doing in Wyoming?"

"Business." She snorted, though she kept her eyes closed. "Another bastard. Always making me take jobs he doesn't want. N-not anymore. I'm going to quit."

Zane smiled despite himself. "You might feel differently once you get warm."

She shook her head, then leaned it against him. "You're warm."

"Cady," he said, gently shaking her when she grew quiet. "Talk to me. What do you do for a living?"

"I'm a bloodsucking lawyer." She issued a soft bark of laughter at that, then sighed. "That's what everyone says behind my back."

Zane wasn't sure what to make of this woman. She could irritate him and then make him smile the next second. "I'm sure not everyone calls you that."

"Everyone who isn't a lawyer."

He glanced at the sky. "I'm afraid you won't get home for Christmas. The storm is supposed to be a big one."

She shrugged. "Don't want to be in the house by myself anyway. Bastard."

That was the second time she had said that after talking about home. "Who's the bastard?" It was none of his business, but damn if Zane's curiosity wasn't piqued.

"Jared," she answered without hesitation. "Cheating bastard."

Ah. Now, he understood. "You're better off without him."

"I wasn't enough."

"With people like that, no one is ever enough. It has nothing to do with you."

She snorted. "Maybe."

"Without a doubt. There's no excuse for cheating. If you want to be with someone else, then end things with whoever you're with and move on."

She lifted her head and opened her eyes long enough to say, "I agree."

Zane didn't want to like Cady, but he found himself leaning in that direction. Or maybe he just felt sorry for her.

"He was never really good in bed anyway. At least, I don't have to deal with his clumsy attempt at foreplay anymore."

Zane wasn't sure whether to laugh or tell her that he was sorry she'd had to suffer through that. He debated how to respond for so long that he realized she hadn't spoken again. "Cady," he said, shaking her. "Cady, wake up."

"Why won't you let me sleep?" she asked grumpily.

"Because it isn't good. Wait until we get to my place. You can warm up and sleep for as long as you like."

She sniffed him. "You smell good. All . . . something. I can't think of the word."

This time he did chuckle. "I'm sure it's horse."

"No," she said after making a sound in the back of her throat.

"Why don't you like horses?"

"There was an *incident*."

She drew out the last word as if it were some kind of secret. Zane smiled despite trying not to. "And what was the incident?"

"Everything is so white."

"That's what happens when it snows."

"And cold," she continued as if he hadn't spoken. "How does anyone live in this climate?"

He guided Brego around a fallen tree. "I could ask the same of your Texas heat. Do you even get snow in Austin?"

"It's very rare."

"You've never had a white Christmas?"

"I've worn shorts at Christmas."

Zane chuckled as he shook his head. "I can't even imagine." Thankfully, the cabin came into view then. "We're here, Cady."

But she didn't respond. He tried to shake her awake again, but she wouldn't reply. The moment Brego reached the cabin, Zane gathered Cady in his arms and swung his leg over the horse's head, sliding to the ground. She didn't stir at the impact. Zane rushed up the two steps to the porch and opened the door.

He laid her on the sofa until he could get the fire going. Once it was roaring, he piled blankets and pillows on the floor before carrying her near the fire. He removed her boots and rubbed her icy feet with his hands. Then he covered her with blankets before going back out to see to Brego brushed down and put up in the stall with feed for the night.

Zane hurried back into the house and threw off the blankets to quickly and methodically remove everything but Cady's bra and panties. He then tore off his clothes and lay down beside her before covering them both. He turned her onto her side and curled around her to give her as much of his body heat as he could.

He barely got settled before he heard the wind begin to howl, signaling the beginning of the storm. Zane had spent the morning getting ready for the blizzard. All the horses were in the barn and fed. There was nothing for them to do other than wait out the storm.

His gaze lowered to the blond locks of the female pressed against him. Tightly. He tried not to think about the fact they were practically naked. He thought of anything and everything, so his thoughts dwell on the fact Cady's skin was the softest he'd ever felt.

But he failed miserably.

There was a woman in his arms. A beautiful, irritating woman. His cock stirred to life. Zane ground his teeth together and begged his body not to respond, but it was too late. Things got worse when she made a soft noise and wiggled her ass against him.

Zane fisted his hands. He would not touch her. It didn't matter that his body responded to her because he knew what kind of woman she was. He'd been down that road once and had the scars to prove it. Nothing in the universe could get him to walk that path again.

No matter what his brain told his body, his cock had other ideas. Then again, his rod had never bothered to listen before. Why would it start now? It had a mind of its own and had proven that time and time again.

Zane closed his eyes and listened to the fire and the building storm. Eventually, it lulled him. He'd been up in the wee hours of the morning, getting everything ready before visiting his neighbors, the McCrackens, to help. The older couple had been surrogate parents to him for years, and though they said they didn't need his help, he'd ignored them. They were in their early eighties, but neither wanted to sell the ranch. Unfortunately, none of their five kids wanted anything to do with it.

Once the McCrackens died, a big corporation would come in and snatch up the land for pennies on the dollar. Zane had seen it happen too many times. If things were different, he'd buy the place himself. But nothing had turned out like he had expected. He planned, and then life yanked the rug out from under him. So, he had stopped planning.

The next thing Zane knew, he woke. The cabin was dark, and the storm was in full swing. He extracted himself from Cady and rekindled the fire. He rubbed his hands together as a chill settled around him, then he crawled back under the covers with his unexpected roommate.

She hadn't moved since he'd curled around her. He saw her breathing, so he knew she was alive. He checked her hands and feet, thankful he didn't see any frostbite. She made a disgruntled noise and tugged at the covers. He grinned and resumed his position. Within moments, he was asleep again.

Zane only rested for short periods. He woke about every forty minutes to throw more wood on the fire. This last time, he yawned and checked his phone to see that it was nearly six in the morning. He tucked the covers around Cady to keep her warm before walking to the bathroom to dress.

When he came out, she had rolled to her other side. Her hair was mussed, and her mouth was open slightly. Zane heard the soft sound of a snore and grinned as he made coffee. A look outside told him that the storm wasn't nearly finished yet. That meant he got to spend the day in the cabin with a city girl.

He'd rather stand naked in the snow.

He eyed the black liquid steaming inside his cup and contemplated adding liquor. It was probably a good thing he didn't have any because he suspected the only way he would come out unscathed from all of this was if he were drunk.

Chapter 3

The dream was amazing. Cady never wanted it to end. She was the warmest she had ever been. Cozy, in fact.

She was drifting in that beautiful, calm spot between sleep and wakefulness. Cady couldn't remember the last time she had been in there, and she was loath to leave. Because in this tranquil place, she felt as if she were connected to the entire world. There was no stress, no bills to pay, no meeting she had to attend.

No project she was behind on because someone didn't do their job.

Cady quite liked the hard body pressed against her. And the strong arms. It was too bad that man was only in her dreams because she could find herself falling for a guy like that. Unfortunately, she was coming to accept that there wasn't a man out there for her. No matter what her sister always told her, she knew there wasn't someone out there for everyone.

Sadness threatened, but Cady refused to allow it. Not in this magical place. Not now. That emotion, along with a slew of others would cascade upon her the moment she opened her eyes. She wanted a few more seconds of the bliss while wondering if she could find this place more often—like every day. She might not feel so stabby around people if she could get this mellow. Then again, the problem was where she worked and who she worked with.

A sound pulled her closer to consciousness. Cady fought against it. She tried to cling to her dream man, but she realized that he was gone. Instead, her hands clutched blankets and not the hard sinew of before.

Then, just like that, her perfect place vanished as she came awake.

Cady found herself staring at the bottom part of a well-loved leather sofa. A fire crackled behind her, and she heard someone moving around not far from her. Confused and disoriented, she sat up. That's when her eyes landed on a tall man in a plaid button-down shirt and jeans with his back to her.

His light brown hair curled slightly at the ends from being a tad too long. His shoulders were broad, the kind that gave the impression that he could withstand a heavy load. Her gaze drifted to his trim hips encased in Wranglers.

She frowned. Wranglers? She didn't associate with anyone who wore those kinds of jeans. Usually, Wranglers were reserved for cowboys. The minute she thought the word, her eyes widened, and her mouth dropped open as she recalled being stranded in the snow and the cowboy who'd stopped to help.

Zane.

Cady found it difficult to breathe. She looked around frantically before a shiver took her. She glanced down at herself to see her black bra and matching panties. She grasped the blanket and wrenched it up to her chest as she tried to remember getting to . . . wherever it was he had brought her.

"Nothing happened," Zane's deep voice filled the space.

She swallowed, her head jerking to him. He hadn't turned around. Did he have eyes in the back of his head? Cady was about to ask how he knew what she was thinking when she met his gaze in the glass of the microwave.

Zane turned to face her. "I had to get you warm. I was worried about frostbite and hypothermia, and the qui—"

"The quickest way to warm someone is skin to skin," she said over him with a nod. "I know."

He looked at the mug in his hand. "Good."

Cady couldn't help but wonder if the dream man she had believed nothing more than her imagination had been, in fact, Zane. "Oh, please, no," she murmured.

"What's that?" Zane asked as he lifted his gaze to her.

She quickly shook her head and lay back to cover herself more fully since she was beginning to freeze. "Nothing."

"I've got plenty of food, so make yourself at home."

"I don't plan on being here any longer than it takes to get to my car and have it towed."

He released a long sigh filled with frustration. "If you listen closely, you'll hear the storm is still going strong. Even if it stopped now, it would be hours before anyone could get out in this. The blizzard was supposed to dump about sixteen inches."

She closed her eyes, trying not to let the situation get to her.

"Not to mention," he continued, "it's Christmas Eve. Unless it's an emergency, I don't think anyone is leaving their homes."

There was no way she was going to spend Christmas with a sullen, broody cowboy who couldn't stand the sight of her. It was just one more unfair thing to happen to her in a shit-tastic year that had gotten worse with each month.

Zane cleared his throat. "I'm sorry you're stuck out here."

He almost sounded sincere. Cady took a deep breath and released it. "I'm sorry you're stuck with me."

"The clothes you have aren't really suitable for this climate. I've got some you can borrow."

"Sweats?" she asked hopefully.

"Afraid not."

Cady rolled her eyes. What was it about Zane that irritated her so easily? It had to be his attitude. Though she was sure hers wasn't the best, either. She remained lying down because the minute she sat up, everything that wasn't covered became instantly cold.

She heard Zane rummaging nearby. She craned her head to see that his place was much smaller than she originally thought. His bed wasn't in another room. It was right there, along with the dresser. Cady took a closer look at everything and saw the log walls. She was in a cabin. A very small one that didn't afford them much privacy, let alone anywhere to go to get away other than the bathroom.

While Cady tried to think about how not to go absolutely stir-crazy with Zane in the cabin, he kept opening drawers and shifting through them. Her hope that this might have been the closest shelter when the storm hit was soon dashed as she came to understand that he was looking through his clothes.

"These might work," Zane said as he set something on the sofa near her.

She had been so deep in thought that she hadn't heard him shut the last drawer. Cady grabbed the clothes, thankful to have something warm to put on. She grabbed the item on top to find it was a faded, worn sweatshirt. She slipped it on, sighing at the warmth it offered. It was huge, but she didn't care. When she reached for the second item, she was surprised to find a pair of sweats after Zane had told her he didn't have any.

It wasn't until she pulled them on beneath the covers that

she realized they weren't nearly as big on her as the sweatshirt. Cady put on the socks and got to her feet. When she looked down, she saw that the pants were women's, while the shirt was definitely a man's. It never dawned on her that Zane might be involved. She hadn't seen anyone else in the cabin, but maybe they were out somewhere.

"Is your girlfriend or wife around so I can thank her for the pants?" Cady asked with a smile.

Zane had returned to the kitchen to lean against the counter. He didn't look up at her. "I don't have either a girlfriend or a wife."

"Oh. Sister, then?" she offered, hoping to make the awkward situation a little less so.

"No sister."

Cady turned her back to Zane and began folding the blankets and setting them on the sofa. She was starving, but first, she really needed the bathroom. Since she saw only one door slightly ajar, she assumed that was it.

Zane didn't look her way as she walked to the restroom and relieved her bladder. She gasped at the sight of her hair sticking up everywhere. Cady raked her fingers through the shoulder-length tangles. She managed to get most of them out and tame all the strands sticking up at odd angles.

When she walked out, she nervously looked around. "Can you show me where the mugs are?"

Zane pointed to a cabinet to his left.

So much for trying to start a conversation. Cady walked to the cabinet and took out a mug. She didn't particularly care for coffee, but she needed caffeine. It should be fine after she doctored it a bit with a lot of milk and sugar. Her mother used to call it coffee milk, but no matter how many times—with all different flavors—Cady couldn't get used to straight coffee. Or coffee in general.

After only pouring half a mug, she returned the pot to its home and went to the fridge. There, she found some milk that she smelled first to make sure it was good. She added that to the mug and began searching for the sugar. It took going through several cabinets before she finally found it. Then she had to search for the spoons to put the sugar in and stir. After all of that, she could barely get the liquid down her throat.

Cady put in more sugar, which helped. Some. And the hot liquid assisted in warming her, as well. She pulled out one of the four kitchen chairs and sat at the table.

"I hope you don't have any dietary restrictions, and I really hope you aren't a vegan."

His condescending tone instantly irritated her. She looked at him and sweetly said, "I don't, and I'm not."

He set down his coffee and licked his lips. "I'm sorry for that. There's no excuse for my sarcasm."

"I think there's a story there."

His lips twisted ruefully. "Yes, there is. Same as your story about being terrified of horses."

She gawked at him, then closed her eyes in embarrassment. "What did I do?"

"Nothing," he said with a small laugh.

She cracked open one eye. "No. I absolutely did or said something."

He shrugged and sat across from her. "You got on Brego."

"I remember you telling me his name." She flattened her lips while trying not to recall that she had not only gotten close to the horse but had also sat on top of Zane. "You read the books. Did you not watch the movies?"

"I haven't, no."

"You're missing out."

His gold eyes watched her. "I saw how terrified you were of my horse, and you overcame that."

"I wouldn't call what I did overcoming it. It was a life-or-death situation. I chose life. Unfortunately, that meant I had to get close to the beast."

Zane laughed at her comment. "However you see it, you survived."

"I don't remember much after you pulled me up on Brego." And onto Zane's lap with very strong, capable arms wrapped around her, but Cady wasn't going to mention that part.

"You were pretty out of it. The cold was getting to you quickly. I tried to keep you talking so you wouldn't sleep."

She winced. "If I said anything disparaging, I apologize. Profusely."

"You kept calling someone a bastard. I thought it was me, but I'm not sure because you also called Jared a bastard."

Cady put her head in her hands for a moment. Then she looked up at Zane. "I must have been talking about David. He's my boss."

"The one who sent you out here?"

"I told you that, too?" she asked with wide eyes.

Zane wrinkled his nose and nodded. "I did get a few things out of you."

She turned her mug around on the table as she looked at it. "And I mentioned Jared?"

"Yeah. The one who cheated on you."

Cady looked into Zane's beautiful eyes. "Damn. I told you that, too. He worked in my field, though at a different firm. We had lived together for three years when I surprised him at work and found him fucking one of his colleagues. That was right before Thanksgiving."

"Ouch," Zane said in a soft voice.

She shrugged and sat back in the chair while wrapping her cold hands around the mug to warm them. "I took the rest of the day off. I paid extra to have movers come that day and pack his stuff. Everything was at the curb by the time he decided to come home at six. He didn't say anything to me, didn't attempt to call after I found him or after I threw him out. I've not seen or talked to him since."

"That's probably for the best."

"I would agree."

Zane caught her gaze. "I'm sorry you had to go through that."

"I survived," she said with a smile. "Or I *am* surviving it."

"You'll get through it and come out stronger on the other end."

Chapter 4

He knew all about being deceived. Zane wished he didn't, but there was no denying it.

"You're nothing like I expected," he told Cady.

She smiled as she lowered the mug to the table. "Hmm. I'm afraid to ask who you thought I'd be. I'm guessing it has to do with the *city people* remark."

"Yeah, I deserve that," he said with a grin.

Cady tugged the arms of his sweatshirt down to cover everything but the tips of her fingers. Then she lifted the mug to her lips again. "You certainly do."

Zane liked that she didn't hesitate to say what was on her mind. Was it because of her profession, or was that a personal trait? Oddly, he wanted to find out.

"What?" she asked with a frown.

He blinked. "What?"

"You're staring. Is my hair sticking up again?"

"Your hair is fine."

She reached up and smoothed her shoulder-length blond locks down anyway. "Then why are you staring?"

"I'm trying to figure you out."

"Oh. Well, I can help you out there. I'm simple."

"There isn't a woman in the history of the world—past, present, or future—who is simple."

She gave him a flat look. "That isn't true. And I am simple."

"Tell me how you think you're simple," he urged as he sat back and crossed his arms over his chest.

"All right. If you insist." Cady took another drink of the coffee and set a socked foot on the chair, her knee near her chin. "I treat people the way I want to be treated. I also love the way I want to be loved. It's a Capricorn trait."

Zane didn't know what he expected to hear, but it wasn't that. "You're going off a zodiac?"

She rolled her eyes. "No. But it is a trait, and I am a Capricorn. Other traits of my particular zodiac that fit me to a *T* are hardworking, ambitious, responsible, stubborn, sensitive, and practical."

"That doesn't sound simple in the least."

She grinned, shrugging. "I suppose you'll tell me you're simple."

"Without a doubt."

"Simpleminded?" she asked with an innocent look, then ruined it by smiling.

Zane laughed. "Good one."

"Tell me how you're simple."

He thought about that before he said, "I'm honest, and expect honesty in kind. I don't keep secrets, I'm not unfaithful, and if I have a problem, I talk about it instead of letting it fester until it rots me from the inside."

"So, you treat people the way you want to be treated. And you love the way you want to be loved."

He'd never thought about it that way, but she was right. "I suppose I do."

Cady's lips curved into a smile. "I would call that simple. Wouldn't you?"

"Indeed, I would."

At that moment, her stomach let out a loud growl. They both erupted into laughter.

"Well, that was embarrassing," she said.

Zane was still chuckling when he rose to his feet. "I've got plenty. Tell me what you're hungry for."

"Peanut butter."

He jerked his head to her, surprised by her comment. He had expected something elaborate.

"I told you I was a simple girl," she said.

He jerked his chin to her luxury boots, purse, and clothes. "Not based on what you have."

"Those are just things."

"From my experience, those *things* can drive a wedge between people."

She cocked her head at him. "Are you implying that because I can afford nice things that I shouldn't buy them?"

"I didn't say that." He wished he'd never said anything, but since he'd found the sweatpants, memories of the past had flooded him.

"There's a story there."

He got out the peanut butter and set it on the table along with a knife. "Would you like bread? Crackers?"

"Toast, if it's possible. And one of the bananas, please."

He got out the toaster and put the bread in before bringing her a plate and the banana. "What couldn't wait until after the holidays for your boss to send you here?"

She quirked a brow at him, letting him know that she was aware he hadn't replied to her comment about the story. Cady lowered her foot to the floor and peeled the banana before using the knife to cut the fruit into thin slices.

"I work in business law. I had to finalize negotiations with a company for another corporation who's buying them out."

The toast popped up. Zane grabbed it and brought it to the plate. "A lot of roads are closed during the winter."

"I found that out," she said with a twist of her lips as she spread the peanut butter on the toast before placing the banana slices on top.

"Will you get credit for the work?"

It was only after she had taken a bite, chewed, and swallowed that she answered. "Not likely. Even though there were complications I managed to get resolved. It's what put me a day late getting on the road."

"The fact that you got it done before Christmas is impressive."

Her blue eyes met his. "Yes, it is. I had an epiphany while here. I've worked my ass off under David for the last few years and received no recognition for my contributions that have advanced the firm. I've gotten one promotion. Other firms have shown interest, but I believed I was with the best in Austin. I've come to realize that it's time I find somewhere else to work."

"Good for you. You have to know your worth in life."

"That's so true. I can't believe it's taken me this long to come to that conclusion."

He finished the last of his coffee. "I take it your plane was headed out of Cheyenne?"

She nodded as she took another bite.

"How in the world did you end up here?"

"Spotty GPS. I turned in the wrong direction."

"Hmm. Fate had you go the opposite way you needed to. Maybe it was time you overcame your fear of horses."

Her mouth was full of peanut butter and banana, but she shook her head emphatically.

Zane laughed as he rose to get more coffee. He looked out the windows to see how high the snow had piled and how thickly it was still coming down.

"Maybe I was sent here to show you that not all city people are the same," she said.

He doubted that, but he kept that comment to himself as he poured fresh coffee and returned to the table. "Maybe so."

"We've talked about me plenty. Time for you to open up," she said and began fixing another slice of bread, peanut butter, and banana.

He twisted his lips. "Not much to tell, really. I've spent my life right here in Wyoming."

"You never left? Never visited other places?"

"I have. My parents were adamant that we know more of the world than our little piece."

Her brows raised. "We?"

"My parents tried for years to have children. Nothing ever worked. After twelve years of marriage, they decided to adopt. The week they were to finalize, my mother found out she was pregnant."

"I take it the adoption went through?"

He nodded as he glanced at the table. "Charlie and I are eleven months apart in age. My parents had their hands full, but they couldn't have been happier."

"And your brother now?"

"He's in politics, actually."

Shock filled her face. "That's not something you hear every day. Does he aspire to become president?"

"He has his sights set on governor."

"Do you support him?"

Zane nodded. "Of course."

"Does he hold office now?"

"He holds one of the representative seats."

"What's his last name?"

Zane hesitated. He didn't want to say it because then everything would start the way it always did. It was why he was out in the cabin so far from others. He was tired of it all.

"Zane?" Cady urged. "You don't want to tell me your brother's name? Your name?"

He drew in a deep breath and slowly released it, preparing himself. "It's Taylor."

"Charlie Taylor," she said, thinking. "I don't think I've heard of him. Then again, I'm not from here. Though, I'm not up to date on who holds office in my own state."

He couldn't believe it. Could she really not know the Taylor name? Or was she playing him? Had the car in the snow all been a ploy? No, he didn't think that. Maybe in any other season, but not winter when it was so cold. Cady had been in real danger. She'd had no idea that he or anyone else would come upon her. Had he not, she likely wouldn't be alive now.

So, if that hadn't been a setup, then she might really not know who he was.

"I'm Cady Adams, in case you didn't remember," she said with a smile and stuck out her hand.

It took him a second to realize what she had done and shook her hand. "Nice to meet you, Cady Adams."

"So, Zane Taylor, I take it you're a real cowboy."

He nearly spit out his coffee, he was so startled by her comment. He wiped the dribble from the corner of his mouth. "As a matter of fact, I am."

"Do you enjoy it?"

"Unequivocally."

"Even in weather like this?"

He glanced out one of the windows. "There isn't a season in Wyoming I don't love. In spring, you have everything blooming and breaking free of winter. Summer, everything is alive, and you can enjoy the warm temperatures. With fall, you have the leaves changing and crisp morning air. Then there's winter and the wonderland of white that blankets everything."

Zane swung his gaze back to Cady to find her staring at

him with an odd expression. He'd never said anything like that to anyone before.

"You make me wish I could see every season," she said in a soft voice.

His gaze lowered to her lips, and he recalled how she had fit against him so perfectly. How smooth her skin had been. How she had smelled of lavender. He hadn't allowed himself to look at her breasts when he'd disrobed her, but he had glimpsed the black satin and lace of her bra.

And damn if his balls didn't tighten at the thought.

Chapter 5

With one look, the atmosphere in the cabin shifted. The air was rife with tension—the sexual kind. Cady licked her lips to get the last of the peanut butter from them and saw Zane visibly swallow, his gaze locked on her mouth.

She had never felt such a rush of . . . hunger before. It took her by such surprise that she didn't know what to do. She ended up on her feet, putting everything away from her snack. She felt his eyes on her the entire time. How she wished she knew what to say in a situation like this. She knew what she wanted—Zane.

Cady wasn't sure when she had comprehended that fact, only that the truth was there. And she accepted it. Maybe it was because she knew she'd never see him again. She'd never had a one-night stand before. That could be the appeal.

Or perhaps it was because of the situation that'd put them both into forced confinement when they would have otherwise never stayed in the same room together.

The whys didn't matter. So many times, she had done what others wanted or would approve of. That hadn't gotten her very far. It was time to do what she wanted, to follow her heart. And right now, everything screamed at her to take Zane. To let him know that she wanted him. Wanted whatever it was between them. It would be her Christmas present to herself. A way to close out one year and start the new one fresh, with a different outlook on everything.

Cady turned around to find that Zane was on his feet. She hadn't heard him rise. She rested her hands on the counter on either side of her. Even with the heat of the fire warming the place, the cold seeped through the floor into the thick socks on her feet, causing her to shiver. Or maybe that was because of the way Zane stared at her.

"I-I don't have a right to ask this," she said.

"Ask it," he said before she finished.

Cady licked her lips again, unsure of how to put it into words.

Zane's hands clenched at his sides. "Ask it," he urged again.

If you're going to do it, then do *it. Stop being a ninny!*

Cady lifted her chin. Action was better than words. She pushed away from the counter and started toward him. She didn't stop until she reached him. Then she rose on her tiptoes, put her hands on either side of his face, and brought his head down to her lips.

The moment their mouths touched, he let out a groan and wound his arms around her. Cady was unprepared for the onslaught of passion. He teased her lips, lightly pressing small kisses over and over, lingering longer and longer as his hands ran over her back. Then his tongue slipped between her lips to tangle with hers. He let out another low moan and grabbed her butt with both his hands, pulling her tight against him so she felt the length of his arousal.

Cady melted against him, her body throbbing with desire so intense, she wasn't sure she could stand on her own. Going for what she wanted had flipped some switch. Need and hunger for Zane unlike she had ever experienced before overwhelmed her, drove her.

Consumed her.

Her fingers slipped into the cool locks of his light brown hair. His breathing matched her ragged breaths as they clung to each other. He deepened the kiss, igniting flames of desire that threatened to scorch her. She eagerly reached for them, sought them.

He spun her, pressing her back against the fridge. She couldn't stop touching him. Even through his shirt, she felt the hard muscle beneath. And she couldn't wait to see it.

She ended the kiss, pushing him back just enough that he opened his eyes. Confusion filled the golden depths. She smiled and winked at him as she started to the bed. Cady removed her shirt and glanced over her shoulder to find him watching her, his eyes dark with desire. The socks and pants went next. When she reached the bed, she turned and crooked a finger at him.

His strides were long and powerful, eating up the short distance between them. He yanked her against him, kissing her as if his very life depended on it. She started to unbutton his shirt when he broke the kiss and shoved her hands away. Then he quite literally tore the shirt off.

Buttons went everywhere, but neither noticed. The thermal ripped when Zane tugged it off. When Cady saw his rock-hard chest and washboard abs, her mouth slackened. She was taking all of that in when he yanked open his jeans and pushed them, as well as his boxer briefs, down his legs before stepping out of them.

All the breath left her when she saw his cock. It was long, thick, and hard. She had felt it against her stomach earlier, and she couldn't wait to feel it inside her. She roamed her gaze up and down his body, slowly taking in every defined inch of him. He was the most gorgeous specimen she had ever laid eyes on.

"Oh, yes," she murmured and reached for him.

They came together in a heated kiss as they fell sideways onto the bed. With just a flick of his fingers, he managed to unhook her bra. It sagged between them. She rolled him onto his back to straddle him as she sat up and tossed it aside.

Only in his wildest dreams did he think he would get to know Cady's taste. He'd never seen a woman look so enticing or beautiful as when she walked to him and kissed him that first time. But it was when she walked to the bed while taking off her clothes that he knew he was in big trouble.

He didn't just want her. He yearned for her.

Craved her.

With each kiss, every touch, his desire grew, stamping out all thought, all reason. Until there was nothing but the two of them and the passion that wouldn't be denied.

He gazed up at the stunning woman above him. Her blue eyes were bright with need, her skin flushed with desire. He moved his hands from her hips up to her bare breasts. Her pink nipples were taut, waiting for his mouth. But first, he wanted to know the feel of her breasts.

He cupped them in his hands, gently massaging them. She sighed, her eyes closing as her head dropped back. He didn't know what he'd done to deserve such a gift this Christmas, but he would make sure Cady was well pleasured.

Zane sat up and wrapped his mouth around one turgid nipple before gently suckling. Cady's breath hitched as her hands grabbed his shoulders. He wrapped one arm around her to hold her against him. When that wasn't enough, he flipped her onto her back and settled between her legs so he could move from one breast to the other at his leisure.

When she ground her hips against him, he knew it was

time. He kissed down her stomach until he reached the edge of her panties. Only then did he lift his head to glance at Cady. Her blond hair fanned around her. Her nipples glistened from his kisses. He hooked his fingers into the waistband of her underwear and gently slid them over the gentle flare of her hips and then down her legs.

He ran his hands up her legs from her ankles, taking in the beautiful sight of the woman laid bare before him. Her breasts filled his palms perfectly, the orbs falling softly to the sides with their weight. Her pale skin was silky smooth, begging for his touch. But he was dying to learn another part of her.

Zane pushed her legs wider. Her eyes fluttered open to watch him as he settled between her thighs once more. Then he tenderly ran his tongue across her sex.

It was too much.

It wasn't enough.

Cady was locked between the two, unable to do anything but *feel* everything. Zane teased her clit with his tongue, doing things she had never known were possible. Just when she thought it couldn't get any better, he pushed a digit inside her.

She dug her fingers in the comforter. With one movement, he had flung her to the edge of climax. She sat, waiting, silently begging him to send her over the edge. As if he knew his power, he pulled back just enough to keep her from reaching the final pinnacle but still on the brink.

"Please," she begged.

Instead of answering, he began moving his finger, his tongue swirling around her swollen clit in the same tempo. She cried out as he once more slowed. The orgasm was so close. She just needed a little push.

Again and again, he brought her to the threshold, only

to pull back at the last minute. Cady's entire body shook with her need for release. She flung her head from side to side, words no longer possible. He owned her body, and she wouldn't have it any other way.

Once more, his mouth was on her sex, licking and laving. His finger moved inside of her, stroking her steadily. The familiar feel of desire tightened in her belly. Her body stiffened in response, and she waited for him to pull back again. But this time, his tongue kept flicking over her clit, and his finger kept moving within her.

When the climax hit, she screamed her release as it enveloped her. Waves upon waves of pleasure flowed through her, each one more intense than the one before. She had no idea how long the orgasm lasted. Seconds or centuries. It could've been either. As she floated back into herself, she felt . . . utterly content.

And wildly uninhibited.

She opened her eyes and found Zane rising to look at her. She caught sight of his cock, and her stomach fluttered in excitement at having him inside her. He moved over her, the smooth head of him brushing against her flesh.

Cady bit her lip in pleasure when he guided himself into her.

She was hot and wet. Zane had nearly spilled his seed when he finally allowed her to climax. The sound of her, the *sight* of her had been spectacular. He had pushed her to the very limit, and she had let him.

But in the process, he had pushed himself too far. He wanted her too desperately, but there was no turning back now. He had to be inside her. He had to feel her clutching his rod as she had his finger. He would accept nothing less.

The sight of her biting her lip made him moan. The woman used seduction as easily as breathing, and it set him aflame.

He gradually pushed inside her, letting her body stretch

to accommodate him. She sighed, her eyes rolling back in her head. Then he began slowly moving his hips. It wasn't long before he was thrusting in and out of her faster and faster, deeper and deeper. She opened her eyes to look up at him. He became lost in the sea of blue, in the desire and seduction he found there.

A storm raged outside, but inside the cabin another kind of storm raged, one that Zane never wanted to end.

He pumped his hips faster when he felt his orgasm approaching. The feel of Cady's tongue on his nipple caused him to let out a shout as he climaxed.

Chapter 6

Was this state of total bliss and utter contentment what it was supposed to feel like after sex? A smile pulled at Cady's lips as she stared at the ceiling above her. Zane had moved off her to lay next to her. Her entire body hummed as if every neuron had been given a large dose of happiness.

She heard Zane turn his head to her. Cady slowly turned hers to him and met his gold gaze. They shared a smile.

"Damn, woman," he murmured.

A small laugh escaped her. "I could say the same. I've never felt anything like that."

"Me, either."

"You don't have to lie."

He rolled onto his side, propping his head up with his hand. "I'm not. I don't say things I don't mean. And I'm telling you right now, that was . . ." He paused as if searching for a word.

"Epic?" she offered.

His lips curved into a sexy smile. "Epic."

She sighed serenely. "It certainly was. We can do that again, right?"

"I was hoping you'd say that."

Cady lifted her hand and smoothed a lock of his wavy hair out of his face. "I've never done anything like this before."

"Why now?"

"I have no idea." She dropped her hand and rolled onto her side to face him. "Maybe it's this place. It could be because it's Christmas. I don't know. And, honestly, I don't care."

"Just as long as you don't regret anything."

She gave him a flat look. "With as great as I feel, there is no way I could have any regrets or anything close to it."

"That's good. Come here. I can see chills rising on your skin."

Cady eagerly scooted next to Zane as he lay on his back and moved the covers so they could put their legs beneath it. His body heat warmed her instantly. But what she really enjoyed was lying on his chest. She had always loved cuddling, but none of her boyfriends had liked it. So, not only did she have mind-blowing sex, but she was also cuddling.

"I've never had such a great Christmas Eve before," she said as she stared at the fire.

"I concur."

"You are rather comfortable."

His arm tightened around her. "And you fit quite nicely."

"Not bad for two strangers forced together."

His chest rumbled with laughter. "Not bad at all."

"One thing can spoil all of this."

"What's that?"

"I didn't get a chance to call my family. They have no idea I didn't get on the plane. They'll be worried sick."

Zane's fingers caressed up and down her back. "Were you spending Christmas with them?"

"I made up an excuse about work. I didn't want everything to be about me and the breakup."

"Spending the holiday alone sounded better?"

She snorted. "You'd understand if you knew my family. They're great, but they're very up in my business. Every ten seconds, one of them would ask how I was doing. If I needed a cry or some such thing."

"They care about you."

"I know. I just . . ."

"Needed time," he offered.

She nodded slowly, her eyes closing as his fingers moved into her hair. She absolutely adored when someone played with her hair.

"How big is your family?" he asked.

"My parents, of course. They got divorced when I was ten. It was amicable if you can believe it. So much so, we still have holidays together. My dad eventually remarried, and my mom has been with the same man for fifteen years but refuses to get married again. All four of them get along great."

There was shock in Zane's voice as he asked, "You're kidding."

"I'm not. It's a little weird when I tell people, but being around it for most of my life, it's just normal. I adore my stepmom and stepdad. They're amazing people. I feel like we got lucky and have two amazing sets of parents. Though it isn't the norm, by any means."

"It sounds lovely."

She smiled, thinking of her parents. "Mom and Dad love each other very much, but they realized they were better as friends than spouses. As they told us when it first happened, their paths diverged some, but they would always be together for us. And they have been."

"And your siblings?"

"There are three of us. I have an older sister and a younger brother. We're all two years apart, so we were pretty tight growing up. Though the arguments were fierce."

Zane laughed at that. "I know about that. Charlie and I were best friends, but we could be at each other's throats, as well. Usually, you hear of divorces that are contentious and difficult for the kids. I admire your parents for going another route."

"Neither cheated or anything like that, which is why some divorces happen. They just wanted different things. I've had so many people ask me how they could divorce if they still loved each other. I tried to explain that you can love someone deeply but not be *in love* with them. My parents vowed to each other that they would do whatever was necessary to keep our family together, even if they weren't. It hasn't always been easy, but they managed. It took a lot of work on their parts—and ours, to some extent."

"They sound like remarkable people."

"I think you'd like them. Even though they're from the city," she teased.

He tickled her, which made her jerk away and roll onto her back. He followed, their laughter filling the cabin. Their eyes locked, and the smiles died as desire took hold once more.

They reached for each other at the same time, their lips crashing together as they shoved away the covers, and he buried himself inside her with one thrust. Their bodies rocked against each other as their tongues dueled.

To Cady's shock, it wasn't long before the tightening in her belly that was fast becoming familiar started again. Suddenly, he pulled out of her and flipped her onto her stomach, raising her hips. Then he was inside her once more. She closed her eyes in ecstasy as his movements became rhythmic.

A gasp tore from her when he reached around and found her clit, slowly stroking it. She was powerless against the orgasm that descended upon her. As she let out a cry of pleasure, she heard Zane reach his climax.

They fell forward together and lay like that for several minutes until their breathing evened. Cady turned to Zane when he pulled out of her, and they resumed their previous position. Her eyes started to drift close. Her body was sated, her mind quiet. It would be so easy to sleep, but she didn't want to. Whatever was happening, whatever this . . . rift in time . . . was, she wanted to take full advantage of it. Because once the storm ended and she returned to her world, she would likely never see Zane again.

"Do you like your life?" she asked.

He was quiet for a few moments before saying, "I do. It's grueling and chaotic, but at the same time, therapeutic and steadying."

"What is it that you do?"

"I ranch."

She thought about that for a moment. "What exactly does that entail?"

"A little of everything," he said with a smile in his voice. "There's the cattle. Selling and buying, the feeding and worming that goes along with it. We're strictly grass-fed, which means we don't supplement with grain or anything else during the winter months. We have to tag and brand the cattle, ensure that they're pregnant, and then there's calving season. Don't even get me started on the vet bills if any of the cattle get sick."

"Wow," she said.

"There's the horses, which require a lot more time and money. The fences and gates that have to be mended, and the regular day-to-day management and administration that any business has to do."

She glanced up at him. "And I thought my job was hectic."

"You have to deal with people. I'd rather have the animals."

Cady laughed at that. "I don't blame you there. People can be assholes."

"What about you? Are you happy with your life?"

"I'm not sure. I love my house, or I used to. I worked so hard to save up to buy it. It doesn't give me the same satisfaction anymore. And my job, well, you know my thoughts on that."

"Is it your job or who you work for?"

Cady drew in a deep breath. "It's who I work for. I like what I do. I'm good at it, too."

"I bet you are," he said and squeezed her.

Something about talking like this with someone after such amazing sex was soothing. "My world got rocked last month, and while it sucks how it occurred, I think it needed to happen. I didn't realize until he was gone how unhappy I'd been. He wanted me to change everything about who I was."

"If you're with someone, you take them for who they are. Not try to change them."

"I agree. Though I've never understood why some women always want to change men."

He chuckled. "You got me there. I mean, I'm perfect just the way I am."

Cady tried to hold in her laugh, but she couldn't.

"What?" he asked with a smile in his voice. "You don't even know me, and you think something needs to change? Let me guess, the cabin? You think I should be in something nicer."

There was an edge to his voice that she couldn't ignore. She had inadvertently hit a nerve. Cady pushed up onto her elbow and met his gaze. Zane still wore a smile, but it wasn't as easy as before. "This cabin suits you perfectly. Any woman who is with you must understand that. If she doesn't, then she isn't for you."

"Not everyone thinks like you," he said and tucked a strand of hair behind her ear.

"That's because I'm awesome."

His eyes crinkled at the corners as he grinned. "That you are. But you would change something."

"I might take you shopping after having a look in your closet, if for nothing else than to update some shirts."

"Work shirts don't need to be new. Trust me, I can dress with the best of them."

"Now that, cowboy, I'd like to see."

He winked at her. "Maybe you will."

Chapter 7

They talked all day and into the night. Zane had never had that kind of connection with anyone before. They spoke of their families, friends, stories from their childhoods, dreams of the future, and everything in between.

And only stopped long enough for food and more sex.

He couldn't get enough of Cady. She was in turns fierce and tender, passionate and relaxed. She never held back. She laughed with such joy and openness that it took Zane aback. The fact that she had suffered greatly so recently wasn't apparent. If she hadn't told him the story, he never would've known that someone had broken her heart.

It made him wonder why, after so many years, he held onto his anger that had turned to bitterness.

"Why the frown?" Cady asked.

He gazed at her reclining at the foot of the bed with pillows behind her. Zane was propped against the headboard. They were nude, their legs intertwined. He put a hand on her feet and felt the coolness of her skin. "Just thinking."

"Thinking that caused a frown," she said with raised brows

as she gathered a handful of popcorn from the bowl between them and put a kernel into her mouth.

"I'm not the person I used to be."

She shrugged. "No one ever is. We all change, every day. Sometimes, it's incremental, and we don't notice until much later. Other times, it's a great big leap that alters our lives in an instant."

"How did you get so wise?"

She grinned devilishly. "I'm just that good." She swallowed her bite and said, "My dad is a big proponent of meditation and awakening the mind. When I was growing up, he listened to a lot of audiobooks on those subjects. He never forced us to listen, but some things just stuck."

"And now?" Zane asked.

"I meditate. It used to be every day. The more hectic my life got, the less I did it, which is the exact opposite of what I should've done. I miss it." She narrowed her gaze on him. "Don't start calling me a hippie, though."

He was taking a drink of beer when she said that and nearly spit it out. "I would never. Charlie meditates, and he's always told me to give it a try."

"You should. We've gotten off topic. You were talking about how you aren't the person you used to be. I take it you don't like who you are."

Zane wasn't ready to go down that particular road with her. At least, not all of it. "I don't like some of the things that have changed."

"Change them back," she said with a shrug.

"You make it sound simple."

She gave him a hard look. "Because it is. I've come to realize that I don't like my current employer. I'm going to change that. I don't like that I've stopped meditating. I'm going to change that."

"I'm not talking about things like that."

"It's still simple. If there's a certain attitude or thought process you don't like, then figure out why you're doing it. Once you do that, then you can trace it back to what changed. That's when you can set about reversing whatever it is. I'm not saying it'll be easy, but the brain is a powerful organ. It can do astonishing things once you decide on it."

Zane set aside his beer. "Is that how you go through life so carefree?"

"Carefree?" she repeated and then snorted. "I overthink everything."

"I've never met anyone like you." He was shocked at himself for saying something like that to her when he had only just admitted it himself.

A slow smile pulled at Cady's lips. "I'm not so bad for a city girl, huh?"

"Not bad at all."

She poked his chest with her big toe. "I'll admit that you certainly aren't bad for a cowboy."

He laughed and leaned forward to crawl over her until he hovered near her face. Then, he slowly lowered his head and placed a lingering kiss on her lips.

"Did I mention handsome?" she asked.

Zane raised his brows. "Handsome, you say?"

She nodded and ran her hands over his chest. "Exceedingly so."

"Is that right?"

"Very much so," she said as she tugged him down atop her.

He braced himself on his forearms and stared into her blue eyes. "You're the most unusual and amazing woman I've ever met. On top of that, you're absolutely stunning."

Her eyes softened as she smiled sweetly. "Keep talking like that, and I may never let you leave this cabin."

"I'd be okay with that."

He rolled to the opposite side of the popcorn bowl and brought her with him. They grew quiet as they lay in each other's arms. Zane listened for the storm, but to his surprise, it had tapered off sometime during the day as they were otherwise engaged. When the storm passed, there would be no reason for her to stay.

Sure, they had said a lot to each other, but the truth was that they had different lives in different states. This chance encounter was simply that. It didn't mean anything more. It couldn't. He wouldn't move from Wyoming, and Cady wouldn't move from Texas. And why would they? They barely knew each other.

"You're thinking."

Her words startled him. "What?"

"I can literally hear your brain," she said with a smile. "I bet if I looked at your face, you'd be frowning."

Zane instantly smoothed his expression. "I might have been frowning."

She laughed.

"Do you not think?" he asked.

"I did admit a few minutes ago that I overthink everything."

"Do you mind if I ask what you're thinking about?"

She was silent for a heartbeat. "I'm thinking how weird it is that I was irritated to be holed up here with you, only to find that today has been the most incredible day of my life. I'm not just saying that, either. It's like a reset button was pushed. So much has become clear to me, and it isn't just about my job. It's about me in general."

"I'll admit, meeting you certainly has changed my way of thinking. I've dreaded this holiday for years, but you've made it special. You've made it something I've not only enjoyed but will also remember for the rest of my life."

Cady lifted her head to smile at him. "Really?"

"Really," he stated emphatically.

She smiled as she leaned forward to kiss him. "I'm glad you found me."

"Me, too," he said as he hugged her tightly.

They remained like that for several minutes. When Cady got up to get something to drink, Zane decided he should go check on Brego.

"I won't be long," he told Cady.

She lowered the water bottle. "I think I might jump in the shower."

It felt natural for Zane to walk to her and kiss her before heading out. It wasn't until he was in the barn petting Brego that he realized what he had done. He might have only met Cady a little over twenty-four hours ago, but he felt as if he'd known her for his entire life.

Once he was satisfied that Brego was fine, Zane walked back to the cabin. Snow flurries still fell, but the wind had died completely. By morning, the snow would have likely stopped. Zane could make an excuse to keep them there on Christmas day, but he didn't want to do that to Cady. Not only would it be deceptive, but it was also unfair. She hadn't asked to be trapped in Wyoming. She wanted to go home, and he would see that she got there.

He stomped his feet to get the snow off before going inside and removing his boots, hat, and coat. The shower was still on, so he tended to the fire and picked up the beer and water bottles from earlier, as well as the bowl of popcorn.

Zane was contemplating dinner when the water cut off. It wasn't long before Cady came out in the sweats he'd loaned her earlier and a towel on her head.

She smiled when she saw him. "I feel better."

"I'm going to jump in."

"Everything okay with Brego?"

"He's cozy and well fed," he replied.

Steam still hung in the air of the bathroom. He let the water heat before he got in and washed his body and hair. He didn't linger since the water heater wasn't a large tank, and he didn't want to be caught in a cold shower.

The instant he opened the door, a delicious aroma assaulted him. Zane walked out with a towel around his waist and looked into the kitchen. Cady's blond locks hung damp around her as she hummed while chopping garlic.

"It smells great," he said.

She glanced at him, then did a double-take when she saw his towel. "The least I can do is cook for you."

"I certainly won't complain."

Zane put on clean clothes and hung his towel before joining Cady in the kitchen. He looked over her shoulder onto the stove to see that she had the iron skillet out with steaks on one side and potatoes on the other.

"What are you cooking?"

"Garlic butter steak and potatoes."

His stomach growled in hunger at the smells. "Is it nearly done?"

"Depends on how you like your steak," she said with a laugh.

"The rarer, the better."

"Then they're done."

She had to use both hands to move the heavy skillet to another burner. Zane got out the plates and utensils while she finished turning the potatoes and let the meat rest. She plated his food, giving him the biggest steak and a large helping of the diced potatoes.

"Thanks," he said as he took the plate. If it tasted half as good as it smelled, it would be one of the best meals he'd had in a long time.

Once Cady had her plate and sat, he cut into the steak and took a bite. He shook his head in amazement. Next, he tried a potato.

"Well?" she asked, watching him.

"Can you cook for me again?"

She laughed and touched his arm with her hand. "Gladly. I'm happy you like it."

"Like it? This is amazing. Are you sure you aren't a chef?"

"I don't mind cooking. Usually, I'm too tired after a long day, but I know how. Growing up as we did, we helped Mom out by taking turns cooking. It got to the point that we kept trying to outdo each other. My brother loved it so much, he *is* a chef."

Zane continued to stuff food into his mouth as she spoke. The more he learned about her, the more impressed he was with her and her family. It would be hard to say goodbye to her, that was for sure. She had left her mark on him without a doubt.

"Before we part ways, will you tell me your horse story?" he asked.

She swallowed her bite, nodding. "Only if you return the favor and tell me why you hate city people so much."

"I think your story will be better."

"If you want mine, I want yours."

He sighed loudly. "I want your story enough that I'll agree to that."

"Perfect," she said with a smile.

When they finished dinner, they cleaned up together before making their way to the sofa. Their conversations moved easily from one topic to the next. There were silences, but they weren't uncomfortable. Zane didn't feel the need to fill the silence with anything, and that was a rare gift indeed.

"It sounds like the storm is done," she said as she reclined against him.

Zane dreaded this. "There are still flurries, but it should be finished sometime in the night. Clear skies are in the forecast for tomorrow."

"Christmas Day."

"That's right."

"Do you have to be somewhere?"

He glanced down at her to see her gaze directed at the fire. "I don't."

"You said my rental car is probably buried in snow."

"It will be."

"It wouldn't be very nice of me to call someone away from their family on Christmas Day just so I can sit in an airport, trying to get on a flight."

Hope sprang in Zane's heart. "That would be the . . . neighborly . . . thing to do."

Her head turned to him. "You don't mind?"

"I was hoping that's what you'd want."

"What about your family?"

Zane lifted one shoulder in a shrug. "My parents passed away some years back. Charlie is in Cheyenne with his girlfriend and her family. It's just me."

"What are the odds that neither of us would have plans for the holiday?"

"About as unusual as you taking a wrong turn and ending up on the very road I travel after seeing my neighbor."

Cady looked away pensively. "I don't believe in coincidences like that."

"You think we were destined to meet?"

Her blue gaze swung to him. "Do you have another explanation?"

"Nope. I just know I'm enjoying myself. With a city girl," he added with a grin.

She rolled her eyes while smiling. "Just for that, you're going to have to have sex with me again."

"Oh, the torture," he said as he bent to kiss her.

Chapter 8

They talked into the wee hours of the morning. Cady didn't remember falling asleep, but how could she not when Zane held her and kept her warm. When she opened her eyes, she was smiling. And happy.

So very happy.

She couldn't honestly remember the last time she had felt such joy and elation. And contentment. Some might say it was because of all the sex. That probably had something to do with it, but Cady knew there was more. Something deeper, something more profound had occurred over the last couple of days.

Not only had she been in mortal danger, but she had also faced one of her greatest fears and been more honest with herself—as well as Zane—than she had ever been. And she had let go of all the rules she had always placed on herself. What that had given her was one of the most incredible experiences of her life—one she didn't want to end.

She lay on Zane's chest, listening to the beating of his heart and his even breathing. It was quiet, the only sound a log falling in the hearth. It was the first holiday she hadn't thought about gifting anyone presents or receiving any. This Christmas, she had gotten something even more special—herself.

And Zane.

She knew without a doubt that if they lived near each other, this could turn into something real. She had a horrible habit of trusting too much, but she saw the raw honesty in Zane's gold eyes. She knew that he wasn't leading her on or giving her false promises. Neither had spoken any kind of oaths.

Because they knew this was just a holiday romance—something that wasn't meant to last.

The problem was, she really wanted it to.

He took a deep breath and tightened his arms around her as he rolled her onto her back. Zane smiled down at her. "Merry Christmas."

"Merry Christmas," she said and brushed her hand over his two-day growth of whiskers that gave him an even more rugged appeal.

Not that he needed any help. The man was heart-stoppingly gorgeous. She would've noticed it the moment she saw him, but she had been freezing and scared. Cady didn't want to be depressed this morning. She would have time for those feelings on the plane back to Austin. For now, she planned to enjoy every second.

"Hungry?"

She eyed him. "For food?"

He grinned. "Either. You pick."

"Food first. I need energy before I have my way with you," she teased.

"Ah, woman, you know the way to my heart."

He rolled off her before she could respond. Cady told herself that it was just a joke, something someone might say in response to her comment. And yet . . . a tiny part of her wished there might be some truth to his words.

Cady instantly missed his warmth. She covered herself as she watched Zane tug on jeans and a shirt before walking to the kitchen. He glanced at her over his shoulder and blew her a kiss. She smiled but didn't move from the bed. Too many thoughts filled her mind.

Stop this, she told herself. *You live in Austin. He lives in Wyoming. How in the world do you expect things to work? Not to mention, he works on a ranch.*

There were ranches in Texas. Some very profitable ones. Perhaps he could work on one of those.

Oh, God. Don't. Don't go down this road. It won't end well. You know *this. You're just feeling lonely.*

She wouldn't call what she felt lonely. She would call it . . . happiness. Joy.

Ecstasy.

It's a holiday fling. Something you can look back on years from now and smile. You two come from different worlds. He wouldn't move to Texas, and you wouldn't move here. You despise the cold. And last but not least, there hasn't been any kind of talk about this . . . fling . . . turning into something more.

You're reaching.

How could she not after having such a life-altering time?

Cady slipped from the covers and grabbed her clothes as she made her way to the bathroom. After she closed the door, she turned on the faucet and looked at herself in the mirror. "What am I doing?" she whispered.

The fact that she didn't have an answer was answer enough. She needed to stop thinking about tomorrow and the day after and accept the few hours she had left with Zane. Ironic that she had originally felt as if this trip had been some kind of penance. Instead, it had become the best thing that had ever happened to her.

By the time she dressed and combed her hair with her

fingers, her smile was back in place. She opened the door, ready to help Zane with breakfast. Instead, she found him talking to a woman in a police uniform.

"You must be Cady," the older woman said with a smile.

Cady nodded and glanced at Zane.

"This is Sheriff Charlotte Smith," Zane told her in a soft tone.

Gone was the smile and teasing from before. Cady knew instantly that their time was finished. Their winter fling had been disrupted.

"Your car was found late last night," the sheriff said as she put her hands in the pockets of her thick jacket. "It took us until about an hour ago to dig it out of the snow. I can't tell you how relieved I was not to have found a body inside."

Cady forced a smile, her heart sinking with every second that passed. She wasn't ready for this to be over. She wasn't ready for any of it. Her gaze slid to Zane, but his eyes were on the floor. He wouldn't look at her.

"I held out hope that someone might have found you," the sheriff continued. "I knew this cabin wasn't far. It was the first place I checked. You're very fortunate that Zane ran across you when he did."

"Yes. Fortunate," Cady heard herself say as if from a great distance.

She wanted to turn, rush back to the bathroom, and lock the door. Maybe then the sheriff would leave, and she and Zane could pretend that their refuge hadn't been disrupted. Cady took a step back, thinking of doing just that.

"The car is being towed. There's another rental place about twenty miles down the road. One of my deputies can drive you there to get a new vehicle so you can get back on the road."

"I can take her," Zane said.

Cady was thankful for his offer. That would give them

more time together. But was that wise? She didn't care if it wasn't. She wasn't ready to return to her life in Texas.

Sheriff Smith smiled at Zane. "Appreciate that. The roads should be plowed by now. Oh, one more thing." The sheriff left the cabin. A few moments later, she returned with Cady's carry-on luggage. "I think you might need this."

"Thanks," Cady said.

"Well, then," the sheriff said, looking between the two of them. "I'll be off. Happy holidays."

"Be careful," Zane told her as he followed her to the door and gently closed it behind her.

Cady stared at Zane's back as he remained there, unmoving. She didn't know what he was thinking, but she couldn't wrap her head around what had just happened. She believed she had most of the day, if not all of it.

"It's still early," Zane finally said as he pushed away from the door. "The skies are clear. It won't take the airports long to clear the snow and ice from the runways. I'll cook breakfast as planned, then we can get on the road."

Her lips parted, but no words came out. She wanted to tell him that she wished to stay for the day. What held her back was the knowledge that he might not want her to. They had been trapped. That was no longer an issue. This could be Zane's way of letting her know that she should leave.

Cady took a deep breath and resigned herself to the fact that the best holiday of her life was essentially over. "Can I help?"

"I've got it," he said, keeping his back to her.

It hurt that he wouldn't look at her, but she didn't press him. Cady retrieved her luggage and brought it into the bathroom with her. She opened her bag and got out some clothes before begrudgingly removing Zane's sweatshirt and folding it neatly to set on the counter. The pants followed next, and she tucked them beneath his shirt. Then she rummaged for clean underwear and hastily pulled on wool socks before stepping into jeans, a thermal undershirt, and a thick, black sweater.

If she was leaving Zane, she wanted him to remember her at her best.

Chapter 9

No matter how Zane tried, he couldn't stop time.

Nor could he reverse it to keep the sheriff from knocking on his door.

The moment the knock had sounded, his stomach sank. He'd known before he opened the door who it was. He'd tried to get the sheriff to leave before Cady emerged, but even that plan had failed.

Zane couldn't look at Cady for fear that he'd see elation on her face at finally being able to go home. Sure, she'd said that she'd had the best holiday ever and that she didn't want to bother someone to get her vehicle on Christmas, but that didn't mean she wouldn't be happy to get home. She'd never let him think otherwise for an instant. The only thing he could think to do to prolong things was to drive her and cook breakfast. Maybe during all of that, he could think of something, anything to keep her here.

If only for one more day.

But he knew it would always be *one more day.* There would never be enough time with Cady. If he got the day, he'd want another one, and another, and another. But how could he not when he was so happy?

He heard the bathroom door close softly. Zane rested his hands on the counter and hung his head. He'd known that this time would come, but he hadn't realized it would hurt so damn bad. It was the kind of pain that never healed, the kind that would remain with him for a lifetime. He'd been waiting for a girl like Cady. How could he let her walk out of his life?

How could he get her to stay?

There was one way, but he simply couldn't do it. It went against everything he believed in. And if she wanted to stay with him for that reason, then it would never work. Yet, he couldn't think of any other way.

He'd lived alone, bitter and angry for too many years. Cady had washed all of that away with a kiss. She'd mended wounds he believed could never be healed. And now, she was about to walk out of his life as effortlessly as she had appeared.

Somehow, Zane managed to cook pancakes. His mind went over every second he had spent with Cady. How he managed not to burn the pancakes or himself was a miracle. By the time she emerged from the bathroom, he was on the last pancake. He put it on the plate and turned to set it on the table when he caught sight of her.

She took his breath away. She'd brushed her blond hair, and it fell gently against the black sweater. The jeans molded to her legs, making him recall how she had wrapped them around his waist.

"I love pancakes," she said with a smile.

He cleared his throat, mentally shaking himself. "Please, sit and eat."

Zane got them both some coffee before sitting across from

her. Whereas the conversations before had been easy and simple, he couldn't think of anything to say now, making it awkward. They each tried to start an exchange a couple of times, but eventually gave up.

All too soon, the meal was finished.

"Let me do the dishes," Cady said as she got to her feet.

Zane rose and put on his boots. "I'll go see to Brego."

He took his time with the horse, but Zane knew he could only put off the inevitable for so long. After giving Brego a final pat, he returned to the house. Cady's suitcase was near the door, along with her purse. She sat at the table, waiting.

"Ready?" he asked.

She glanced at the bed. "If you are."

"I thought I'd drive you to the airport."

"Is that out of your way?"

He shrugged. "I don't mind."

"Thank you."

With nothing else to do, he made sure the fire was out in the hearth, then he grabbed her suitcase and his keys. She put on her coat and looped her purse over her shoulder. He followed her out of the house and closed the door behind him, locking it. She trailed him around the side of the cabin where his truck sat under a covered area.

The drive was excruciating. The closer they got to the airport, the more his mood soured. Cady seemed just as content not to talk. She spent the drive looking out the passenger window, seemingly lost in thought. He called himself ten kinds of fool for not telling her what was on his mind, but each time he said the words to himself, they sounded crazier and crazier.

He'd had his heart broken before. He wasn't afraid of putting it out there again. He was scared of Cady saying no. If he never asked, he would never get the answer he feared more than anything. It was idiotic, but there was a chance—however slim—that he *could* get the answer he wanted.

But he knew the odds, and right now, they were stacked heavily against him. No one in their right mind gambled against such odds. Not even a man like him.

The drive went by too quickly. When he pulled up to the curb at the airport, he put the truck in park and turned off the ignition as Cady got out of the vehicle. Zane got her luggage out of the back and set it before her.

"Thank you," she said, her gaze meeting his. "For everything. I can't tell you how much the time meant to me."

He touched his knuckles against her cheek. "I'll never forget you."

"This ended much quicker than I was prepared for."

"We could only hold off the world for so long."

There was a ghost of a smile. "You never told me your story."

"You never told me yours."

"Zane, I—"

He grabbed her and kissed her, pouring all of his passion and yearning into it. When he finally ended it, they were both breathing heavily. "Goodbye, city girl. Take care of yourself, okay?"

Zane walked away, hoping she would call out to him, tell him to stop. But there was nothing. His heart had never ached so badly before. He started the truck and pulled away from the curb. When he could stand it no more, he glanced in the rearview mirror to see her standing there, watching him.

He pointed the truck toward Cheyenne and didn't stop until he arrived at his destination. Zane walked up the path and knocked on the door. Charlie's surprised smile dimmed.

"What happened?" his brother asked.

"I think I fell in love."

Chapter 10

Her chance was gone. Cady hadn't had the nerve to stop Zane. The first tear fell down her cheek before he got in the truck. They were falling freely as he drove away. She stood in the cold, crying long after his truck had disappeared.

A baggage porter came over to see if she was all right. Cady was anything but, yet she pulled herself together. Or she tried to.

"I saw it all," he told her, his blue eyes filled with kindness.

That made her cry even harder.

"Do you have a ticket?"

She shook her head, wishing with all her might that she was back at the cabin with Zane.

"Where are you headed?" he asked.

"Au-Austin," she answered with a sniff.

He took her luggage. "Come. We'll find you a ticket."

Cady wasn't used to letting anyone do things for her, but at this moment, she was grateful that someone had stepped in since her mind was otherwise occupied. At the ticket counter, he and the airline employee found her a seat on a flight, leaving in thirty minutes. She gave them the information they wanted, then headed to security because that's what she was supposed to do.

On the flight, she sat in a middle seat between two burly men with screaming kids around her and didn't care about any of it. Her thoughts were back in the cabin. Yet, the longer she was away from Zane, the more she wondered if it had all been a dream. He had suddenly been there, and then he was gone in a blink.

When she landed in Austin, she turned her phone on and saw the dozens of texts and calls from her family. She should've sent them something before the flight, but her mind had been occupied with thoughts of Zane. She quickly sent a reply on their group text and gave them a brief explanation of what had happened and that she was home. They would want more, but she would give it when she was ready, and not before.

She drove to her house and found herself missing all the snow. Once inside, she dropped her purse and keys on the table near the door and left her luggage. She poured some wine, then got her phone from her bag and turned it off because her family wouldn't stop texting. She curled up on the sofa and turned on the TV.

But she couldn't concentrate on anything. She daydreamed about Zane, his kisses, and their conversations until around midnight when she finally went to bed. Sleep, however, was impossible.

The next morning, she showered and dressed and went into work, where she put the files from her trip on David's desk, along with her resignation letter. Then she cleared her desk and carried everything to her car without speaking to anyone. She returned home, only to discover that she didn't know what to do.

Cady found herself sitting in front of her laptop. Without

knowing what she was doing, she typed *Charlie Taylor Wyoming* into the search bar. She found Zane's adoptive brother easily enough since he was in politics, but it was the mention of the Z Bar Ranch that got her attention. When she read a short bio of Charlie stating that he had grown up on the ranch, she had to know more about it.

A search of the Z Bar Ranch made her mouth drop open. The more she read, the more shocked she was. The ranch itself was successful, but it was the family connected to it that stunned her. The article she read called the Taylor family *Wyoming royalty* because of the silver mine on the property that netted the family billions.

Cady had to know more. She searched anything and everything having to do with Zane and his family. That was how she discovered that his great-grandfather had first bought the land and found the silver mine. It was only after the silver that he acquired more land and got into the cattle business.

As she scrolled through pictures of the ranch and family, Cady paused when she found one with Zane and a tall brunette who could've passed for a model. They were holding hands and dressed in formal attire. The next picture was of that same woman, published in a Wyoming newspaper, as she attempted to cover her face. The caption read: *Caught Cheating.*

Hours later, Cady finally rose from the chair and closed the laptop. That's when she called her mom.

"I'm okay. Really," Cady said.

"I birthed you, honey. I know you're not."

Cady swallowed. "You're right. I'm not."

"Want to talk?"

"Yeah."

"Want me to come to you?"

"Please," Cady said. "And bring ice cream."

Less than thirty minutes later, she let her mom in. They sat facing each other on the sofa in silence, each with their own carton of ice cream.

"You don't have to talk."

Cady scooped some ice cream onto her spoon. "I quit my job."

"Thank goodness."

She was taken aback by her mother's response. "You and Dad always taught me not to quit before I had another lined up. You two drilled that into us."

"There are some exceptions," her mother said with a knowing look. "You're financially responsible, you have no bills, and you've been miserable for some time now. I thought it was just the job. Then I thought it was just the jackass. Now, I realize it was both."

Cady tried not to laugh at her mother calling Jared a jackass, but she had to admit, the name fit. "I thought the firm was what I wanted."

"It was. When you first started out. But everyone changes."

She thought back to the conversation she'd had with Zane about change. "I clung to the same idea I had when the firm first hired me. Why couldn't I see that I had changed?"

"It wasn't just you. It was everything else that changed, as well. And," her mother said with a little shrug, "sometimes, we can't see the forest for the trees."

Cady ate another bite of ice cream.

"What are your plans now?" her mom asked.

"I have no idea." But there was a smile on Cady's face. "I'm actually looking forward to it."

Her mother grinned in response. "That's my girl. You've always had big dreams. Go out and chase them."

Cady looked around at her house. "I fell in love with this place the first time I saw it my senior year."

"I remember," her mother said with a chuckle after a bite.

"How many times did we drive out here? How many times did you talk your dad into driving you out here?"

The memories brought a smile to her face. "So many. It annoyed both of y'all tremendously, but neither of you said anything."

"I remember when you called us, screaming in excitement when the house finally went up for sale. It was meant to be yours, that's for sure."

Cady set aside her ice cream and looked into her mother's blue eyes. "I don't know if it's still meant to be mine."

Her mother's smile was sad as she nodded and set aside her ice cream. She folded her hands in her lap. "You've always done things to the beat of your own drum. You and your siblings. Your father and I, and our significant others, have fostered that. After things went sideways with you and the jackass, you seemed rudderless. But now . . . well, honey, whatever happened in Wyoming changed you."

"Yes, it did."

"I have to say, I was worried sick about you."

Cady twisted her lips. "For a bit, I was worried. You know how I feel about the snow and the cold in general. I packed the warmest things I had, and it wasn't enough."

"You couldn't have known the GPS would fail you."

"Mom, do you believe in destiny?"

Her mother gave her a flat look. "Of course I do. You know that. I was destined to marry your father so we could bring three amazing people into this world. And I was destined to find the love of my life years later."

"I'm not sure I really believed in any of that until recently. I sat in that car for hours. I had no cell service, no way of starting the engine to warm up, and no way of getting anywhere out of the elements. I was stuck. Then, out of nowhere, Zane showed up."

"Didn't you hear his vehicle?"

"He was on a horse."

Her mother's eyes bugged out. "You're kidding."

"I wish I was." Cady shook her head, smiling. "He was as patient as he could be despite the storm moving in while trying to get me on the horse. He knew instantly that I was from the city, and he wasn't impressed in the least."

"Did you get on the animal?"

Cady wrinkled her nose. "I was so cold. I could barely feel my legs, and I just wanted to get warm. In the end, I was more afraid of the cold than Brego."

"Brego?" her mother asked with her brows raised. "Like from *Lord of the Rings*?"

"Yep. Except he read the books."

Her mother's mouth formed an *O*. "Interesting."

"He had a not-so-flattering first impression of me, and I had one of him as a cowboy. I couldn't have been more wrong. He took care of me, Mom. Brought me to his cabin, got me warm and fed."

"Seems I owe this man a lot for looking after you."

"The storm kept us locked in. We couldn't get out, couldn't use phones. We were shut away from the rest of the world, and, for some reason, that changed my outlook on everything. I set aside the person I'd been and decided to try to be the person I was."

Her mother grinned. "How did that go?"

"It was the most incredible two days of my life."

"He a good lover?"

Cady smiled as she hugged herself. "You wouldn't believe it if I told you."

"Those men are rare, honey. *Very* rare."

"We spent hours talking and hours having sex. It was . . ."

"Life-altering?" her mother offered.

Cady nodded. "Yes. I've never been so open with anyone. And I think he was the same. I was just myself."

"As you should always be."

"That isn't easy to do all the time. Yet, it was with Zane. Then, the storm stopped. I wasn't ready to get back, even though I knew all of you would be concerned. We decided to have Christmas day to ourselves. We had just woken that morning, and he was making breakfast as I went to freshen up. When I came out, the sheriff was there. They found my rental car."

Her mother sighed as her lips pressed together. "And the bubble that protected you two from the world burst."

"Yeah. In an instant. Zane wouldn't look at me the entire time the sheriff was talking. I kept waiting for him to give me a sign that he wanted me to stay."

"Did you tell him you wanted to stay?"

Cady glanced away. "I was too afraid he'd say it was time to get back to the real world."

"Oh, Cady," her mother said dolefully. "Both of you agreed to have the day, even though either of you could've said to get back to the world. Why would the sheriff arriving make a difference?"

"When you put it like that, it makes perfect sense. But, Mom, it was a weird situation."

Her mother shook her head, her face lined with disappointment. "You wanted him to ask you to stay. And he wanted you to ask to stay. Both of you are idiots."

"You might be right."

"What happened after that?"

Cady tucked her hair behind her ear. "Zane drove me to the airport ninety minutes away. We didn't talk at all. Before, we had so much to say. I wanted to say so much during those last miles, but nothing came out. Then we reached the airport."

Tears stung her eyes. She tried to blink them away, but they fell down her cheeks.

Her mother leaned forward and put her hand on hers. "Oh, honey."

"I thanked him for everything. He told me he'd never forget me and kissed me. Then he told me to take care of myself and drove away." By the time the last word fell, she was sobbing.

Her mother scooted closer and wrapped her arms around her, holding Cady as she bawled.

"Why d-didn't I s-say something?" Cady asked.

Her mother rubbed her hands over her back. "That doesn't have to be the last time you talk to him."

Cady sat back, blinking. She sniffed and wiped at the tear streaks on her face. "What?"

"It's evident that your heart is in Wyoming."

Cady considered her mother's words, wondering if it was possible . . . if she dared . . .

Her mother took her hands in hers and smiled. "You asked me about destiny. I think you were meant to feel like your life was falling apart. How else would you be open to new possibilities with a man like Zane?"

"I wouldn't have been."

"Exactly," her mother said with a knowing smile. "Jared had to hurt you so you'd see that he wasn't meant to be in your life. You had to realize how crummy David was at the firm so you'd decide whether to stay or go. You had to be put in a situation that forced you to face yourself and the future that awaits. If you're bold enough to take it."

Cady couldn't believe what her mother was saying. "You think that I should, should . . . ?"

"Get your ass up to Wyoming and see if there is anything between you and Zane? You bet I do. It might turn out to be nothing. It might be something that fizzles in a few months or years. Or . . . he could be the love of your life."

"But I hate the cold. He's a rancher. With horses."

Her mother laughed. "He got you on Brego."

"Mom. He owns a huge ranch. Based on what I discovered today, his family is considered Wyoming royalty. He's rolling in money."

She shrugged. "So?"

"He didn't tell me any of that."

"There's a reason for that, I bet."

Cady thought about the picture she'd seen of Zane and the woman. She hadn't told him about every ex-boyfriend she'd had. Why would she expect him to tell her everything in the time they'd had?

"New Year's is coming," her mother said. "You're in between jobs."

Cady couldn't believe what she was thinking.

Her mother gave her a nod, smiling. "Come on. I'll help you pack."

Chapter 11

Zane ran a hand down his face and blew out a nervous breath. He had driven around the block six times, and he wasn't any closer to getting up the nerve to get out of the car than he had been when he first arrived.

He looked at the charming house nestled in the Austin foothills. He could imagine Cady living there. It had a quaint, old-world appeal, mixed with a modern air that shouldn't work but did. He'd hoped to see movement inside, but the house was quiet.

After reaching his brother's place, Zane had spent the rest of the evening telling him all about Cady and their time together. Charlie had asked him point-blank what Zane was doing at his house instead of going to see Cady. After that, it was all Zane could think about.

He drove back to the ranch, but he didn't go to the cabin. He couldn't. Not without Cady. He threw himself into work for a few days, but not even that worked. The next thing he knew, he had booked a flight to Austin and boarded it just a few hours later. It didn't dawn on him until he was on the way to Texas that he had no idea where Cady lived in Austin.

It took some digging and a few phone calls before he got her address. Once he had the rental car and was headed to her, he went over and over in his head everything he wanted to say. Then he got there, and his mind went blank.

Zane decided he needed to sleep and start fresh in the morning. He put the car in drive and headed to his hotel.

Cady's hand shook as she pressed the button on the intercom at the entrance gate to the Z Bar Ranch.

"Can I help you?" a woman's voice asked.

"I, um, I'm here to see Zane Taylor."

There was a brief pause. "Your name?"

"Cady Adams."

Her heart pounded in her chest. Would he refuse her? Would they tell her to turn around? Wou— Her thoughts halted as the gate began to swing open.

"Get a hold of yourself," she said as she drove through.

The pictures on the internet didn't do the ranch justice. It was sprawling and blanketed in white. Black fences were in direct contrast, and she tried to imagine what the place looked like in the summer when everything was green.

There was no mistaking where the house was. Though she wouldn't call it a house. It was more of a mansion. A castle, even. But with Western architecture so the abode didn't stand out against the beauty of the land but added to it.

Cady's mouth was dry as she parked behind three other vehicles. She didn't see the beat-up truck Zane had driven her to the airport in, but maybe that was at the cabin. This was the craziest, most ridiculous thing she had ever done. But her mother had been right. What if . . . ? That question hadn't left her mind since her mother had put it there. No matter what the answer was, Cady had to find out. Otherwise, this new leaf she had turned over would be for naught.

She had played it safe for so long. It was time to take the chances she'd once taken, to follow her heart without worry of consequences.

None of that, however, helped to calm the nervousness that made her shake and her palms clammy. She put the vehicle in park and turned off the ignition. She opened the car door and stepped out. The sight of a cowboy hat moving among the vehicles made her heart rate kick up a notch. She looked expectantly, thinking it was Zane.

Only to find a man in his fifties coming her way. He smiled at her in welcome. As he drew closer, she noted his dark skin, hair, and eyes that denoted him as a man of indigenous descent. "Hello," he said in a deep, even voice.

"Hi."

"Zane isn't here."

All her hopes melted away in an instant. She tried to hide her disappointment, but she knew she failed. "Oh."

"So. You're Cady."

That made her frown. "I'm sorry?"

"I heard about your car getting stuck before Christmas and Zane finding you."

"Yes, he did."

The man stuck out his hand. "I'm Jacob, the ranch manager. Would you like a tour?"

"Uh . . ." She looked around, confused. "I'm not sure I should."

He grinned at her. "Why? Do you have somewhere to be?"

That made her laugh. "I don't, actually."

"Then let me show you around."

How was she supposed to say no to that? Besides, Cady was curious to see more of Zane's life. Jacob didn't take her directly to the house. They walked around to the back and down another drive to a barn. It was a good thing Cady had bought better clothing, a coat, and boots. Otherwise, she'd be shivering. Well, she was shivering, but it wasn't as bad as it could be. When they reached the barn, she refused to go in once she saw the horses.

Jacob chuckled, shaking his head. "You really are afraid of them, aren't you?"

Cady wondered if there was anything Zane hadn't told Jacob. Just as they were walking away, a horse stuck its head over the stall door. She recognized Brego. A small part of her wanted to see the horse, but she quickly disregarded it.

Jacob took her back to the other side of the house, where they went into a side entrance. "I would bring you through the front, but this time of year, Zane rents out half the house to others."

"He what?"

Jacob shrugged and briefly met her gaze as they stopped in a solarium. "It's a big house, and with Zane here by himself, it's too much. About three years ago, some rich guy who wanted to pay him an enormous sum of money to bring his family up here for Christmas contacted him. Zane accepted his offer, but with stipulations. Guests are prohibited from entering certain areas of the house. We got to work and put locks on the doors to the rooms that Zane wanted kept private. Six months later, Zane was inundated with calls from others asking to do the same thing. From mid-November until the first of January, he rents the house to whoever wants it."

"And stays at the cabin," she surmised.

"That's right," Jacob said with a nod. "Something to drink?"

"Anything hot." She unzipped her coat and loosened the scarf around her neck as she looked around at the beautiful home.

Jacob returned a short time later, his coat removed, along with a mug of coffee and a little tray that held cream and sugar. “He didn’t tell you any of that, did he?”

“He also didn’t tell me about this ranch.”

“I’m not surprised. He’s a very private man. Please, sit,” Jacob said as he motioned to the chairs.

Cady chose one and wrapped her hands around the mug before taking a sip. “He didn’t want to tell me his last name. That was because he thought I’d know who he was.”

“Yeah,” Jacob said with a nod. “He’s been burned by that.”

“I can imagine. Women after all of this,” she said with a wave of her hand.

Jacob stretched out his legs and caught her gaze. “So, Cady. Why are you here? Is it because you found out who he was and wanted to see if you could get your hooks in him?”

“No,” she said with a smile and a shake of her head. “I make a good living. Nothing like this, but I’ve never needed a man for anything, especially financially.”

Jacob’s smile was wide. “I like you.”

“I’m here because I didn’t say everything I wanted or needed to say to Zane. I want the chance to do that.”

“You came all the way back from Texas for this? You could’ve called. Texted,” Jacob offered.

Cady glanced at the mug in her hand. “This is one of those things that needs to be done in person.”

“I wish I could help you, but I didn’t lie. Zane isn’t here.”

“Will he be back today?”

Jacob twisted his lips as he shook his head. “I don’t expect him back for a few days.”

“He isn’t out at the cabin, perhaps?” she asked hopefully.

“I would’ve taken you straight there if he was.”

Her hopes thoroughly dashed, Cady wasn’t sure what to do.

“Where are you staying?”

She hadn't gotten a hotel because she had hoped that Zane would ask her to stay.

Jacob sat forward. "Stay at the ranch. I'll even take you to the cabin if you'd like. Zane would want you to remain for as long as you'd like."

"I don't want to put anyone out."

"Trust me, you won't," he assured her.

Zane took it as a sign that he wasn't meant to find Cady when he finally knocked on her door and she didn't answer—two days in a row. He even left a note in her mailbox, but she still hadn't answered the door. He gave it one more day, and when she still didn't respond, he checked the mailbox to find his letter gone.

He took that to mean she had gotten the note and simply didn't want to see him. She wanted to leave what'd happened between them in Wyoming. And now, so would he.

Zane was weary when the flight landed in Cheyenne. The drive to the ranch was even more exhausting. It was dark when he pulled up the drive, and he was surprised to find Jacob waiting for him.

"How'd it go?" Jacob asked.

Zane grabbed his overnight bag and closed the truck door after getting out. He walked past, Jacob falling into step with him. "I'm here. That should tell you everything you want to know."

"Your house guests haven't left."

"I noticed that when I saw their vehicles still here," Zane stated. He paused and looked at his friend. "Sorry. I'm in a foul mood."

"No need to apologize."

"Everything good here?"

Jacob nodded. "Like always."

"I'm not in the mood for company. I'll be in my room for a few days."

Jacob made a sound in the back of his throat.

Zane quirked a brow. "What was that for?"

"Listen."

Zane took a second and listened. That's when he heard the loud music and laughter. He closed his eyes. The one thing he hated about letting others stay at the house was that they disturbed his peace. It was why he always went to the cabin. He'd go there now, except . . .

"I think it'd be wise if you didn't stay here," Jacob said.

Zane turned on his heel and retraced his steps. "You know where I'll be. Only contact me if there's an emergency."

"I've got things covered!" Jacob hollered.

Zane got back into his truck and slammed the door in irritation. He started the engine and backed up before putting the vehicle in drive and heading to the cabin. On the way there, his thoughts turned again and again to Cady. The more he thought of all the things he should've said to her before he left her at the airport, the angrier he got at himself.

They'd had something real. He was sure of it. How could he have been so stupid as to let it go?

He pulled up alongside the cabin and turned off the engine. Zane sat there for a moment, steeling himself for what he would find when he walked in. The bed would still be unmade. The sheets would still smell like Cady.

"The city girl who hadn't minded the cowboy," he murmured. "At least, for a time."

He briefly closed his eyes as he blew out a breath. Then he grabbed his bag and got out of the truck. As he walked around the cabin, he saw the smoke from the chimney. He clenched his teeth. The last thing he wanted to deal with was some hunters who had inadvertently gotten onto his land and decided to make themselves at home in the cabin.

Zane threw open the door, ready to demand that whoever was there get out when his gaze landed on a familiar petite blonde, her blue eyes locked on him.

"Cady," he said, feeling as if he'd just been kicked in the gut. He dropped his bag, shock causing him to blink to make sure he wasn't hallucinating. "What are you doing here?"

"Waiting for you, cowboy. You took your sweet time."

Chapter 12

He was there. Cady fought not to run to him and throw her arms around him. His stunned expression told her nothing as he stood in the open door. She shifted her feet nervously. The instant she'd heard the truck, she had gotten to her feet, waiting anxiously for his arrival.

"I was out," Zane said offhandedly.

"Somewhere nice?"

His Adam's apple bobbed as he swallowed. "Austin. Looking for you."

She was so shocked, she could only stare at him. Then she rushed to him and threw her arms around him. He caught her, holding her tightly as his mouth descended on hers. They kissed as if they had been apart for years instead of days.

Zane kicked the door shut behind him and tore off his coat. He lifted her so that she could wrap her legs around his waist. Cady knocked off his Stetson as he walked to the sofa and sat on the edge. He ended the kiss and pulled back to look at her.

She ran her hands down his face. "You went to Austin?"

"You came here?"

"I had things I needed to tell you."

He quirked a brow. "Oh?"

"I did promise to tell you why I'm scared of horses."

"You did."

"And you promised to tell me your story."

He shifted her so that she sat sideways and could lean against the arm of the sofa. "I suppose you know who I am, who my family is?"

"I do now."

"I should've told you."

She shrugged. "Maybe."

"I was with someone once. I fell pretty hard for her, and it was only after I learned of her cheating that I found out she was only with me for my money."

"It made you distrust women," Cady said softly. "I understand that. I would do the same."

His gold eyes held hers solemnly. "That's my story. As simple as it is."

"There's nothing simple about that. She deceived you on multiple fronts. That is a lot for anyone to take."

He linked her hand with hers. Cady looked at their entwined fingers.

"Your fear?" he prodded.

She smiled and lifted her gaze to his. "I was thirteen. A friend, Amy, had several horses and had a party one weekend. The girls stayed over, but the boys left at midnight. There was this new kid in school, and I liked him."

Zane chuckled. "You wanted to impress him."

"I did. When he asked if I could ride, I said yes, knowing I'd never sat on a horse before. A girl I didn't get along with heard me and dared me to get on one. At that point, I was stuck. I couldn't get out of it without looking a fool and admitting that I'd lied—which is what I should've done."

"Instead, you got on the horse, didn't you?" he asked with a smile.

"Amy took pity on me and got one of the oldest horses they had. Getting up on that tall horse took everything I had, but I did it. All would've been fine, but the girl I didn't get along with knew I lied, and she wanted to prove it. After I was on top of the horse, she slapped his back leg, and he took off running. There hadn't been a saddle, so there was nothing for me to hold onto. All I remember is the wind in my face and screaming. Next thing I knew, I was on the ground."

"I'm really not liking the girl who did this. What's her name? We should pay her a visit."

Cady laughed and kissed him. "It's fine."

"It isn't. You could've been seriously injured, or worse."

"I know. Trust me. After my parents made sure I was safe, I got a stern lecture from them as well as Amy's parents. We all did."

Zane brought their hands to his mouth as he kissed the back of her hand. "Yet you still got on Brego."

"Because of you. I knew even then that you'd never let anything happen to me."

"I wouldn't. I won't," he vowed.

Cady licked her lips and glanced away. "I don't know what this is between us. What I do know is that it felt wrong being away from you."

"It did," he said with a nod.

"We've both been hurt. It would be easy to walk away and close ourselves off to any possibilities. But I want to see where this goes. I want to know if this could be a forever love."

He ran the back of his finger down her cheek. "I feel alive when I'm with you, and I know that I would rather be with you than anywhere else. In a few days' time, you've captured my heart and soul. You've given me a glimpse of what life could be, and I want more. With you."

"I quit my job," she said.

"Start a practice here."

She laughed, excitement building. "It isn't quite that easy."

"I don't care what it takes. I'll move to Austin if that's what you want."

Cady shook her head. "I'm starting to like winter. As long as I have you to warm me."

"I'm all yours, city girl."

"I was hoping you'd say that, cowboy," she said as she began unbuttoning his shirt.

Zane moaned and took her mouth with his as he grabbed her and moved them to the floor in front of the hearth. "Here's to us," he whispered.

She gazed into his gold eyes and smiled. "To us."